CHRISTMAS SPIRIT

THE WANTLAND FILES

BOOK 5

LARA BERNHARDT

Christmas Spirit

Copyright © 2022 by Lara Bernhardt

Print and eBook editions published by Admission Press

All rights reserved.

This is a work of fiction. Names, characters, organizations, places, events, and incidents are either products of the author's imagination or are used fictitiously. Any resemblance to actual persons, living or dead, or actual events is purely coincidental.

No part of this book may be reproduced in any form or by any electronic or mechanical means, including information storage and retrieval systems, without written permission from the author, except for the use of brief quotations in a book review.

eBook ISBN: 978-1-955836-14-2

Print ISBN: 978-1-955836-15-9

Hardcover ISBN: 978-1-955836-16-6

LARA BERNHARDT

CHRISTMAS SPIRIT

ADMISSION PRESS

"No space of regret can make amends for one life's opportunity missed."—Charles Dickens

MACY DIDN'T CARE what her boss thought, she loved Christmas. He could bah-humbug all he wanted but she wouldn't let him ruin the happy season for her. She sang along to "Winter Wonderland" as she opened the storage closet door. She ran a hand down the boxes, foot tapping in time to the tune playing through the hotel. Finally, she caught sight of the scrawled label she searched for: *Christmas decorations*. She yanked the box loose and noticed another one with the same label. She'd have to make multiple trips. She hoisted the box onto her hip and pushed the door to, then headed for the lobby.

A new employee, Cristal, worked the front desk, singing along with "Baby, It's Cold Outside." Macy smiled before she realized she would need to give the young woman some pointers on how to navigate Christmas around their boss. She dropped the box by the desk. "Oof. That's heavier than it looks." She pointed to a corner by the front door. "I always set up the tree there, so it's visible through the windows."

Cristal clasped her hands and squealed. "Working on Thanksgiving is worth it to start decorating for Christmas."

Macy thought about her daughter home alone and silently begged to differ. "Isn't your family missing you?"

The girl rolled her eyes. "Nah. When I left for college, they were like, good riddance. Besides, I'm a vegetarian, and they refuse to accommodate."

Parents who didn't care if they spent holidays with their children? Macy shuddered at the thought. Too many holidays went by with her working and dreaming about being able to spend more time with her daughter, Abby, who was growing up entirely too fast. Macy felt like she was missing it all. But she had bills to pay—a lot of bills—and what could she do? "You're welcome to join my daughter and me this evening. It'll be a late dinner but better than nothing."

"Awww, thanks, Ms. Crawford. I have plans with some friends though. It's cool."

Macy heard a low moaning sound and spun toward the hallway. Cristal turned with a frown.

"Sick guest?" she wondered. *Great.* A hotel guest probably overdid it on Bourbon Street. Last thing she wanted to do was clean up vomit. "I'll go check. You listen for the phone." Even though no one ever called on Thanksgiving.

Her business casual heels, second-hand from a consignment shop, clicked rapid steps on the tile floor.

The hallway was empty. Strange.

She returned to the storage closet to wrestle the tree from the back as the musical track switched to "Sleigh Ride."

The closet door stood open.

I know I closed that. She approached slowly, watching for movement, and peeked inside, heart hammering.

Nothing. No sign anything had been moved. *Huh. Someone must have . . .*

But who? She and Cristal were the only two employees on the clock today. Mr. Flint complained bitterly as it was about being forced to pay time and a half on holidays. He wasn't about to schedule more employees than the bare minimum.

Weird. Maybe she hadn't closed the door all the way and it blew open.

She grappled with the boxes, playing Tetris until she finally managed to extricate the tree box with a huge heave and a grunt.

This time she made certain the door closed all the way, then shuffled back to the lobby, the box banging against her with each step.

Cristal waited anxiously, phone in hand, and waved her over. "Was someone sick?"

She shook her head. "I didn't see anyone. Don't know what that noise was."

"Thank goodness! I have a guy on hold."

"Really? Someone actually called today?"

"It's a guest. He says the Wi-Fi isn't working. What do I do?"

Macy took the phone and pressed the HOLD button. "Good afternoon. Trouble connecting to the Wi-Fi? Go ahead and type in the passcode for me again. That got it? Good! Yes, probably fat-fingered a key. No problem. Glad it was an easy fix."

She hung up and opened the box, lifting pieces of the tree and trying to remember how it went together.

"I should have thought of that!" Cristal said.

"You'll learn. No one knows everything when they start."

"You know how to handle everything. Mr. Flint is so lucky to have you."

"Wish he felt that way."

"He must! He trusted you with his hotel today so he could be home with his family on the holiday."

"He doesn't have a family. Well, one nephew. But I guarantee he's not spending the day with him."

"Oh."

"Yeah. Here, you work on figuring out the tree while I go grab the other box of decorations. We want everything done today so it'll be finished when he comes back tomorrow. That way it would be too much work to take back down, and he'll let us leave it all up."

"Take it down? Why would he take down the Christmas decorations?"

"Technically, he wouldn't. He'd demand we take it back down. He's not really—"

Another moan, longer and louder, filled the hallway.

Cristal jumped. "What *is* that?"

Macy hurried down the hall and rounded the corner—

The storage closet door hung open. And this time a pasty, bloodless face peered out at her.

She opened her mouth to scream but only gaped, incredulous.

This cannot be happening. This cannot be happening.

Chalk-white fingers curled around the edge of the door and widened the gap.

The black pit of a mouth opened, and another agonized moan ensued.

The figure of a man emerged from the closet, a decaying, rotten man, weighed down with chains and dragging heavy boxes padlocked onto his shackles. The chains rattled with each agonized step.

He moaned again, then stared at her with empty eyes that seemed to offer a view of the depths of the universe.

She couldn't move, couldn't even back away as the rattling, wheezing, dusty bones clanked toward her. He leaned low and moaned one word.

"Flint."

CHAPTER ONE

KIMBERLY WANTLAND PEERED up at the quaint building in front of her, knowing her latest foe resided inside. The Cardinal hotel, nestled between other centuries-old buildings, stood out along the street because it alone drooped sad and unadorned. No garlands or strings of lights festooned the front, as though the building was ashamed of its secrets. Whatever lurked inside couldn't hide from her, however. That's why she was here.

"No Christmas decorations, huh?" Sterling joined her. "Wonder what's up with that."

"At least we're right here in the French Quarter," Stan said. "Easy to check out all the sites."

"I've always wanted to see New Orleans," Rosie said. "I have the best job."

Kimberly loved seeing her crew so pleased with their investigation location. They slogged through plenty of rough days when no one considered this the best job.

Michael took off his sunglasses. "Dismal old place. Why can't ghosts haunt a state-of-art, brand new building with all the luxury amenities we can imagine? Just once?"

Well, at least most of them were happy. She draped an arm

around Michael's shoulders. "Nothing ever goes your way, does it?"

He curled his lip and hung his head. "Sadly, no. Ah, well. You getting anything?"

Clutching her quartz, she breathed deeply and focused, opening her sixth sense and hoping whatever had impeded her last investigation had cleared her system. She waited for her skin to prickle, the hair on her arms to stand on end, or a voice out of the past to whisper in her ear. Anything that might indicate a spirit wished to connect.

"Nothing. Let's try inside."

Sterling pulled her into a selfie. She beamed, and it wasn't faked. She truly appreciated that Sterling handled the social media posts so she could focus attention on the investigation.

Rosie looked up and down the street, her little black bag of chakra stones, essential oils, and loose-leaf teas at her side. "Where will they set up your trailer?"

Michael answered. "No room for trailers. The hotel set us up in suites, though. We can make do with them for footage review and makeup, no problem."

"This building dates back to 1845," Elise said, eyes drinking in the historic old building nestled between other historic old buildings. "Built in Vieux Carré style, renovated as a hotel."

"This building belonged to a single family?" Michael asked.

"Yes. Most of these buildings have been repurposed but were family dwellings originally."

"Everyone wealthy back then? I don't get it. Something this massive would cost a small fortune. How?"

"The area unfortunately has an antebellum past. Slave quarters were incorporated into most renovations, combining the separate quarters into a single building."

Kimberly looked on the building differently, the white pillars stretching from the brick porch with its wrought-iron, filigreed railing all the way to the top of the five floors more menacing than they'd seemed before.

"Shall we?" Michael asked.

Sterling opened the door, gesturing the crew inside.

A chill swept over her as she crossed the threshold, her stomach lurching. She curled a hand around her quartz. The necklace she wore every day helped her focus energy on all her chakras, each corresponding stone related to one of the seven chakras. The quartz, most critical, hung as a pendant so she could easily access it when she needed to use her sixth sense to bridge dimensions.

Before she could attempt to connect, a woman behind the front desk crossed the lobby to meet them, arms wide. The woman threw her arms around Kimberly as though greeting a long-lost friend rather than meeting a virtual stranger for the first time. Excited energy coursed from the woman and pulsed through Kimberly, setting her chakras spinning. Too much energy.

Still clutching her, the woman bubbled over. "Thank you so much for coming! I've watched your show since the series began and can't believe you're here! Something really spooked me on Thanksgiving."

A strangled squeal from a younger woman hopping and clapping behind the desk kicked up the mood of the room another notch. "I can't believe we have legit celebs here!"

Sterling lit up the room with his brilliant smile and held out a hand. "Another fan? Awesome."

"I'd never heard of you, but I looked you up! I'm Cristal. I just started here. This is awesome!"

Rosie whispered, "Someone who's never heard of Sterling? This is a switch."

"Never seen the show?" Sterling asked.

"I don't watch television. Only YouTube."

"Then you'll be delighted to hear about our brand-new YouTube channel which will be debuting soon," Sterling told her.

"You started one already?" Kimberly asked. "That was fast!"

"I had help. Everyone agreed it was a great idea. Randmeier

approved. Michael had the old recordings from your Albuquerque Paranormal Society investigations. We have a crew working on uploading and prepping."

Cristal took out her phone. "That sounds cool. I'll like and subscribe as soon as it's up! You've seen real ghosts? For real?"

Kimberly nodded. "And I didn't like or subscribe. It just happens."

"I wish I could."

The hugger shuddered, and Kimberly felt her spectrum shift from warm, yellow delight to cold, grey fear. "I wish I hadn't. Really, Cristal, don't wish for that. I'm Macy, by the way. I'm so grateful you came to help. I'm scared to be alone since I saw . . . whatever it was I saw."

"Who else was disturbed by the manifestation?" she asked.

"Well, we've heard thumps, footsteps, voices, that sort of thing for some time. But then I saw a—"

Stan and TJ joined them, lugging boxes of equipment, which they dropped to the floor with a thud.

"We know where to take these yet, Ms. Wantland?" TJ asked, rubbing his hands.

A little gasp from the desk drew Kimberly's attention. Cristal stared at TJ.

She smiled. "Not yet. We're just checking in now."

"I am so sorry," Macy said. "Where is my head? Cristal, let's let them settle in. We can share our experiences later."

"That's true," Kimberly said. "We want to record your testimony and we can do that right before we do a walk-through—"

"I heard it!" Cristal said. "I heard the ghost! On Thanksgiving, right after I started working here."

TJ glanced at the young woman and did a double take. "Oh, hi."

Macy joined Cristal behind the front desk, fingers flying over the keyboard. Cristal tore her gaze from TJ and assisted with the distribution of room keys.

A withered, hunched old man, wispy grey hair limp on his

balding head, shuffled into the room. Kimberly checked her sixth sense for any indication this was a spirit joining them. But she knew he wasn't as soon as the others in the room turned to watch the man's jerking movements. And then he noticed them.

"Hello, Mr. Flint!" Macy greeted him. "This is Jeremiah Flint, the owner of the hotel."

The deep lines etched into the papery skin of the man's face indicated that the scowl he greeted them with was a permanent setting. "What's all the hubbub? Carolers again? This is why I told you no Christmas decorations. They invite in all the sad sack charity cases and the riffraff who think we all—" He jerked his head side to side, beady slits of eyes taking in the lobby. "Have you added *more* decorations?"

"No, sir, Mr. Flint! Nothing since we decorated on Thanksgiving."

Cristal stared at the floor and mashed her lips together in a straight line.

The man looked again. "Are you sure?"

"Yes, sir!"

Cristal either coughed or choked. Kimberly couldn't tell which as the young woman hid her mouth behind her hands.

Flint eyed the young woman, then turned his beady eyes back on Macy, giving her a look that could freeze eggnog. "I know I told you no decorations."

"So sorry, Mr. Flint. I misunderstood. Thought you meant on the outside."

Cristal choked and began to cough.

"Outside! Inside! All the sides!"

"But the guests love them, Mr. Flint. Really! Just today—"

"Aaaaah! Bah!" He waved a hand at her then glowered at Kimberly. "What are you people doing here?"

"You people?" Rosie said. "We're here to help you!"

"You can forget it. You won't get any donations from me."

She looked at Michael who looked as baffled as she felt.

"Seriously?" her director asked. "He doesn't know who you are either? This has never happened."

"They're guests checking in," Cristal said, her eyes gleaming with amusement.

Flint narrowed his eyes more. Somehow. "That's the strangest luggage I've ever seen. You guys hippies?"

Macy kept a tight smile stretched across her face. "These are the paranormal investigators, Mr. Flint."

"Para what?"

Macy glanced at her, expressing an apology without saying a word. "The ghost hunters. To help with the ghost problem we're having."

"Ghosts? What complete rubbish! I said no!"

Macy lifted a piece of letterhead. "But you signed this, giving permission for them to come investigate."

"I did not. Why would I do that?"

Macy handed him the paper, which he squinted at while he scrutinized it.

Cristal snorted.

Macy lifted her eyebrows. "Do you need to get some water, Cristal?"

Cristal nodded and hurried from the room.

"I guess I did." He handed the paper back. "I don't believe in ghosts, though. She's the one who was scared. Which rooms are you putting them in?"

Macy hesitated. "Some of the suites were empty so I—"

"Suites? You're putting these freeloaders in my best suites?"

"Freeloaders?" Michael raised his voice, nearly snarling at the older man. "Excuse you? Do you know how much free publicity you'll be getting by being featured on our show?"

Flint rubbed his gnarled hands together. "Free?"

Sterling stepped forward, holding out a hand. "Completely free. And we don't charge for our investigative services."

"What's that?" Flint cocked one ear and leaned closer.

Sterling raised his voice. "We don't charge anything."

Flint seemed to grapple with something internally. He lifted one eyebrow. "But you're not paying for your rooms?"

"For the love of—" Michael looked on the verge of a fit.

And Kimberly knew he could out-pitch the crankiest of old men when pushed hard enough. She rested a hand on his back, hoping to subdue him with some calming energy. "We don't—"

Sterling yanked out his wallet and slid a card across the desk to Macy. "Put it on that."

Flint nodded once and finally shook Sterling's hand. "Good man. Settles his debts. Doesn't expect something for nothing." He tottered down the hall.

"Something for nothing!" Stan murmured. "Already a crowd out there checking out the van and snapping pics of the place."

Macy breathed a sigh of relief and held out Sterling's card. "Here you go. Thank you for humoring him."

Sterling shook his head. "I told that man I'd pay. And I'm not a liar."

This man never ceased to amaze her. "Really, Sterling, this isn't your responsibility. If we need to pay, the show will pick it up."

Macy shook her head. "I assure you, no one will be charged. He'll never know. And once he thinks about it, he won't care. Those suites are sitting empty anyway. He'll realize how silly he was being. He really is all bark and no bite."

"His bark is pretty nasty," Michael said. "He didn't know we were coming?"

"I may have "

Cristal peeped around the corner. "Is he gone?"

"Yes. You need a better poker face."

"He had no idea we were coming?" Rosie asked. "You set this up without him knowing? Did you fake his signature?"

"She faked the whole letter." Cristal stifled a giggle. "Macy always does what's best for the hotel. She knows how to handle Flint. He's so cranky, I just can't even. He cracks me up."

Michael lifted his eyebrows and sighed. "Well, this will be an interesting investigation. An owner who doesn't believe in ghosts, doesn't want us here, and thinks we're freeloaders. Great."

"We've worked in more difficult situations than this," Kimberly reminded him.

"Not recently. And I'm getting too old for this. Let's get settled so I can call Ian. He ought to enjoy this almost as much as Cristal."

"He will come around, I promise," Macy said. "Let me show you to the elevator—"

"I'll show them!" Cristal raced around the counter to TJ's side. "Can you carry that all the way without help? It looks heavy."

TJ's cheeks pinked. "This? It's nothing." He lifted the equipment case and pumped it up and down a few times to flex. "See?"

"I'm sure I couldn't lift it." Cristal gazed at him.

Stan caught Kimberly's eye and gave her a knowing look, doing his best not to grin.

Macy cleared her throat. "The elevator, Cristal."

"Oh right!"

TJ stumbled after her, face red with exertion, the case clutched in both hands and thumping against his shins.

Stan chuckled as he lifted a case in each hand and followed, the equipment steady at his sides. "Should I tell her he has the light one?"

CHAPTER TWO

THE FRENCH QUARTER hummed with the excitement of tourists and anticipation of the impending holidays. Kimberly had never been to New Orleans and would have enjoyed seeing the famous, historic town even before learning her mother had grown up here. Knowing her family tree had roots here made her that much more excited and anxious to soak up as much knowledge and culture as she could.

Michael had suggested they walk the streets and find food somewhere in the old district, and everyone had jumped at the idea. She turned her head from side to side taking in all the sights as they started down Chartres Street, lined on both sides with mostly two-story buildings, balconies spanning the entire second floor of each, the wrought iron railings swirling up into arcs along the tops. Lush green plants hung along the roofs and balconies, spilling over and down the sides of the buildings. Christmas decorations joined the natural trailing greenery.

"Doesn't much feel like Christmas, does it?" Sterling asked, taking her hand in his. "The humidity makes the temperature almost tropical."

"These buildings are perfect examples of the Creole Style," Elise said, eyes drinking in the architecture. "Also referred to as

French Colonial, it's a mixture of French, Spanish, and Caribbean influences, which blended together here centuries ago. Those hand-forged wrought-iron railings were expensive and thus a sign of wealth. Most buildings have a large, central courtyard hidden behind the walls as well."

"That's cool and all, but I'm hungry," TJ said.

"I'm with Teej," Stan said. "I'd love to hear all about this, but can we maybe table the history lesson until after lunch?"

"Lunch? It's nearly dinnertime!" TJ's stomach rumbled, as if seconding the motion to eat first, learn later.

Kimberly glanced at the time. "I hate to say it, but if we intend to record the interview and walk-through before Macy's shift ends, we need to pick a place quick and get back."

"The light will be more advantageous earlier too," Stan pointed out.

"I have the solution," Elise said. "Napoleon House is just a few more blocks down Chartres Street. The reviews of the food are stellar, and I can fill you in on the history while we eat."

"Then can we come back out for dinner after the—" TJ stared at his phone. "Hey! That girl Cristal followed me on Insta. Sweet."

All thoughts of food appeared to evaporate from her young camera operator's mind.

Sterling grinned. "Excellent! New fans. Gotta keep growing the base. What's her name?"

"Cristal," TJ repeated. "Her username is @cristal_lite. Ha! Clever."

"Let's hope she follows the show too." He flipped through his feed, forehead creasing as if he worried about something.

She rubbed his back. "Hey. You're missing out on some fantastic architecture right here. Maybe a little less screen time?"

"I guess." He thrust his phone back into his pocket. "Just trying to keep a handle on all the media."

She didn't need her sixth sense to know her attempts to soothe him did not assuage whatever irritation plagued him.

"Shall we take some pictures for you to post? Would that help?"

His forehead smoothed, and his lips curled into a gentle smile. He dropped a quick kiss on the top of her head. "Nah, you're right. Plenty of time for that later."

"I can't wait to hit Bourbon Street," Stan said. "Always wanted to check that out."

"That will be better at night, though, for the real experience," Michael said.

The streets teemed with people. Writhing clusters congregated in front of famous buildings while people with other destinations in mind snaked through the obstructions.

A hand patted her shoulder.

She'd been recognized. Only a matter of time. She squeezed Sterling's hand and smiled widely before turning to greet her admirer.

No one stood behind her. Actually, that wasn't true. Plenty of people thronged the street, but they all peeled to the side and passed by. No one waited for her attention or seemed to notice her beyond more than a quick flick of the eyes and a smile.

"What's up, girl?" Rosie asked.

"I thought someone . . . It was nothing. I guess someone bumped against me."

Napoleon House sat on the corner of Chartres and St. Louis Street. Ceramic tiles spelled out the street names at the corner.

"These tiles in the street date back to the eighteen hundreds," Elise told them. "Horse-drawn carriages were the common mode of transportation. Tiled signs in the streets were easier for drivers to read."

The woman who greeted them at the restaurant promised to seat them quickly. "I just need to push some tables together. Give me a minute."

Her crew snapped photos and selfies, documenting the experience. Sterling pulled her close for their mandatory couple selfie. But his smile seemed forced.

"Cristal already liked my post!" TJ beamed, turning his phone, as if any of them required proof.

Sterling frowned at his phone before tucking it back into his pocket. "I'm with Kimberly. Let's all take a break from social media."

Rosie and Michael both shot her a look. She shrugged. He hadn't shared anything with her that would explain this shift in attitude.

Rosie looped an arm through hers and leaned close. "He not getting enough sleep? Maybe you need to let him rest."

"He's getting as much sleep as I am. I think."

"You don't know if he's sleeping?" Michael asked.

"Once I'm out, I'm out. He hasn't mentioned anything."

She shrugged as a waitress approached and directed them, "You can follow me."

She ran a hand over Sterling's back, suffusing him with gentle bursts of positive energy as they wound their way to the table. "Something bothering you?"

Sterling squeezed his temples. "Nothing for you to worry about. I'm the media specialist."

She dropped her arm to her side, confused. "And you do a phenomenal job. And now I don't have that added pressure."

"Exactly," he murmured.

He seemed to think that settled it. But she was still lost. "Exactly what?"

He shook his head and forced a smile, whispering, "Not right now."

Michael pulled a chair out. "Kimmy, sit." He gave her "the look" and gestured, communicating clearly the subtext: sit down, smile, and don't make a scene in public.

She sighed and sat, only then noticing every eye in the place on them. And how many of their fellow diners fumbled with phones. She smiled and waved.

"Are you going to connect with Napoleon's spirit?" someone called out.

She smiled. "Actually—"

Elise piped up, turning to face their fellow diners. "Actually, that would be impossible."

"Here we go." Stan laid down his menu and sat back with a sigh.

"Napoleon House was originally owned by Nicholas Girod, the mayor of New Orleans in the early eighteen hundreds. He planned to offer refuge to Napoleon Bonaparte, who was exiled at the time. He and a group of his friends gathered to discuss the plan regularly over drinks. Sadly, news of Napoleon's death reached them before they actually saw the plan through to fruition."

Stan leaned forward, elbows on the table. "Wait a minute. When did he die?"

"In 1821."

"So for years, they got together to drink and talk about bringing Napoleon to live here?"

"Correct."

"Uh-huh. That plot was just a reason to get together and drink. Just saying. And that's all printed right here on our menus. Which I'd like to order from." Stan looked around for their waitress.

"Do you feel any spirits?" someone yelled from across the room.

She glanced at Michael, who nodded his approval. Why not give her media specialist something to promote? Maybe that would cheer him up.

She stood and several people clapped. Chairs scraped the floor as their occupants adjusted for a better view. Clasping her quartz crystal, she closed her eyes and breathed, tapping her sixth sense and opening it to input from the spirit world. Mindful of her energy, she reached out, feeling for residual energy that could indicate a repeating loop or perhaps even an intelligent haunting.

A gentle nudge on her psyche alerted her that someone answered. She smiled. "Definitely a presence here."

Little gasps and quiet murmurs broke the silence of her audience.

"Nicholas? Nicholas Girod, is that you? Are you still here in your old home? Still hoping to rescue Napoleon?"

The nudge became a pull, as though it honed in. Gently, she opened her senses wider, inviting the connection, which was eagerly accepted. She sensed a thrill from the presence, distant but closing in. Something else thrummed beneath the top, giddy layer of energy that pulsed along the spirit realm. A malignant energy within the excitement. As though something tracked her.

Or hunted her.

With a gasp, she pulled away, closing herself off from the Nightshade. Quickly recovering, she smoothed her features and smiled. "I couldn't ascertain who it is, but we definitely have a spirit nearby."

More clapping filled the restaurant as she sat down and clasped her hands together under the table to hide how badly they shook. She should have told them it was Girod, that the owner continued to plot Napoleon's rescue from exile. But she couldn't bring herself to lie, even for a good story that would delight her audience.

Michael waved. "Thank you. Be sure to watch the New Orleans Christmas special this season to see how she resolves the investigation." He leaned over. "Okay, what was that?"

"The good news is that I seem to be able to connect with spirits again without being pulled into the Nightshade."

"That look on your face was not the result of good news. So what's the bad?"

"Whatever I connected with had . . . bad energy."

"Meaning what? I've never heard you say that before."

"I don't know how else to describe it. It felt ugly and slippery. Like it takes great pleasure in causing misery and suffering."

"Should we leave? We're eating with that hovering nearby?"

"That's the other thing I can't explain. It isn't *here*, here."

"Then where here is it?"

"I couldn't tell you. Somewhere in the Nightshade. And I had the feeling it doesn't know exactly where we are either. But it wants to. It wants to find us." She shivered.

Sterling took her hand. "It'll be okay."

Rosie didn't look convinced. "Maybe I need to keep more protective items nearby. If you're at risk of a psychic attack—"

"Attack?" Sterling shook his head. "She doesn't even know what she felt. Let's not get worked up over nothing."

Rosie wrinkled her nose. "Okay, what gives? You're supposed to be her biggest advocate. Why are you being weird?"

Leave it to Rosie to get right to the point.

Sterling shrugged. "No one worries about her more than I do. But I don't want everyone to get worked up over one foggy, unclear connection. A frenzy like that builds on itself and will only adversely affect her. You'll convince her some boogey-man is after her."

Rosie squinted one eye at him. "Do I look like I'm caught up in a frenzy? I'll stay close, ready to help. I hope you will too."

"That's never a question. Protecting her from imagined danger is still protecting her."

The waitress returned to take their orders. Kimberly hadn't even glanced at the menu but while the others ordered muffulettas, gumbo, jambalaya, and Po' boys, she scanned the options and zeroed in on a shrimp-remoulade-stuffed avocado. "Oh, this sounds delicious. And unique. I'll have this."

Sterling's forehead creased. "That won't be enough. Go ahead and bring a smoked Gouda grilled cheese for her too. And I'll have the seafood gumbo."

She sighed. Grilled cheese sounded heavy.

He nudged her with his leg. "Don't sigh at me. Protecting you from undereating is also a responsibility of mine."

The usual sparkle was back in his eye. She couldn't help but grin.

After the waitress left with their orders, she turned the discussion to the investigation. "I think this should be an excellent Christmas special. Don't you?"

"Yes, but what's up with that Flint character?" Michael asked.

"He's a total grouch," TJ said. "Cristal thinks it's funny how easily Macy handles him."

"But why put up with that?" Stan asked. "Talk about a hostile work environment."

"Cristal says he's all bluster. And always worried about money."

"Poor guy," Rosie said. "The hotel must not be doing well. Imagine working all your life to build up a business only to have it fall apart."

"The place is looking a little sad," Michael agreed.

"And he's too old to find a new job. He must really be struggling."

"If he doesn't have private retirement, you could be right," Sterling said. "People can't live off social security alone. If he didn't invest for retirement, that could be a factor in why he's still working. He clearly isn't there because he loves the work."

"Macy isn't too old," Stan said. "She could find a new job and not have to put up with that cranky old man."

"She must have her reasons," Kimberly said. "I didn't notice any distress on her part."

"And Cristal thinks he's hilarious," TJ said.

"Yep. You mentioned," Sterling said. He'd retrieved his phone and stared at the screen, tipping it away when she glanced toward it. His brow furrowed at whatever he saw.

What was up with him? Mindful of her audience, she pulled her gaze away. This was not the time to push for answers.

"Surely, Macy must—" A tugging at her psychic sense, the feeling someone watched her, turned her attention to the window. Goosebumps broke out across her arms.

A woman stared inside the restaurant, her gaze fixed intently on Kimberly. Blue eyes sent an icy chill down Kimberly's spine as they peered at her, piercing intensely as though the woman could see into her soul. The pale face registered shock, eyes widening as she realized Kimberly had caught her staring.

Without knowing why, Kimberly rose to her feet, drawn inexplicably by this woman's presence. This woman meant something, knew something. She could feel it. Dimly aware of her crew questioning her actions, Kimberly started for the door, eyes never breaking the locked gaze of this woman. She wasn't close enough to read the woman's spectrum or attempt to gauge what her intentions were. But she intended to find out.

The woman turned and moved swiftly away from the restaurant. Kimberly picked up her pace, bumping into a waiter in her haste to catch up with the mysterious woman.

She ran out the door, searching for the tall, pale woman in the crowds of people on Chartres Street.

The woman had disappeared.

CHAPTER THREE

Back inside the restaurant, Kimberly shrugged off questions from her concerned crew. "I saw a woman watching me and went to see what she wanted."

"You normally run *from* fans, not *to* them," Michael said. "What was different?"

"I can't explain it. She seemed to be . . . reading my spectrum. The way I can read others. I've never encountered anything like it. I wanted to see who she was."

"What happened?" Rosie asked.

"She saw me get up and ran off."

"That's weird," Rosie said. "Sterling? Still convinced nothing is amiss?"

Sterling laughed. "A woman saw Kimberly running toward her and ran off? That isn't weird. Who knows what she was thinking. Maybe just that some crazy lady was after her."

"Yes, I'm the crazy one," Kimberly said. "That woman was upset that I saw her watching me. I could tell. And she didn't want to tell me what she was up to."

"She could have been afraid of a confrontation," Sterling said. "No one wants to deal with that." His face clouded as he reached for his water glass.

What was up with him?

"Great," Michael said. "Apparently Kimmy has a stalker we'll need to be watching for while we're here."

"You guys don't know the half of it," Sterling muttered.

"The half of what?" Stan asked. "I, for one, will keep my eyes open for stalkers, Kimberly."

"We don't know for sure she was a stalker," Kimberly said. "After all, she didn't try to speak with me."

"No, she just Michael Myers'ed you. That's *way* better." Michael gave her his patented eye roll from hell.

"Without the knife," she reminded him.

"Or the creepy Shatner mask," Sterling added. "Seriously, guys, let's not blow things out of proportion."

A parade of waiters arrived, laden with plates bearing their food.

Kimberly took in the mountain of food. "Speaking of proportions, I did not need this grilled cheese. I'll try a bite because it looks amazing, but someone needs to share with me." She looked pointedly at Sterling, since he'd ordered it.

"Not sure I can finish all of my own food," Sterling said. "Fortunately, my suite has a refrigerator. You need to eat though."

His suite. A reminder that they did not share the same room this week.

After they'd eaten, too full of the delicious but rich dishes, they decided to take a longer route back to the hotel to walk off some of the calories as well as to see a bit of the city. They dropped a block closer to the Mississippi River and routed through Jackson Square. Edged on one side by a park and on the other by the St. Louis Cathedral, the Square pulsed with people.

Sterling gazed up at the towering spires of the white cathedral reflecting the afternoon sun. Artists drew caricatures and displayed drawings of famous people from history. Teenaged boys sat on the curb near the park, drumsticks clattering rhythms on overturned five-gallon buckets. An older man played the saxophone. Music blared from a stereo while a group of men danced along to the beat.

Stan covered his ears. "This is too noisy to be enjoyable."

"You always wanted to see New Orleans," Michael reminded him. "Here it is in all its glorious, noisy, fabulous, delicious wonderfulness."

"Can you imagine what it's like during Mardi Gras?"

"Oh my gosh, yes," Michael said. "I should bring Ian back for that."

While the cacophony rendered her sixth sense mute, Kimberly was drawn, fascinated, by the sheer number of professed psychics congregated in the square. All her life she'd tried to hide her gift and yet here were women and men at folding tables gladly offering Tarot card readings and palm readings, advice for the future, offering to reach out to loved ones already deceased.

One of them called out to her. "How about a Tarot card reading?"

She couldn't resist, eager to see what the woman would tell her. Taking Sterling's hand, she dragged him over to sit with her.

"Wait a minute, why am I part of this?"

"Do we want a couple's reading?" the woman asked.

"Sure!" she said at the same time Sterling replied, "No."

The woman shuffled her deck of cards. "Anything you especially want to know about?"

"This is nonsense, so I have no expectations of any outcome." Sterling crossed his arms.

The card reader handed the deck to Kimberly. "We focus on you, then. Shuffle the deck and think clearly about what insight you hope to gain."

She took the deck and split the cards in half, ruffling them together again as she wondered about her pregnancy scare.

"And you"—the woman stared down Sterling—"keep your bad juju to yourself."

"He can't!" TJ laughed. "He spews bad juju everywhere he goes."

Kimberly realized her crew had gathered to watch. Stan had a small hand-held camera recording the reading. She sighed. She would have preferred some privacy. That was not her life.

Sterling looked sideways at her. "This is how you want to spend your time?"

"It'll be fun," she said, less convinced it actually would be, now that her crew crowded close and Sterling was annoyed. She searched his eyes for a glimmer of amusement or reassurance, something in those dark depths to communicate his sour attitude was only for the show. But she didn't see it. She handed the deck back to the reader.

The woman spread the cards in front of her, fanning them out. "Let the cards draw you. Pick three cards and hand them to me one by one."

Kimberly did as instructed. The woman revealed her chosen cards and placed them on the table in front of her, then glanced up at Sterling. "Hmmm. Death. The lovers. And new beginnings."

Death? Someone was going to die? She waited for the woman to expand on the interpretation.

"I think the cards are telling you it's time to move on." The woman rolled her eyes toward Sterling and tipped her head, giving Kimberly a pointed look.

"Wait just a minute!" Sterling said.

"I did not choose the cards," the woman said with a shrug. "I only read them."

"You only invent stories about them. You could say anything. I think the cards mean it's time for Kimberly and me to start a new beginning. How about that?"

"You're not factoring in Death," the woman told him. "You're not trained to read."

Further antagonizing Sterling would not help his mood. She

took some bills from her purse and handed them to the woman. "Thank you."

Grabbing Sterling's arm, she turned to go. Walking the line between psychic and skeptic wasn't easy. Some of the things she found fascinating and fun only frustrated him. "I shouldn't have stopped. Let's get back for the interview and walk-through."

A woman passing by nodded a greeting, then did a double take. She stepped in front of Kimberly. "You're a true psychic. I can tell. Don't waste your time here. These are all amateurs capitalizing off tourists. You'll find what you're looking for here." The woman held out a card, then pressed it into Kimberly's hand.

She watched the woman continue on before looking at the card.

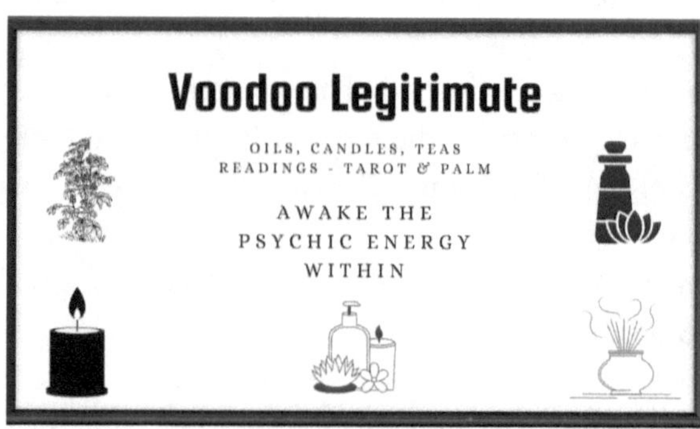

She tucked the card into her purse.

"What is that?" Sterling asked. "I could have told you not to waste your time on this."

"It's a card for a shop. Maybe I'll go by and see it while we're here."

"We can do all the tourist things we want later," Michael said. "First, let's start this investigation."

CHAPTER FOUR

How had that woman known she was psychic? Kimberly could not stop thinking back to that moment. *You'll find what you're looking for here.* She stared at the card. *Voodoo Legitimate.* Although she had no desire to practice Voodoo and honestly knew nothing about it, she rested the card on her nightstand, knowing she would go. Even if she had to sneak off by herself so no one in the crew knew. Maybe she'd see the woman who had approached her with the card there. Meeting and connecting with other psychics tantalized. So much so that she wished she could go right now. But everyone was assembling for the interview. No time.

Though she'd shared a room with Sterling during the last investigation, reservations at this hotel had been made booked prior to their change in relationship status. They each had their own room. That of course didn't preclude them from sharing. But Sterling had taken his room key and luggage and settled without a word. Nothing about changing them to a single room.

They were fine. Right? She had no reason to worry. They still weren't entirely sure she wasn't pregnant. Something must be bothering him, though, and he wasn't sharing it with her.

A knock at the door offered relief. That must be him. She

smoothed her features and smiled, clearing all evidence, she hoped, of the concern weighing her down.

Rosie waited at the door, though not with a matching smile.

"I was headed to your room for makeup," Kimberly reassured her, glancing at the time. "Sorry. Am I late?"

"No. Sterling showed up early and said he'd prefer for me to get him ready first. Didn't say anything else and left as soon as he was ready. You can tell me if it's none of my—"

"So something *is* wrong with him. He's being weird."

"He hasn't talked to you?"

"Not a word." She gestured to the room. "And you can see he's not here. Neither is any of his stuff. I don't get it."

"He said he would wait in his room until call. I hoped he meant here."

"Haven't seen him since we got back from lunch. I can feel something is off though. His spectrum isn't resonating in alignment."

"I suggest then"—Rosie thumped her makeup case on a desk—"that we prep you for the interview and walk-through here. He could be isolating to protect you since you've . . . you know, had some troubles with weakened abilities recently. If he's a mess, he could drain your energy and make things worse."

She nearly hugged Rosie. "Thank you. I hadn't thought about it that way." She sat in front of the mirrored desk, where Rosie spread out her makeup.

"Eh, I have way more experience. At least my years of disastrous relationships can benefit someone."

"Does that mean you and Lorenzo . . ."

"We're still talking. Trying to figure things out. I'm on the road all the time. He doesn't want to leave Eureka. Where does that leave us? Close your eyes."

She followed instructions, their routine second nature after years of working together. She held perfectly still as Rosie applied eyeliner. "What about that guy at the diner in Hannibal? The one who sent over a waffle?"

Rosie switched to a brush and smoothed shadow on her eyelids. "Craziest thing, girl. I went over to talk to him, right? And there I was, sitting across from this super-hot guy who was trying to flirt with me, and all I could think about was Lorenzo. Open for mascara."

Kimberly's heart melted. She held her eyes wide open. "Awww. How about that? You really do like him."

"Yep. I figure it'll work out somehow. It has to. I mean, no, he didn't quit his job and come join the show. But I didn't quit mine to go live in Eureka Springs either. I get it."

"We aren't kids anymore. We have lives. It complicates things."

"True." Rosie dusted her face with powder and dabbed some blush on her cheekbones. "And speaking of jobs, it's time for the interview. You are camera-ready and look fabulous."

She watched for Sterling in the hallway as they waited for the elevator but didn't see him until they reached the lobby. He stood by Michael, leaning close and talking softly, his phone tipped toward their director. Michael frowned. But when they saw her, Sterling hid his phone and moved away.

Her crew had set up around the Christmas tree in the lobby. Light stands with softboxes shone diffuse light on three chairs in front of the tree. Umbrellas hung between the lights. Stan and TJ tweaked the camera angles.

Michael led her to a chair.

"What was Sterling talking to you about?" she asked.

"If he wants you to know, he'll tell you."

Her eyebrows shot up. "Uhhh that sounds like I need to know."

Michael shook his head. "It's Sterling's to share, not mine. Let's put you here in this chair, farthest from the window in case we have sunlight bleeding through. And then Macy here."

"You let me worry about that," Stan said. "I won't let anyone look off from bad lighting. No shadows in my shoots."

Kimberly knew "anyone" referred to her. And she was okay with that.

"Sterling, you sit here by Kimberly—"

"What about me?" Cristal asked. "Where should I sit?"

Michael frowned. "I thought you didn't actually see anything."

"I heard it though!"

"Can't we record her experience?" TJ asked. "I'll grab another chair. You never know what might wind up being helpful."

Michael shrugged. "Whatever. Sure."

Kimberly knew they'd spend more time arguing about it than just letting the girl participate and nodded at Michael. She smiled at Sterling as he settled into his seat. His return smile did not reach his eyes. He looked away too quickly. She had to get him alone and encourage him to share whatever bothered him. His mood affected her own. Not good during an investigation. She couldn't afford distractions.

Michael held out his hands, palms out as if surveying the scene. "Of course, that throws off the balance now, but . . ." He rolled his eyes and adjusted them until satisfied with the arrangement. He stepped back and scrutinized the four of them. Finally, he nodded, stepped out of the shot, and counted her in. "And in five, four, three . . ."

She faced Stan's camera with her gravest look of concern as she introduced the investigation. "We're in New Orleans this week at the Cardinal Hotel. Hotel manager Macy Crawford called us to come help. Macy, tell us what happened."

"I went to the storage closet on Thanksgiving to get out Christmas decorations. At first I noticed the door kept opening by itself. I didn't think too much about it. But then when I went back again, I saw something. A spirit I guess. He—"

"I heard it!" Cristal interrupted. "I heard it saying Flint! Really!"

Kimberly nodded at Cristal. They could try to edit out the interruption if necessary. She'd have to see how the rest of the interview played out. "Flint. Interesting. Macy, please continue. You saw . . ."

"He looked really old. I had the feeling he was restless. Unhappy, you know? I heard chains rattling. And I also heard him say, 'Flint.' I'm positive."

"And Jeremiah Flint is the owner of the hotel?"

"Right! My boss."

"What did he say about the ghost you saw when you mentioned it to him?"

Cristal giggled. "I don't think you want her to repeat what he said."

Macy glanced at Cristal and nodded. "She's right. He doesn't believe in ghosts and basically said it was preposterous nonsense."

"But with different words." Cristal giggled again.

"How long has this activity been occurring? Cristal mentioned earlier that she'd just started working here when the Thanksgiving appearance startled you both. But you reached out to the show before then, didn't you? How long have you been aware of activity?"

"Oh, yes. I've been here ten years . . . wait, maybe it's longer now. Anyway, this was the first time I saw that particular ghost and the first time I heard the name Flint like that. But we always have activity around Christmas. Our guests notice it. It isn't just me. I have reports every year of personal items disappearing or moving, footsteps when no one is nearby. That sort of thing."

That hadn't been shared with them. Or at least not with her. "Wait. You always notice activity around Christmas? *Only* around Christmas?"

Macy nodded. "It starts right after Thanksgiving typically, increases all through December, and then goes quiet again after Christmas is over. And stays mostly quiet the rest of the year. I actually reached out to your show last year, but you were booked. And it didn't make sense to schedule anytime but the holiday season. Otherwise, I don't think you'd witness our haunting."

She kept her facial features smooth and controlled while a little bubble of excitement welled within. "You're telling me this is a recurring Christmas haunting?"

Macy nodded.

She turned to Sterling, oddly silent during the entire exchange. "Isn't that interesting, Sterling?"

"Very. I'm excited to see what we find here."

Well, he did manage to sound somewhat excited, even if his spectrum completely gave away his true feelings. She faced Stan's camera again. "In this truly unique haunting, the restless spirits seem to be targeting the hotel owner during the Christmas season. Stay with us tonight as we investigate the Christmas spirit."

"And cut!" Michael called. He grinned at her, one eyebrow raised, and gave her a thumbs up.

His look of delight confirmed he felt exactly as she did—this would be unlike any previous case they'd investigated.

CHAPTER FIVE

GRASPING HER QUARTZ CRYSTAL, Kimberly cleared her mind and breathed deeply. The walk-through helped her identify hotspots in a building prior to diving into an investigation. Normally. Not sure what to expect with her energy draining quickly and her psychic sense cutting in and out, anxiety spiked, sending her heartbeat racing.

Rosie powdered her face to ensure a soft matte finish. "How you doing?"

No one else in the lobby appeared remotely interested in their conversation. They were occupied with equipment—checking batteries, noting ambient sound and temperature levels for control samples later. Macy remained behind the counter, while Cristal followed TJ wherever he went.

She whispered anyway. "My anxiety is through the roof. What if I can't detect anything?"

"Put that out of your mind. Only positive thoughts to feed positive energy." Rosie draped a hematite necklace over her head. "For protection. And this"—she rubbed eucalyptus oil onto her wrists "to energize."

She breathed in the essential oil while TJ clipped a mic to her blouse.

"Wantland sound check," the younger camera operator said.

"Check one." She complied out of habit, no thought required. "Check, check."

Stan flashed a thumbs-up. "Sound level good."

Michael counted her in. "In five, four, three . . ."

She waited two beats and began, fingertips pressed together at waist level. "The Cardinal Hotel rests in the historic downtown New Orleans district. Every Christmas, a spirit reaches out from beyond, crossing planes to communicate. But what tidings does this spirit so desperately wish to convey? Are they glad? Or something more sinister? And why does this apparition only manifest at Christmas? I hope to reveal something helpful during our walk-through."

Moving slowly through the lobby, she stretched her senses wide, taking note of her energy level. At the first sign of decreasing energy, she would pull back.

Michael followed close behind her, KII in hand. They'd decided he would monitor the ambient room temperature and EMF levels around her so he could warn her immediately of any changes that could precede an apparition.

TJ, Stan, and Elise fanned out with cameras and digital voice recorders.

Elise began an EVP session, inviting the restless spirit to talk to her. "The recording device may capture your message even if we can't hear it in real time."

Kimberly made her way to the storage closet that Macy identified as the place she'd first seen the corporeal, full-body apparition on Thanksgiving. It wasn't much, but it was a start.

Sterling bumped her with an elbow. "I like watching you work."

"Good. Stay close. Just in case."

"You feeling okay?"

"So far, so good." She could've asked him the same question but opted to wait.

The static hiss of the KII trailed behind her as she

approached the closet. Good. Michael stayed close. His proximity comforted her.

Placing both hands on the door, she breathed deeply and reached out.

Talk to me.

The sullen door remained silent. She cracked it open, and an angry squeak filled the room. But the closet harbored nothing more than stacked boxes.

She stepped aside, allowing Stan to film the interior. Maybe in footage review they would discover a spirit lurking in the shadows that the naked eye could not detect.

As they moved on from the disappointing closet, Sterling rested a hand on her lower back. She sensed his emotional turmoil—fear, anxiety, confusion, and apprehension all churning within him. What had him twisted up in knots?

The rest of the crew caught up with them. Quick shakes of the head communicated no one had encountered anything of interest.

"Let's walk the halls," she suggested. "TJ take the lead with the FLIR, please. You'll have a better chance of catching a spirit if we're not contaminating the space with our images."

TJ cleared his throat and nodded, pushing ahead of them as though the fate of the world rested on his shoulders. She couldn't help but smile. His devotion to the show buoyed her spirits, boosting her energy.

Cristal whispered, "So cool!" but was smart enough to stay behind, out of the way.

Down the hall, up the elevator, down another hall. Nothing piqued her sixth sense. As they passed their own suites on the fourth floor, she stiffened, reminded again that she and Sterling didn't share one. Maybe he felt like they'd been moving too fast. And maybe they had. On the other hand, she still could not definitively proclaim herself not pregnant. She was late. And she hadn't told him yet. He'd seemed so happy with the idea of a baby, but maybe with some time and more thought, the harsh reality of what that would mean had—

The moment the elevator doors opened on the fifth floor, goosebumps rose on her arms. A chill passed through her as she felt herself urged forward.

"Kimmy?" Michael asked. The bond between them plus their years of experience meant he immediately recognized when she established a connection.

"Non malicious," she assured him, before she addressed the spirit. "I hear you. I'm listening."

This presence was the polar opposite of the one she'd sensed at Napoleon House. Where that one had struck her as male and inherently malicious—dare she say evil?—this one felt female and gentle, nurturing even. Compassion suffused her. She opened the aperture of her lighthouse, shining the welcoming beacon more intensely—and burning more fuel too.

"Can you hear me? Who are you?"

The soft outline of a woman appeared, a golden glow suffusing the image. The first time she'd seen a manifestation like this one, Kimberly knew exactly why people sometimes believed them to be angels. Her connection wasn't strong enough she could share unresolved memories. She could just make out the silhouette and a hint of the clothing.

"The apparition has slowly developed into a full-body, corporeal manifestation. Clothing indicates possibly 1960s."

Camera lenses whirred as her crew focused on the space she indicated. The area hummed with contained excitement.

The glowing specter came more fully into focus and beckoned her to follow.

"Stay on my six," she told them, following the spirit.

"We're not going anywhere," Stan assured her.

The hazy, golden figure drifted to a door and attempted to knock, but the filmy hand passed through the solid door.

Kimberly raised a fist to rap her knuckles on the door.

"Don't do that!" Cristal called. "That's Flint's room!"

The door flew open. The spirit disapparated.

Flint stood before them in a knee-length nightshirt, scowling. "What's all this noise? I'm trying to sleep!"

Kimberly heard Cristal choking back laughter as she fought a smile herself. Something about the grizzled old crank struck her as too ridiculous to be true.

"At six thirty at night?" Michael asked. "I understand beauty sleep but—"

"Can't a man have any peace and quiet in his own room?"

"I'm so sorry," Kimberly said. "I had no idea. The ghost led us here and—"

"Ghost! No such thing! Bad enough you're in my hotel but I will not have you in my room!" He slammed the door in her face.

Cristal giggled. "See what I mean? He's hilarious!"

"I don't know." TJ scrubbed at the back of his neck. "He must've had a pretty miserable life to be that unhappy."

"This guy doesn't have a house somewhere?" Rosie asked. "He lives here?"

Cristal shrugged. "He says it saves him money."

"His money problems must be worse than we realized."

"So is our ghost problem," Kimberly told them. "Because this room is the only hotspot in the entire building. And we're not allowed in it."

CHAPTER SIX

THE CREW RECONVENED in the hotel lobby after going to dinner. Kimberly, far too full from lunch to even think about food, had opted to stay and rest in her room. She would have preferred to focus this first night investigation on the one place she'd detected activity—Flint's room. But his adamant refusal left them with no other option than to fan out and attempt to engage the spirit elsewhere.

The desk night monitor stood where she'd become accustomed to seeing Macy and Cristal. She'd introduced herself to him but learned nothing more than his name, which he muttered without bothering to look up. "Bram."

At least she thought he'd said Bram. Maybe Brad? She snuck glances at him when he seemed engrossed with his phone. Easy, since he always was. Alarmingly pale with jet-black hair. Frighteningly thin, so undernourished he looked almost sickly. What did Flint pay his employees? Though he seemed distracted and uninterested in them, the young man appeared perfectly content and wide awake.

"You got stuck with the nightshift, huh?" she finally asked. Something about him intrigued her.

He flicked his eyes at her. "I *applied* for the nightshift." His low but silky voice mesmerized.

"You work all night regularly?"

He nodded.

"What's your secret? I'm up all night frequently, but I'm chronically exhausted and have an almost constant headache. And I get breaks between investigations. You look perfectly fine. How do you manage it?"

"Creatures of the night don't manage it. We simply are."

Okay, that was weird even for her. "You're saying you are truly nocturnal?"

"Why not?" He looked at her directly, his black eyes sending a shiver down her spine.

"How do you manage? Shop for groceries, run errands, pay bills? What if you needed to move?"

"I admit accomplishing such things used to present a much greater challenge. These days, everything is online. Grocery stores stay open twenty-four hours. If I desire a new dwelling or companionship, I simply seek out businesses that cater to those like myself." He went back to his phone.

She stood, mouth hanging open, but unable to answer. He spoke as if from experience yet seemed far too young to know how things "used to be."

Rosie shook her head. "Smooth, girl. Nicely done. Handled that like a pro."

"I just—" She went to the desk. "I'm sorry but you've intrigued me. I've always felt more productive during the night. Until I pass out from exhaustion. But I have to get up and function during the day. I have appointments and responsibilities and—"

"Don't." Bram or Brad or whatever he'd said his name was shrugged at her like the answer was so simple a child could see it.

"Don't what?"

"Don't allow your schedule to be manipulated by others. Accommodate only yourself. Make them come to you."

That was easy for this night clerk to say. Of course his customers came to him. No one had another choice, and he served a purpose, taking a shift most people would detest. He didn't have interviews and guest appearances and clients to meet with and a team of people to consult with, many of whom preferred eight o'clock meetings first thing in the morning.

"Kimmy?" Speaking of responsibilities, she turned to find Michael frowning at her. "Maybe we can at least pretend to be productive?"

"Of course. Sorry." She took note of the young man's name tag. Bram. Huh. That was his name.

Bram looked up long enough to lift one eyebrow and tell her, "No one can use you as a doormat unless you lie down at their feet."

Hardly fair. Michael wasn't walking all over her by asking her to focus on the work she was paid to do. He was completely justified.

Right?

She returned to Rosie and whispered, "Oof. I know it takes all types, and I know we ourselves are considered on the fringe, but he seems extreme fringe compared to our highly functional fringe."

Rosie shrugged. "Well, he has nothing to do with our investigation so he can stand there and be as fringe as he'd like. Won't affect you."

Rosie was correct. She turned to Michael. "Okay, task master, what have you found?"

He held out the KII. "Not a darned thing."

"There's nothing down here," Bram murmured, that silky voice soft and sure.

"Why do you say that?" she asked. Did he know something he wasn't sharing?

He stared only at his phone. "You said that. Trust yourself."

What was up with this guy? Was he also psychic? Drawn to him, she moved back to the desk, hoping to get close enough that she could read his spectrum and his aura.

Sterling hooked an arm around hers. "Come on. He's right. Let's go to the fifth floor where you reported feeling activity. I'll text Stan to meet us."

"But—"

"We'll be quiet." He guided her to the elevator and pressed the UP button.

She looked over her shoulder at Rosie, who lifted her eyebrows in a silent question. She shrugged a response, *No idea.*

The moment the elevator doors closed she voiced her thoughts. "It's like that guy knows I'm psychic. How do so many people in this city know that?"

Sterling stared at her like, *Really?* "Gosh, I don't know. Maybe because you're a nationally recognized psychic from a television show?"

"It's not that. None of the people who approached me acted like excited fans. This is something different."

"I don't like the look of that guy at the desk. Please keep some distance. He looks like bad news."

What did that mean? "I didn't sense any negative energy or ill intent." Though in truth, she hadn't noticed anything at all. She should have asked Rosie to recharge her. Again.

"Please? For me?"

She heard genuine concern in his voice and felt a wave of anxiety. Which meant she should have felt something from Bram. Strange. But she wasn't about to share that with Sterling.

"Okay. But I'd like to know what's up with you. Are we okay?"

His eyes churned under a furrowed brow. He took a deep breath. "I—"

The elevator opened. Stan waited for them in the hallway.

She needed to know what he'd been about to say because it obviously wasn't going to be, "Oh, yeah, we're fine! My unusual moodiness has nothing to do with us!" But as she followed him off the elevator and into the hallway, she could tell he wasn't going to continue the conversation in front of Stan.

Especially since they now hovered in front of Flint's room and didn't want to alert the old grouch to their presence.

"Anything?" she whispered to Stan.

"Not a blip. No audio or visual disturbances. You?"

She shook her head. "The building is cold."

"Totally dead," he agreed. "I'm glad you decided to come back to the source. This haunting clearly revolves around Flint."

"Yes, but a lot of good that does us if he discovers us here. He might decide to throw us out."

"He can't be that harsh," Stan said.

Sterling lifted an eyebrow. "You sure about that?"

She sighed. "Based on his previous behavior? I think I'd have to say—"

A muffled moan triggered her senses, setting them on high alert. "Did you two hear that?"

Sterling didn't answer but went straight to Flint's door, leaning close. "That came from his room, didn't it?"

"Can you hear—"

"Shhh." He held out a hand.

Stan stepped back, framing the shot to best capture it in case something of interest unfolded.

Another moan, louder this time, emanated from the room.

"Definitely coming from in here," Sterling confirmed.

She squeezed in beside him. "Does he sound sick? Or hurt?" Had the golden apparition from earlier been trying to warn them of impending doom? She pictured the older man suffering through cardiac arrest, unable to call anyone or even to cry out for help. She grabbed the doorknob and twisted. The stubborn door rattled but refused to budge.

Yet another moan.

"Okay, that's enough. He may throw us out, but I have to know if he needs help."

She raised a fist, ready to beat on the door.

"I'm calling the front desk," Sterling said, pulling his phone from a pocket.

Flint's voice paused her fist. "Don't! Please, I beg you! Leave me in peace!"

"What the hell is going on in there?" Stan muttered. "Wantland crew! Fifth floor stat. Flint's room. We have a problem. Repeat, we have a problem!"

She'd forgotten the others carried walkie-talkies to stay in touch. Crackled replies followed the call for help.

"Roger!"

"En route."

"Already at the elevator!"

Everything happened at once, and it seemed to Kimberly as if time slowed to a crawl.

Flint's door opened behind her. She spun around and her heart skipped a beat. The man, still clad in his nightshirt, shook violently, his face ashen and pale as death. He seemed unable to breathe.

"Help me!" he gasped.

A split-second later, the elevator pinged and opened, and her crew tumbled out.

"Does anyone know first aid?" she screamed. Except she didn't scream. As if in a nightmare, she struggled to make a sound, voice barely a whisper. But the man needed help, and someone needed to check him—

"What the hell is that?" Sterling had not lost his voice.

She whirled again.

A specter loomed behind Flint, dwarfing the tiny man, draped in chains and padlocks and dragging heavy chests behind him. A metal clank echoed through the building with each step as the dusty, chalk-faced, desiccated figure clunked closer.

The jawbone crackled in protest of being forced open. "Fliiiiint."

The gravelly voice set Flint shaking harder, curling further into himself as he turned slowly and peered over his shoulder at the resurrected nightmare behind him.

A moth escaped the cracked, decaying lips, fluttered toward Flint, and landed on his shoulder.

He screamed and collapsed to the floor.

Stunned silent, the crew gathered around him. Stan ascertained he was breathing and found a pulse while Sterling called Bram and instructed him to summon an ambulance quickly.

Michael folded his hands together and pressed them to his forehead. "Oh, thank God. Someone please tell me we got every second of that."

CHAPTER SEVEN

BREAKFAST the next morning was more subdued than it should have been, considering they went to the famous Café Du Monde in the French Quarter. Flint's terror and collapse had shaken them all. Unlike Flint, who recovered enough by the time the ambulance arrived to bluster at the first responders that he was fine and they could show themselves right back out, Kimberly worried about what the incident meant to their investigation. On the one hand, Flint had grumbled he guessed they could stay on and continue their work, but on the other, she wondered how dangerous this spirit they were dealing with would prove to be. She couldn't handle seeing the older gentleman frightened to death again. What if she wasn't strong enough to handle this spirit?

Sterling took her hand. "Hey. What are you thinking about?"

"Last night. When that spirit scared Flint, he looked . . ." She shook off the concern and focused on her surroundings. "Just worried about him."

She, Sterling, Rosie, and Elise sat at tables while Michael, TJ, and Stan had gone to order. A quartet of musicians on the sidewalk entertained the crowded café with jazz music, the singer sounding as much like Louis Armstrong as anyone she'd ever heard.

People packed the open-air coffee shop. But between the couples at tables and the bodies pressed against the rail, clapping and cheering for the musicians, and the new arrivals threading their way to the front to place orders, Kimberly saw remnants of past customers and waitresses, spirits bleeding through from the spirit realm. One dapper gentleman occupied a seat at a table where a young man and woman gazed adoringly at one another, laughing at each other's comments. But the man stared directly at Kimberly and doffed his hat when she noticed him. He knew. He could tell she saw him. She lifted her hand to return the greeting.

Sterling looked over his shoulder. "Did you see someone you know?"

"Oh. No, I don't know him. Just a . . ." Somehow, she didn't feel like discussing her awareness of spirits with him this morning.

The guys returned with trays laden with cups of coffee and small white bags.

"Café au lait and beignets for everyone!" Michael declared. "It's what they're known for so we're all sampling the famous goodness. Kimmy, just eat it. Berries and yogurt are not on the menu here."

She scowled. She'd already intended to try the fried dough sprinkled with powdered sugar. Didn't need the snark today.

As Michael handed out their breakfast, Elise filled them in on the history of the place. "Did you know that Café Du Monde has been in this same place and operational since 1862? The name means 'the café of the world' or 'the people's café' and the owners still use the same recipes that have been in place since the café first opened."

She peeked into one of the bags at the little square-shaped doughnuts, heavily sprinkled with powdered sugar. She reconsidered eating the unhealthy confection but knew everyone would give her crap if she didn't at least try it. She could eat healthy the rest of the day to make up for it.

"The coffee looks like it comes just the way you like," Sterling said, picking up his cup and taking a sip.

"It does have milk," Elise confirmed, "though the coffee is mixed with chicory. They're famous for their blend, which resulted from a coffee shortage during the Civil War. It was a matter of stretching the limited supply as opposed to mixing it up purely for the impact on the flavor. But the combination turned out to be a hit. People liked it, so they kept making their unique blend, and now they're famous for it."

Intrigued, Kimberly tried it herself. She could detect a rich, dark note. Not unpleasant at all. She blew on the hot brew and drank deeply, the caffeine from the coffee and sugar from the beignet coursing through her system. She'd experience a sugar rush if she ate too much. Which would be followed by the inevitable crash.

Her skin prickled and not due to the caffeine or sugar. She sensed someone looking at her and glanced over the rim of her coffee cup. She nearly choked when she spotted a woman standing on the sidewalk staring at her. The moment Kimberly met her eye, the woman startled, turned, and hurried away.

Kimberly set her cup on the table and stood, peering after the woman, nearly confident this was the same woman she'd seen at Napoleon House. She made her way to the rail surrounding the dining area full of tables, then wriggled through a group gathered to enjoy the jazz band. The Louis Armstrong impersonator wailed about Mack the Knife, as she pushed through a throng of tourists.

The woman had disappeared. No sign of her anywhere. She returned to the confused crew.

"What was that about?" Michael asked, helping himself to one of her uneaten beignets.

"I'm not sure. I saw a woman staring at me again, but she ran off when I tried to see what she wanted. Why does that keep happening?"

Michael shrugged as he bit into the beignet and chewed as he answered. "Hello? Famous celebrity. Nothing unusual about that."

"Which is what I told you too," Sterling reminded her.

"No, this isn't anything to do with the show. She isn't an excited fan. Fans want to talk to me. They don't run from me."

"Fair enough," Michael said.

"Besides, she triggered my sixth sense. I felt her there before I saw her. Something is different here. I feel like everyone I encounter in New Orleans knows something about me. But they aren't telling me." She pulled the Voodoo Legitimate card from her pocket. "Like the woman who handed me this card. She told me she could tell I was a real psychic and said I would find what I'm looking for here."

Sterling took the card and examined it. "Well, recognizing you from your show would explain the psychic reference. And maybe that's a marketing ploy, ya know? She may approach lots of people in that square and lure them to this shop with that line. What does Voodoo have to do with being psychic?"

"I still want to find this place and see what they have there."

"It's probably a lot of tourist bait. Exactly what the woman accused the card reader of."

"I still want to go."

Rosie polished off a beignet and rested a sugary hand on hers. "I'll go with you, girl. So what if it turns out to be nothing but a tourist trap? We should do some touristy stuff. It'll be fun! Besides, we want to look into some alternative healing options for you. If this place is the real deal, maybe they'll have something that can help."

"I didn't say I wouldn't go," Sterling said. "I don't want you to get your hopes up and be disappointed. That's all."

Elise took the card and tapped on her phone. "It isn't far

from here. We could walk there right now on our way back to the hotel."

"Let's do it!" Rosie said.

She drained the remainder of her coffee and gathered her things. Sterling held her light jacket for her, helping her slide into it.

"Doesn't exactly feel like Christmas-time here, does it?" he asked.

"No, but I prefer this temperate weather to shivering through a foot of snow. Besides, the whole city is decorated for the holiday. Still looks very festive."

He rested his hands on her shoulders and murmured in her ear. "Cold weather would be a good excuse to curl up by a warm fire, though. We need to do that someday."

She shivered despite the relatively warm temperature. "Sounds really nice."

As if they'd heard them mention the holidays, the jazz quartet broke into "Christmas in New Orleans" and they all stopped to listen, cheering along with the crowd as it ended. Kimberly dropped a twenty into the tip bucket. The drummer nodded to her. "Merry Christmas, ma'am."

"See? Not everyone recognizes me," she told Sterling.

The entire crew joined her when she opted to walk to Voodoo Legitimate.

"I want to see as much of New Orleans as possible," Stan remarked. "Once the baby is born, I don't know how much traveling I'll be able to do for a while."

That sounded like a hint her primary camera operator would be leaving the show in the not-too-distant future. How would they manage without him? She couldn't imagine.

Elise directed them along the streets. "It's only a five-minute walk at most! Just down and over a couple of blocks."

Shops lined both sides of the street. T-shirts, mugs, keychains, and typical souvenirs filled the windows next to more specific items like Mardi Gras beads and masks. Artwork and antiques filled some shops. Candy stores were common too. As they passed a store dedicated to pralines, which the sign proclaimed to be a New Orleans tradition, she made a mental note to come back and try one.

Once they turned off Decatur, old homes sat sedately behind tall walls, hiding from view, but peeking over just enough to make their stately presence known.

And then they found Voodoo Legitimate. If they hadn't been watching Elise's directions on her phone, they could have passed right by without seeing the small sign etched with the name. The old wooden door remained closed, locked.

"It doesn't open until ten o'clock," Elise said. "Sorry. I should have noticed that when I pulled up the directions. Too excited to see it, I guess."

Kimberly peered in the small windows flanking the door, hoping to catch a glimpse of whatever the woman in the street thought she needed and would find here, but the gloomy darkness that shrouded the interior revealed only shadows and vague outlines.

Rosie tried to peek inside too. "I hope they have something healing in there. Wish we could see inside now and know for sure. I'm a little excited. I'd love to learn some new techniques to enhance your senses."

"Me too," she agreed, though she strongly suspected that wasn't what the woman hinted at. As important as healing was, that wasn't what Kimberly needed most.

"We can come back this afternoon," Michael assured her. "After footage review. Okay?"

"Yes, okay." She peeled herself away from the fascinating place, reluctant to leave. No question that she'd come back. Something in that space called to her, and she intended to find out what it was.

Her skin prickled as she walked away. And she knew somehow that her life was about to change.

CHAPTER EIGHT

MACY AND CRISTAL waited behind the counter when the crew returned for footage review, greeting them with wide smiles.

"Hi, TJ!" Cristal waved furiously.

"Hey." Her young camera operator flushed. It was adorable.

"How did it go last night?" Macy asked. "Bram indicated you guys had some excitement."

"We did," Kimberly confirmed. A young girl sat in the lobby, curled in a chair with a book, though currently the arrival of the television crew had won her attention. Warm brown eyes peered over the top of the book. "Flint refused medical attention though. I hope he's okay."

Macy smiled. "This is my daughter Abby. Abby, this is Miss Wantland, the lady I told you about."

Abby closed the book, and Kimberly noticed dark circles under her eyes—very dark circles. "Hello, Miss Wantland." The girl's voice indicated she struggled to speak, as if she couldn't catch her breath.

A health issue. Out of nowhere the words crossed her mind, and somehow she knew this was a very sick little girl in front of her. Interesting. That was a new development. She didn't normally go around diagnosing illness with her sixth sense.

Macy glanced at the clock. "Mr. Flint will be down soon, Abby. Go ahead and shift behind the desk, please."

Abby nodded, unfolded her legs, and stood. A sudden cough racked the girl's frame, a thick, wet cough that left her bent over, wheezing for air.

Michael's features scrunched into a frown. "Is she okay? Is she—"

"Not contagious," Macy assured them, hurrying to Abby's side. The woman thumped her back a few times. "Take your time."

Abby settled into a beanbag behind the counter, nestling in with her book. The girl coughed again, sounding like she might bring up a lung.

"You're sure?" Michael asked.

"Michael, please." Kimberly remembered how awkward she'd felt, ostracized as a girl, never feeling like she fit in. She stepped closer to Macy. "Can I help? Do you need anything?"

Macy shook her head. "She's having a rough day. Wasn't sure she'd make it through school. She's quiet, won't disturb anyone."

Abby caught her breath and spoke over the top of the counter. "I have primary ciliary dyskinesia."

"That's a mouthful," Sterling said, joining Kimberly at the desk.

"Managing it takes some effort," Macy said. "With any luck, she won't develop an infection and need a trip to the doctor this time. Or, God forbid, a hospital stay."

"This happens a lot?"

Macy nodded. "She was frequently quite ill as an infant— sinus infections, ear infections, chronic cough. Fortunately, my pediatrician took it seriously and sent us to a specialist who diagnosed it. Unfortunately, there's no cure, we can only—"

The elevator pinged and Flint stepped out.

Abby gave a short gasp, curled low into her beanbag behind the counter, and opened her book wide. As if to hide.

"Mr. Flint!" Macy greeted him. "How are you this morning? I hear you had some excitement last night."

"Hmph!" Flint glared at the *Wantland* crew. "You people are still here, I see."

Michael lifted an eyebrow and scowled like, *Can you believe this guy?*

Kimberly went to his side. "We wanted to make sure you were okay. And of course finish the investigation."

"Investigation. Bah! No such thing as ghosts!"

Cristal giggled.

"You seemed pretty upset last night when—"

The door opened and a young man strode into the lobby. "Hello, Uncle Jeremiah!"

Flint squinted in his direction. "Oh. Jeremy. Hello."

Jeremy threw his head back and laughed deeply. "Whoa, now, Uncle! Don't get too excited to see me."

Flint shuffled his feet. "Yes, well . . ."

Jeremy pulled his crabby uncle into a hug. "I know you're secretly delighted to see me! You just don't want anyone to see how happy you are."

Flint scowled and leaned away. "All right, now, get off me."

"Ahhh, my favorite curmudgeon. And quite a big crowd here for the holiday season. Good, good." The young man's eyes stopped when he saw Kimberly.

"Wait. Aren't you—"

"How are you, Jeremy?" Macy asked. She lifted her eyebrows and glanced beside her, appearing to be signaling the young man. "Ready for the holidays?"

"Indeed I am! Christmas is the most wonderful time of the year!" Jeremy, dressed in slacks and a button-up, twirled in a circle as he crossed the lobby and leaned on the counter. "How are you, Miss Macy? Oh! And Miss Abby too! Hello down there!"

Macy closed her eyes. Kimberly understood what Jeremy had not. And he had given away the hidden girl.

Flint stepped behind the counter. "What is this? I've told you not to bring your daughter. This is a hotel, not a daycare!"

"Mr. Flint, please. She's having an episode today and I couldn't send her to school. I need to keep an eye on her in case she gets worse and can't breathe. She won't—"

"Then you should have stayed at home with her!"

"Mr. Flint, you only give us a few days of sick time each year, and you know I already used my days up when Abby was in the hospital."

"Then stay home and use sick leave with no pay."

Stan muttered, "Old guy or not, I'm about to drag him outside and kick his ass. What is this?"

"Mr. Flint, I'm still struggling to pay off her hospital bills. I cannot afford to miss a day of work. Please, she won't—"

"What have I told you? No children at work! I could fire you right now and—"

Jeremy's mouth dropped open. "Uncle! It's nearly Christmas! Don't threaten to fire your best employee! You know you don't mean that."

"I do mean it! I'll do it! What difference does it make if it's Christmas or not? Anyone who won't work deserves to be fired. And then you can come work for me instead."

Jeremy laughed his big belly laugh. "Thanks, but no thanks, Uncle. I'll stick to designing webpages. Miss Macy is here working, so stop threatening to fire her. You need to be nice to her and appreciate her, or she may come to her senses and leave you. I don't know anyone else who would tolerate you the way she does."

"Right?" Michael whispered.

"Abby won't disturb a soul, Uncle. You know that better than I do. Have some compassion for once in your life."

Flint grumbled, "Compassion never paid my bills."

"It never cost you one cent either, I'd wager. Leave Abby be. You know you don't really want to send Macy home." When Flint replied only with a pinched mouth, Jeremy nodded as if the entire thing were settled. He turned to Michael, then stared at Sterling and Kimberly. "You . . . you guys are—Why is *The Wantland Files* staying at my uncle's hotel?"

"They're investigating, Jeremy," Macy told him.

"Investigating? You mean ghosts?" Jeremy laughed. "Nothing haunts my uncle except the ghosts of his bad decisions. Speaking of which. Uncle, I'm here to invite you to Christmas dinner with Nomi and me. She's a fantastic cook, and we'd love to have you join us."

"Christmas dinner. Bah. I'll be busy working. I don't have time for frivolous nonsense."

"Uncle, of course you do. That's only an excuse, and you know it. I know you never warmed to Nomi, but that's because you didn't give her a chance. If you'd only spend time with us and get to know her—"

"I said no! I'll stay here on Christmas like always."

"Doing nothing, like always, when you could be with your only family. Family who loves you, despite everything."

Flint mumbled again, but Kimberly couldn't tell what he said. She could feel the heightened emotions simmering in the room, however—frustration and remorse and eagerness all floating over a heavy undercurrent of sadness. Flint especially struggled with his emotions, pulled between a desire to connect and years of cold indifference. Why couldn't he simply accept the gesture? No one needed to work every day of the year. Perhaps embarrassment at his financial situation kept him from connecting with his family. If he saw the holiday meal and gifts as a gesture of charity, pride could hold him back.

Jeremy smiled and hugged his uncle again. "I couldn't catch that, but I'm going to assume you've said you'll think about it. The offer stands, Uncle, and nothing would brighten our Christmas more than you spending it with us. Goodness knows how many Christmases we may have left."

Flint grumbled again.

"And now I must be off," Jeremy announced with a wave. "Good luck, ghost hunters."

"Nice to meet you," Kimberly told him, because that seemed like the right thing to say.

"Good luck, Saint Macy. I know my uncle appreciates you, whether he says so or not. Who knows, maybe he will even leave the place to you some day. If you can last that long."

Flint spluttered. "Leave my hotel to . . . You know I'll never do that! Why would I? You'll come around some day and take over—"

"No, Uncle. Let that idea go. I don't know the first thing about running a hotel and have no desire to learn. You must learn to appreciate what you have instead of longing for what you don't."

"Thank you for stopping by, Jeremy." Macy waved in return, though her smile struck Kimberly as more forced than genuine. She muttered, "Great. Now he'll be in a mood the rest of the day."

"You mean this *isn't* him in a mood?" Michael asked. "He gets worse?"

Flint hobbled to the counter after his nephew left and stared at Abby, quivering in her beanbag. "Hmph!"

Michael clapped his hands together. "Great. Shall we start on footage review? Let's see what images we captured last night. And voices if we got lucky."

Flint turned away from Macy and Abby and pulled himself to his full height. "I'll come with you. I want to see what you consider 'proof' of ghosts."

Michael rolled his eyes. "Oh, lovely. This ought to be great fun."

"It's my hotel," Flint said. "I want to know what's happening."

Michael held out a hand to the elevators. "Let's get to it then."

Kimberly patted his arm as she passed him. "We've lived—"

"—through worse. I know. You keep saying that, but I'm not so sure. This guy is definitely trying to make this the worst investigation ever."

Thinking about the mysterious woman who seemed to be watching her for some reason, Kimberly suspected it would definitely be one of the strangest.

CHAPTER NINE

THE CREW SET up footage review in Michael's suite, which proved the perfect spot for it. The space held a long table, suitable to hold all the equipment, plus a small kitchenette off to the side. Michael's bedroom and bathroom were beyond the communal gathering space, allowing privacy if he should need it.

Rosie had searched cabinets and discovered a kettle, which she promptly put on the stove to boil while she dashed back to her room for tea.

Kimberly circled the table, watching snippets of footage, waiting for them to reach the point in the night when Flint cried out for help. She'd seen a spirit menacing him. Would anyone else be able to see evidence of that though? And could they determine what the spirit wanted?

For that matter, she remained unclear which spirit to focus on. No one had mentioned a female spirit, yet she'd seen a woman with a golden aura. Maybe something in footage review would give her a clue to that spirit's identity.

Flint sat in a chair, arms crossed, grunting periodically. He seemed unlikely to cooperate with them as they pieced together how to offer resolution so the spirit could rest in peace. Frankly, she wondered why anyone hung around the crabby old man, though if anyone deserved to be haunted, it would be Flint.

TJ called her over. "I may have something."

"Ha!" Flint scoffed. "Stuff and nonsense."

Stan threw a glance at Flint and apparently couldn't hold his tongue any longer. "Didn't seem like nonsense last night when you called for help. You looked pretty scared then." Her camera operator played the recording of Flint, shaking and terrified, when the door to his room had opened.

"Pah!" Flint waved a hand. "I must've had a nightmare. Probably had indigestion. I'll take an antacid before bed tonight."

"Indigestion, huh?" Stan chuckled. "That why you passed out from fright?"

"I didn't!" Flint insisted.

Stan replayed the segment that contradicted Flint's statement. "Yeah, ya didn't, which is why we panicked and called an ambulance. Cuz we all imagined this."

"Pah! It wasn't a ghost!"

Sterling looped an arm around Kimberly's waist. "Please tell me I didn't used to look like this."

She considered, bobbing her head as if deliberating. "Well . . ."

"Hey, now!"

"Even on your worst days, right at the beginning, you were never that bad or that grumpy."

"Pinkie swear?" He held out a crooked little finger, his eyes seeking something in hers. Understanding? Forgiveness?

She curled her little finger around his, wishing he would talk to her. "Pinkie swear."

Stan yanked the headphones off his head. "Whoa. Got something. Listen!"

"Wait," TJ said. "We didn't listen to what I—"

But Stan clicked PLAY on the isolated audio.

"Fliiiint . . ."

Every head in the room swung in the direction of Stan's computer.

"Was that one of us?" Sterling asked. "Maybe calling his name or . . ."

"That sound like one of us to you?"

She leaned over Stan's shoulder. "Play that again? What happens when we hear the voice?"

She focused on the visual recording carefully. As the prolonged, raspy voice crackled the name, she saw a pair of wings flutter briefly. "There! Isolate that for me?"

"What is that?" Michael squinted at the screen.

"Looks like a blip on the recording," Sterling said. "Nothing."

"I hoped the cameras would capture more," she admitted, "but I saw an apparition in his room. It was in a state of decay and dragging chains. I also saw a moth fly out of its mouth—"

"You saw that? You saw the moth?" Flint sat forward, the blood draining from his face.

She nodded. "It landed on your shoulder."

"You couldn't have . . . but I imagined that. Or dreamed it!"

"So, you did see a ghost," Rosie said. "And then you told Kimberly she was full of poppycock. Which I assume means what I think it means."

Flint jumped to his feet. "She couldn't have. I couldn't have seen him."

"Him? You know who the ghost is, and you won't tell us?"

"Because it can't be, I tell you! He's been dead now seven years."

"Who?" she asked.

"Bo. Short for Ichabod. My old partner, Ichabod Morley."

"And he went by Bo?"

"He couldn't very well go by Ichabod, could he? Kids and adults alike tormented him viscously, cursed with a name like that. What else could he shorten it to? Ich? Bod? At least Bo sounded like Beau. French. No one thought twice about it around here."

"Your . . . partner?" Michael asked.

"Right. For decades. But he died seven years ago. Couldn't have been him."

"It absolutely could have been his ghost. Did you two have any unresolved business? Did he die suddenly, perhaps without the opportunity to put his affairs in order?"

"Sudden? Yes. You can ask Macy. He had a heart attack while yelling at her. That baby of hers was sick again or some such nonsense. You know people try anything to get out of working. Something for nothing."

Kimberly stepped closer. "Nonsense? You do know her daughter has a potentially fatal illness that needs to be monitored and managed, don't you?"

He looked directly at Michael, then tipped his head at Kimberly. "You know what I mean."

Michael's upper lip curled, his brow twisted into knots. "No. I have no idea what you mean."

TJ intervened. "Macy saw Bo. Ms. Wantland saw Bo. Mr. Flint saw Bo even though he doesn't want to admit it—"

"And I believe this is the moth," Stan said, gesturing to his monitor. "This is the best frame, and I isolated and enlarged the image. Even Sterling will have to admit—"

"That's a moth. I'll give you that. But a moth in the room doesn't mean much."

"Except when it disappears a few frames later." Stan advanced the recording. Once the phantom moth lit on Flint's shoulder, it disappeared. And Flint fainted.

Sterling shook his head. "Except the camera pans to follow Flint. The moth could have simply flown away, and you missed it."

Stan sat forward, clicking the mouse rapidly, zooming in on Flint's shoulder.

TJ inserted himself into the silence. "Could you guys just—"

"Look!" Stan said. "This frame, moth. The next frame, no moth. It doesn't fly away. It vanishes."

Sterling squinted and leaned over Stan's shoulder. "Play it again?"

Stan obliged, over and over.

Flint leaned sideways, craning his neck, apparently unable to resist. Wasn't that about par for the course? Even the staunchest skeptics turned into rubberneckers anytime her crew managed to record something impossible to explain. Didn't mean they'd acknowledge it or admit to possibly being wrong though.

"What do you think, Wakefield?" Flint asked. "It was just a moth, right? Flies away?"

"Well . . ." Sterling rubbed his face. "I'm tired. My eyes hurt. I don't think I can—"

"Oh come on," Stan said, playing the recording again. "It's here. It's gone. He collapses. In that order. Yes, I had to enlarge and go frame by frame. Not any different than using a microscope to enhance something too small to see with the naked eye—"

"I don't agree with that," Sterling said.

"Big surprise. Nevertheless—"

"What if I concede?" Sterling asked. "If I say I see a moth that does appear to vanish, then what? How does that forward our investigation?"

TJ lost his cool. "Guys! Stop bickering and listen!"

Her younger camera operator played an isolated audio clip, mostly a garbled hiss of static. She recognized the questions she'd asked in front of Flint's room, before the golden spirit had appeared.

"That's what you've been fussing about? More poppycock!" Flint huffed.

"I heard an anomaly, so I slowed it down." TJ clicked again.

She heard her voice on the recording.

"Non malicious. I hear you. I'm listening."

Nothing.

"Can you hear me? Who are you?"

A soft voice broke through the white noise between Kimberly's slowed-down questions.

Maud.

Flint fell back in his chair, clutching at his chest. "Maud?" The older man's eyes searched the room as if expecting a reply.

Stan lifted a hand-held camera, no doubt to focus on Flint's reaction and supplement the wide shots currently being recorded by the sta-cam in the corner. In an incredible feat of alchemy, footage they'd expected to be worthless just transformed into story gold.

Kimberly moved closer. "Who is Maud, Mr. Flint?"

Flint shook his head. "It can't be. It just can't."

"Who is Maud?"

"She's my . . . was my . . ." He turned away and sniffed. "She would have been my wife if I hadn't mucked it all up."

"Your wife?" Michael asked. "But I thought—"

Flint stood. "If you'll excuse me. I'll leave you to this nonsense. If it makes Macy feel better."

Flint shuffled from the room, clearly shaken.

"I'm sorry, did I misunderstand something?" Michael asked after the door closed behind him. "Did he not refer to Bo as his partner?"

"Just business partner, I think," Kimberly said. She looked around the room. "Well, we have a name. Maybe that will help me connect tonight. Do we think his old girlfriend's ghost is haunting him?"

"Macy saw a guy. Heck, Mr. Flint said he heard Bo calling him."

She clutched her quartz. "We need to figure out exactly who Maud was."

But first, she wanted some answers to her own mysteries— who was the woman who kept following her and what did she want?

CHAPTER TEN

THE MOMENT KIMBERLY opened the door of Voodoo Legitimate, the heady scent of incense put her at ease. In a way she didn't remember ever experiencing, a sense of calm settled over her. Candles, anointing oils, and herbs combined with the assortment of incense into the most welcoming atmosphere she'd ever stood in.

For a minute, she stood still and simply breathed, luxuriating in the ease that assuaged her constant anxiety.

Home.

She'd never been here yet felt as if she'd come home after a long absence.

"Well, hello," a voice greeted her.

The woman from Jackson Square who'd extended the invitation to come sat behind the counter.

"It's you!" Kimberly said, holding out the card the woman had given her. "I—" She touched her head, feeling slightly woozy. "Sorry. I—"

"You've never been in an atmosphere so perfectly tuned to a psychic's comfort zone? It can be a bit disconcerting the first time or two." The woman smiled.

"That must be it."

"That or the heavy cloud of weed in here," Stan muttered.

The woman held out a hand. "Zorastra. But please call me Zorrie."

Kimberly clutched Zorrie's hand. A jolt of electricity shocked her. She gasped and pulled away.

Sterling was at her side in a moment. "What happened?"

Rosie and Michael were close behind. "You okay?"

"Oh, my," Zorrie said. "You are highly charged psychically. Enough to throw off sparks. And yet . . ." The young woman held out her hands, palms facing Kimberly, and closed her eyes. "And yet you are weakened, unable to tap your energy. There's a disconnect—"

"Yes!" Kimberly said. "How did you—"

Zorrie opened her eyes. "You are a mess. You need to see Marissa. But she works at night. You'll have to come back. You could schedule a Tarot card reading with—"

"But I work at night," Kimberly said. This close to an answer and she was getting sent away and told to wait? "Can't you just tell me why I'm . . . disconnected?"

"Sorry. No. But we may have some strengthening oils and healing herbs that could help."

"Of course," Sterling said. She could hear the eyeroll without even looking.

Zorrie smiled wider. "Walk around and see what draws you. You're psychic. You'll sense what you need."

"So her psychic powers, which she's looking to heal, will lead her to the product she should buy in order to heal her psychic powers?" Sterling shook his head. "Come on, Kimberly. Let's get you some lunch—"

Rosie pushed passed them to the counter. "I care for Kimberly and keep her in the best health I possibly can. If something is going on with her, I need to know about it."

"That is awesome," Zorrie said. "She's so lucky to have you."

Rosie's forehead crinkled. "Y—yes. So what's wrong with her?"

The woman shrugged. "I don't know. But Marissa will. She's incredible."

"Maybe she can make an exception for Kimberly Wantland and come in early to—"

"Thank you, Rosie," Kimberly said. "I don't want special treatment." That was a blatant lie, but what could she do? This Marissa woman wasn't here, and she didn't want to leave a bad impression. "Let's just look around."

"Let me know if you need anything," Zorrie told them.

Rosie threw her some side-eye. "We just did."

"Okay, listen," Zorrie said. "I'm not supposed to do this. I'm still training."

"Go on," Rosie encouraged.

Zorrie stood and leaned on the counter, looking around at the other customers. "You're worried you might be pregnant, aren't you?"

Kimberly sucked in a breath. That was the last thing she'd expected. "I . . . yes, a little concerned. How did you know that?"

"You're still worried about that?" Sterling asked. "Why didn't you tell me? Let's stop at the drugstore and put the issue to rest."

"Oh, I can tell you!" Zorrie rose onto her tiptoes and grinned like the Cheshire cat.

Sterling lifted an eyebrow. "You have an ultrasound machine in the back?"

"Here. Choose a pendulum. Find one that responds to you. Then we can ask the spirits."

"Ask the spirits? Kimberly, let's go. This is ludicrous."

"She did know what's troubling me," she pointed out, lifting the stone pendulums one at a time, looking for one she connected with. "She has to have strong abilities to sense that."

"You're going to let her use a necklace to predict if you're pregnant or not?"

She pinched a silver chain between her thumb and forefinger, allowing the conical, tan stone to dangle freely in the air. This one pulled at her. As she watched, it began to swing slowly forward and backward, gaining momentum until it swung wildly.

"That one is meant for you!" Zorrie said. "Look at that. I've never seen such a strong connection. Here, sit!"

"This is known as the ideomotor effect," Sterling said. "You're subconsciously making that move."

Zorrie held the pendulum over Kimberly's stomach. "Forward and backward will mean yes, okay?" The stone quivered, then gently rocked back and forth. "Excellent! And side to side will mean no. Can you demonstrate 'no' for me?" The stone stopped swinging forward and backward and switched to gentle side-to-side movements. "Fantastic! You picked a good one! Spirit, is this woman pregnant?"

The stone held perfectly still, then slowly began to swing side to side.

Kimberly breathed a huge sigh of relief. Thank goodness. A baby right now seemed like a terrible idea. Too sudden. Stan hinted at leaving the show when his little one arrived. What would happen if she had a baby? Could she juggle both responsibilities? Better to push that to the future. "Thank you. I feel better now."

The pendulum shifted, turning in a circle, spinning round and round.

Zorrie frowned. "Hmmm. Interesting."

"What is it?" Rosie asked. "You didn't ask it to spin in a circle."

"You're not pregnant. But you will be! Want me to ask if it'll be a boy or girl? Or want me to schedule a Tarot card reading for you? See what the cards say? I can give you a discount on any product in the store if you schedule a Tarot reading."

Sterling pushed off the counter he leaned against. "For the love of—Look, let's just—"

"Sterling Wakefield?"

He looked over his shoulder to see who spoke to him, then stood and whirled around. "Hi!"

"Oh my gosh, that is you! What are you doing here?"

Kimberly turned to see a tall, buxom, very attractive woman beaming at Sterling. The woman wore slacks, a button-up shirt, and a jacket, all business. Kimberly glanced at her own outfit, a loose, flowing blouse with billowing sleeves and soft, flared pants. And noted Sterling's sudden inability to form a complete sentence.

"Oh . . . you know. What are you doing here?"

"Writing an article on the underground supernatural beliefs."

"Oh, yeah? You're into the supernatural too?"

"Into it? You're still hilarious." The woman rested a hand on his arm. "I'm researching the fringe network and how the industry takes advantage of the poor people who fall prey to false promises. Can I interview you?"

Kimberly tugged at the fringe on her sleeves as she suddenly felt too warm in this small, stuffy space.

Sterling cleared his throat and shuffled his feet. "Interview me?"

She waited for Sterling to set this woman straight, eyeing her hand resting on his arm again.

"Of course. *SpookBusters* was the best. I'm here to uncover frauds taking advantage of people susceptible to outlandish claims of spirits and magic and spells. I mean look at this." The woman gestured to an altar to Marie Laveau. "People still go to her grave or to these altars to ask her to intercede for them and grant their requests."

Zorrie stiffened, and Kimberly realized she wasn't the only one feeling insulted. This woman had all the nerve.

"How is that any different than someone praying in a church?" Stan asked, a hard edge to his voice.

"Oh, I didn't say that it is." The woman laughed.

She pressed passed the tongue-tied Sterling and thrust out a hand, her bangles jangling. "Kimberly Wantland. And you are?"

The woman's eyes narrowed as she accepted the offered handshake. "I know who you are, of course. Love that Sterling managed to get onto your show and debunk your psychic nonsense."

Nonsense? She glanced at Sterling again, but he wouldn't meet her gaze. And didn't speak up. "You saw that episode?"

"Oh, no. I'd never support your show by watching it. But I know Sterling, and I'm sure he exposed you and all your chicanery. What are you doing here in New Orleans, Sterling?" The woman looked back and forth between her and Sterling and something seemed to click behind her piercing eyes. "Are you here *with* Kimberly? Another guest appearance?"

Sterling still wouldn't meet her gaze. He stared at the floor, a strange grin she'd never seen before across his face.

He's embarrassed of me.

He made no attempt to deflect or correct this jarring woman's insults.

She heard a foot tapping and discovered Rosie scowling, hands on hips. "Who did you say you are?"

Sterling jerked his hands from where he'd stuffed them into his pockets. "Kimberly, this is Georgia Jones. We went to school together, kind of like you and Michael."

Still not telling this woman he was her cohost.

Georgia Jones—could that even be her real name?—rustled through her purse and extracted a business card, which she thrust into Sterling's hand. "Here. Call me. Let's arrange a time when I can interview you for my story." With one last, lingering look, Georgia capped her pen and left.

Sterling stuffed the card into his back pocket. What she wouldn't give to rip that thing to bits. Did he intend to call that abrasive woman? She turned to Rosie when her hands began to shake.

Sterling recovered his voice. "We should go find your grand parents' old house." His spectrum trumpeted guilt.

What exactly had that woman meant to him? And what did her appearance mean for them now?

CHAPTER ELEVEN

STILL SURE STERLING had been embarrassed to be associated with her, Kimberly climbed into the van with the rest of the crew.

"I have the address of your grandparents' old house," Elise said. "Are you ready to go see it?"

Kimberly felt the camera lenses on her as she nodded and swallowed hard. "I want to see where my mother grew up."

Michael drove them out of the French Quarter, though remained on surface roads, allowing TJ and Stan to record the majestic old buildings and homes along their way. Huge live oaks, roots breaking sidewalks into ragged chunks, towered above them, leafy branches forming a canopy over the roads. Spanish moss clung to branches, hanging in fuzzy veils and shawls, as if the trees had donned their lacy best for her homecoming.

Because once again, despite never having been to New Orleans, she felt as if she'd come home.

"Notice how narrow the fronts of the homes are," Elise pointed out to them. "At the time these were built, one theory suggests, real estate taxes were based on linear footage that faced the street rather than total square footage. Therefore, the homes are narrow, but deep, extending far back onto the property.

These 'shotgun houses' included open spaces and tall ceilings to help dissipate the extreme heat of the summers. But no one can actually find that tax code. Possibly this style of home was brought by immigrants from their countries of origin. However the style began, it's unique to New Orleans."

That was what had been catching her interest, Kimberly realized, though she had not pinpointed the unique architecture until Elise drew attention to it.

"Coming up," Elise continued, "is Saint Louis Cemetery Number One, the oldest cemetery in New Orleans, where famed Voodoo Queen Marie Laveau is believed to be interred. This one is no longer open to unaccompanied tourists, due to the large amount of traffic at her tomb. Vandalism was the final straw, though concerns about the extensive accumulation of offerings contributed as well."

"That's who Georgia mentioned," Sterling commented. "Something about requesting favors?"

"Yes, not unlike praying for guidance or a favor, believers flocked to her grave, drew an X, offered a gift, and asked a favor of the powerful Voodoo priestess."

"I would argue it's very unlike praying," Sterling said, eyebrows bunched above his dark eyes.

"Not for someone who practices Voodoo," Kimberly said, bristling at the mention of Georgia's name as well as her myopic views. Sterling had been opening his mind to new ideas. Who was this woman to come along and shake things up? "Just because someone adheres to different beliefs doesn't make their ideas wrong."

"Come on. Drawing an X, leaving an offering? In hopes a favor will be granted?"

"And how many times have you lit a candle or burned incense," she asked, "while praying for the intercession of a saint?"

Sterling clamped his lips together and turned away, staring out the window.

Elise cleared her throat. "Anyway, I suggest we tour at least one cemetery while we're here so you can see the unique tomb style utilized in New Orleans to bury their dead."

Over the top of the concrete wall surrounding the cemetery, Kimberly could just make out triangular roofs of tiny buildings covered in moss and assorted vegetation. "Do you think you could find my grandparents' tombs?"

Elise ducked her head. "I already looked it up and found them. I wasn't sure how you'd feel about it, so I didn't mention it. The cemetery they're buried in is on the other side of town."

"I'd like to see them. Let's make time for that."

Michael glanced at her. "You got it."

"Are you sure you're up for that, girl?" Rosie rested a hand on her arm. "You're in a weird place emotionally right now. And psychically."

"I appreciate the concern, really, but I can't pass up the opportunity while I'm here. I'll be fine."

Elise's map app instructed, "At the next light, turn left."

"We're nearly there," her researcher said.

Butterflies jittered in her stomach, which seemed silly. It was only a house. Nothing but an empty shell and certainly nothing to get worked up about.

"Here. This one on the right."

Michael pulled to the curb. All of them hunched over, peering out the windows.

"That one?" she asked. "It looks like something out of a fairy tale."

"Queen Anne style," Elise told her.

The small, two-story home with a wide porch hid behind a hedge, a rusted gate across the entrance. A turret jutted from the side of the second story, spindle-like. Painted baby blue and yellow, the house truly seemed unreal, like something she was imagining from a fantasy story rather than a real place. Her skin tingled. She rubbed her hands over her arms, suddenly chilled. "I can't believe my mom lived here."

But it was more than that. Her mother had grown up in this house, learned to walk inside its walls, toddled through the hallways, celebrated holidays, presumably giggled with friends in a bedroom, achieved milestones, dreamed, suffered disappointments. Which room had been hers?

She clicked the seatbelt release and slid free, reaching for the door handle.

"Whoa, Kimmy," Michael cautioned. "This is an occupied dwelling, not an abandoned site we can just waltz right into."

"I know," she murmured. But she had to get as close as she could.

Doors opened and closed behind her as she crept forward, watching the house for signs of . . . what? Recognition? Did she imagine the building had taken a deep breath, swelling and relaxing as if preparing for an inevitable confrontation it had known would someday come to pass?

Movement at an upstairs window stopped her.

Rosie plucked at her elbow. "You're creeping me out, girl, so I can only guess what anyone inside might be thinking. Come on back."

But the house bade her come closer. She heard it—felt it—as clearly as she heard Rosie continue to cajole her. At the gate, she gripped the iron bars in fists wet with nervous sweat and sent out a psychic beacon.

I'm here.

Could one or both of her grandparents' spirits wait inside? The house shimmered before her, changing color, the curtains morphing, a rocking chair appearing on the wide porch.

A sharp pain in her temple left her doubled over, clutching her head.

Her phone rang. Angela's ringtone.

"Angela, hi," she answered.

"Something strange is happening. All the curtains are blowing around, but the windows aren't open and there's no air moving in the house. And . . . I swear I just heard a growl from the attic."

She glanced back at the house in front of her—the curtains shimmied in a macabre dance, taunting her, daring her closer. "The curtains . . ."

The image of a terrified little girl huddled in a closet accompanied another sharp stabbing pain.

Rosie bent beside her. "What is it?"

The door opened and a man stepped onto the porch. "Can I help you?"

Rosie waved and answered in her friendliest tone. "Just admiring your beautiful home."

Angela's voice took on a note of concern when she spoke again. "Are you okay?"

Kimberly answered through gritted teeth. "Be safe. I'll have to call you back, but be safe." She hung up and eyed the man on the porch.

"You filming something?" he asked, taking in her camera operators. "A movie or television show like that *American Horror Story?*"

"Ever watch *The Wantland Files?*" Michael asked.

"Can't say I have. But I will if my house is on it."

"Then, yes. You'll be featured in our New Orleans investigation."

The man opened his door wide. "You need to see inside?"

Michael beamed. "That would be wonderful!" He turned to Kimberly and whispered, "I do not have the paperwork for this. You owe me one."

Rosie frowned. "I don't know if she should—"

"Oh, she's going inside," Michael said. "I've promised this man his house will be in the episode, so now we're doing it. Kimmy may not have grown up here, but she has family ties to it which should pique interest. With any luck, she'll connect with something."

He didn't realize she'd already connected with something. And she wasn't sure it was a good thing.

Rosie tried again. "But something is—"

"It's okay, Rosie." Kimberly pressed fingers to her temples. "I'll be okay. And we can't waste an opportunity like this."

"I happen to have paperwork on me," Elise said. "Consent to feature on the show, waiver of liability, all the usual."

Michael pointed at her. "I owe you." He turned back to Kimberly. "You still owe me."

Rosie linked an arm around hers. "Be careful. Speak up if things get to be too much."

She squared her shoulders. Nothing would keep her from taking advantage of the opportunity to learn something about her mother. "I will."

Arm in arm, they climbed the steps toward the gaping mouth of the door, the homeowner smoothing his virtually nonexistent hair, eyes glued to the cameras following them inside.

Giggles assaulted her the moment she crossed the threshold. Footsteps pattered up and down the stairs, the halls, skipping from room to room.

The residue of past experiences thrummed through the old dwelling, the house breathing in her presence. In welcome?

Or warning?

She closed one fist around her quartz and prepared to reach out, to connect with the spirit realm. She sensed equal anticipation from the other side. Someone longed to tell her something.

Rosie gripped her arm. "I don't think you should, girl. Not here. Something seems off about this."

"I know I'm not at my strongest, but . . . she lived here, Rosie. I can feel her. Her residual energy coats this house."

"You're sure? Sure it's her? I don't want you getting pulled into the Nightshade again. You were so vulnerable during the last investigation."

Vulnerable? Weak was more like it. She never wanted to feel so powerless again. Rosie was right. She wasn't sure. She wanted it to be her mother so badly, but so far she couldn't prove who or what she felt moving through this old house. An echo of her mother? Or something more sinister? "Okay. Let's look around first and see what happens."

Moving through the house, aware of camera lenses, curious homeowners, and a pull on her sixth sense, she remained guarded.

"Elise? Did you happen to find pictures of them in your research? My grandparents?"

"I did!" Elise hurried to her side, rifling through a file folder. "Here."

Obituaries. From a local paper. They had moved back to New Orleans after her parents moved from Oklahoma to New Mexico. She relished the articles, learning about the grandparents she'd never known. While she savored each word, she also wondered why more details weren't included, more history provided. Her grandfather had passed first, then her grandmother not long after. She scrutinized the accompanying photographs, seeking a family resemblance while searching for a hint, some clue as to why they'd disappeared from her life. They looked perfectly average and normal, Henry and Gladys LeBlanc, gazing out from the thin paper, smiling at her, the granddaughter they'd never known about. Did her mother have Gladys's eyes? Henry's mouth? She realized her memories of her mother had grown hazy, more basic shapes, less detail, mostly supplanted by the image of her mother's spirit reaching for her at the very end.

Survived by daughter, Veronica LeBlanc.

Interesting. Her mother's birth name, not her married name or pseudonym she'd apparently adopted somewhere along the way, Vanessa.

And by one granddaughter.

Her hands formed fists, scrunching the edges of the paper.

Rosie dug through her little black bag. "Hang on. I have some peppermint oil in here. And some sweet orange oil somewhere."

"They knew," she whispered. "They knew about me."

Disbelief rumbled through her, followed by bursts of betrayal and fury. The storm lit up her psychic spectrum.

The air around her sizzled. The hair on her arms stood on end. The room crackled with energy, buzzed as past images fought for her attention.

Clapping and giggling turned her attention to the living room. Grainy images of a Christmas tree in a corner hummed in and out of focus like a sickly neon sign that couldn't quite manage the strength to fully light. Two adults—her grandparents—sat on the couch watching a little pajama-clad girl clap and squeal that Santa came.

Her mother.

She sucked in a gulp of air but choked as the world around her blurred, hazed into a distorted melding of past and present. Hands held her arms and seemingly distant voices urged caution.

The image disappeared and the room snapped back into focus, twinkling tree and former residents gone. She clasped her quartz, ready to exhaust every shred of psychic energy to bring back the image of her mother on Christmas morning.

Until a cry for help pealed from upstairs, followed by a scream.

She tore upstairs, never once having set foot in this home and yet knowing exactly where to go—up the stairs, to the right, into the room that once belonged to her mother.

She yanked open the closet door, where the cries for help emanated.

A bright blue light greeted her, the brilliance blinding her but not before she spotted a tiny hand disappearing into the portal, which then closed with a pop.

Dropping to her knees, she ran her hands over the floor, the walls, the static air, begging it to open again. She slammed her eyes closed and fought to control her percolating emotions, forcing every ounce of energy into the space, searching psychically for a crack, a fissure she could take advantage of, force wide, and peek inside, into the spirit realm.

Hands, warm living hands, pulled her from the closet, held her still, massaged her hands and arms with lavender oil. Voices murmured softly, urging her to relax.

"This part of the show?" she heard the older homeowner ask.

"Most definitely," Michael answered.

She wished it wasn't also her reality.

CHAPTER TWELVE

THEY KNEW ABOUT ME.

Though the second-night investigation needed her full attention, that one thing dominated Kimberly's thoughts. Her grandparents had been aware of her existence. And for some reason had been perfectly content to go about their lives never meeting her, never creating a relationship with her. What kind of grandparents—what kind of people—could do that?

"Kimmy?"

She met Michael's eyes and found them full of sympathy. Not good. Her personal issues could not be allowed to impinge on the show.

Forcing a smile, she nodded. "I'm fine. I'm ready."

He lifted an eyebrow, silently calling out her BS, but pointed to Stan and TJ, then counted them all in. "In five, four, three . . ."

Two fingers. One. He pointed, turning it over to her.

"We're on the fifth floor, location of previous paranormal activity, to see if the restless spirits are willing to talk tonight."

Flint stood with her crew, still mumbling about "stuff and nonsense" but no longer insisting they stay away from his room. In fact, he'd drifted downstairs while they'd been preparing in the lobby, on the pretense he'd needed to check up on Bram, then sauntered closer and closer until she took notice.

"Acting exactly like a cat," Stan muttered, "when it wants attention but doesn't want to ask overtly for it."

Kimberly had caved and acknowledged him. "I'm so sorry, Mr. Flint, if we disturbed you. Are we making too much noise?"

"Nah, nah. Had to check on . . ." He waved a dismissive hand at Bram, who rolled his eyes and went back to his phone. "You'll probably need inside my room tonight, won't you?"

She'd glanced at Michael, unsure if this was an invitation or a trap. "Well, we wouldn't want to disturb your sleep—"

"I can't sleep anyway. Better keep an eye on all of you."

Her entire crew turned away, hiding smiles and suppressed laughter. She was starting to see why Cristal found Flint so amusing.

She'd kept her face serious, pretending to contemplate before answering. "Yes, I think you're right. That would be better."

Of course it was better. His grudging cooperation was a huge improvement over being barred from the room where all the activity was. But no harm allowing him to believe this was his idea, she thought, watching Flint eye the equipment while attempting to veil his obvious curiosity. They all took care not to pay too much attention lest they spook him.

"Like a cat," Stan repeated quietly, laughing to himself.

She clutched her quartz and breathed deeply, allowing her sixth sense to reach out into the hallway, where she'd encountered the golden entity before. "Maud? Are you with us tonight?"

The smell of roses engulfed her, accompanied by a gentle warmth. She cocked her head. "Did Maud wear rose-scented perfume?"

Flint inhaled deeply as if hoping to catch the scent himself. "Maud? No. She always smelled of lilacs and . . . fresh green meadows. Of new beginnings and endless possibilities."

"This guy secretly a poet?" Rosie asked. "And how could any

woman resist a guy who described her like that? I might go out with him if he talked to me that way."

She gave Rosie "the look" and continued. "Who has joined us? Maud? Someone else? Can you make yourself known to us?"

"I told you Maud didn't—" Flint suddenly sucked in a breath and pressed a hand to his cheek. He spun around as if looking for someone. "Who—? How did you—? Violet?"

"Who is Violet?" she asked at the same moment a gentle tug urged her toward Flint's room. "I believe I've made a connection, though I'm not certain who is reaching out to me."

With cautious steps, fearful of Flint's possible reaction, she crossed into his room. The sitting area was furnished with only a couch. In the kitchenette she saw empty counters. But the bedroom was what drew her, so she continued on into the side room. The bare space, sparsely decorated, held only a bed, a nightstand with a lamp, and a dresser.

"Did he literally just move into a hotel room?" Sterling asked. "I know guys don't decorate like women, but this place is completely empty."

The one bit of decoration in the entire place turned out to be the item drawing her—a hinged photo frame, one side displaying the photo of a smiling little girl, the opposite a brooding, dark-eyed boy. She touched the glass over the boy's picture. "This is you."

Flint nodded.

"A grouch even as a boy," Michael noted softly. "EMF reading over one hundred, Kimmy."

"Yes, I have activity. Someone is communicating. May I?"

Flint lifted the frame and handed the photos to her.

The moment she closed her hands over them, images bombarded her. A young boy and an even younger girl, sitting, legs tucked under them, shaking packages beneath a tiny tree decorated with tinsel and homemade ornaments.

"I hope it's shoes," the girl said. "I can barely squeeze my feet into these anymore."

"I hope so too, Violet." The boy smiled at her warmly, sadness in his eyes. "Mother and father do the best they can, of course."

"Of course."

Kimberly opened her eyes. "It was . . . Christmas Eve, wasn't it? And a little girl was hoping for new shoes."

Flint stared at her. "I've never told that to a soul. Not a soul. I never would have believed it if I didn't see it myself. You really can see my memories, can't you? You a mind reader?"

She shook her head. "It isn't like that. A spirit, your sister I think, is sharing memories, visions, with me. I can't explain it. I've always been able to connect with spirits this way."

"I've never seen such a thing. What else can you see?"

"You . . . made the ornaments on the tree." She heard laughter, saw craft supplies, smelled glue and paper.

Flint cracked a smile. "We had so much fun making those. Toothpicks and construction paper. And a little glitter. We could make anything out of those! Our gifts that year weren't much better. She didn't get those shoes she was hoping for. Our parents were so poor."

The images melted, swirled, and reformed into another setting, the two children alone in an empty room. Violet clutched him. "It's Christmas, Jeremiah, presents or no. As long as we're together, that's all that matters."

Horrible grief tightened her throat. "You lost your parents. When you were very young."

Flint's typical scowl flew back into place, replacing the short-lived smile. "That's right. It happens. Violet and I spent years in foster care. No one much cared if we stayed together or didn't."

"Bastards," Stan said. "Who could do that? Separate a brother and sister?"

"How many orphans have you taken in?" Flint asked.

"Same number you did, from the looks of it. But if I did, I wouldn't separate families."

The shared vision continued, and in it, Kimberly watched

young Violet pulled, screaming and reaching for her brother, away from Jeremiah.

The scene fogged, blurred, like a watercolor caught in a rainstorm, and reformed. An older Jeremiah sat before a desk in a stark office. "I'm eighteen. Why can't I assume guardianship of her?" he demanded.

Violet sat in a chair, eyes down, fingers clenched in fists resting on her lap.

A severe man behind the desk adjusted his glasses. "Sorry, my boy. You can barely support yourself. How would you care for her?"

"But no one is caring for her! No one! She sits here in this sterile, sorry excuse for a home—"

"I'm sorry, but—"

Jeremiah leaned forward. "I'll work two jobs—three if need be—if I can take Violet with me!"

"I'll work too!" little Violet piped up. "I'll work as hard as Jeremiah."

The man shook his head. "You're not old enough to work. You need to finish school. I'm sorry, but this simply isn't possible."

When the vision ended, Kimberly compared the young boy to the man he'd become and saw the same deep sadness and loss reflected in his eyes, now heavily lined with years of hardship. She knew Flint relived these memories, that Violet's spirit shared the images with both of them.

"He was right," Flint said softly. "I couldn't care for her. I tried for guardianship again a few years later, once my income had increased, but . . . And then she married young and was pregnant soon after."

Kimberly saw Violet beaming at Jeremiah with a sleeping infant swaddled in her arms. "I named him for you, Jeremiah. Finally we have a chance to have a family. We can give him all the love we never had."

The pieces clicked. "Your nephew. Jeremy."

Flint nodded.

Then another realization hit her hard. "She's . . . Violet is . . ."

"Dead." Flint spoke in a monotone. "That husband of hers was no good. Shiftless, alcoholic asshole. She never admitted it, but I think he abused her physically, in addition to criticizing her endlessly and destroying her spirit. Never wanted me around because I saw him for the no-good trash that he was and called him out on it, tried to get Violet to leave him. She deserved so much better."

"How did she . . ."

"The first Christmas Jeremy was in college, Violet and Mark went to a party, and he got stinkin' drunk like always. He'd never let her drive, and he was a mean drunk. He'd cuss at her and fight to keep the keys. I told her over and over to call me anytime she needed a ride. I would have picked her up! That man—" He pulled a handkerchief from his pocket and covered his eyes. "I loved my sister! She was the only one who ever showed me a bit of kindness. But I couldn't save her. Died far too soon. And Jeremy . . . he looks . . . looks exactly like her. Especially the smile. Every time I look at him, I see her smiling face." Flint rubbed his chest, as if massaging an ache that never went away. "I failed you, Violet! I'm so sorry!"

A soft soughing traveled through the room, lifting tendrils of her hair. A chill shivered through her, and bitter remorse filled her lungs.

"But no, Jeremiah, I failed you." Kimberly didn't recognize her own voice and when she looked into the mirror, another woman's reflection stared back at her. *Violet*. "She's so sorry, Mr. Flint."

Flint tucked the handkerchief back into his pocket. "Please, Violet, no more. I can't bear it."

She felt a soft susurrus again, and the room went quiet. "She's gone. I'm so sorry. I wish—"

The dresser pulled at her, commanded her attention as clearly as if a hand grasped her sleeve and tugged. The mirror reflected her own image again, but something—someone—demanded to be heard.

She closed her eyes and held out her hands.

Guide me.

"Kimmy?" Michael asked. "I'm seeing a sharp spike in EMF. What's happening?"

"Hot. Something is radiating heat." She ran her hands over the dresser. Whatever she was looking for, it wasn't on top. She opened drawers, nothing in the top two. "TJ? Can you see anything on the FLIR?"

"No, I don't—Wait! Middle drawer on the right side. I have a heat source!"

She opened it and rifled through the pressed and folded shirts, neatly stacked in perfect piles. Buried beneath them, at the very bottom of the drawer, a small, hinged box pulsed with energy, nearly burning her hand as she closed her fingers around it. She knew the psychic energy she felt as heat could not truly burn her skin. A malevolent force had once caused her actual injury, but she didn't sense that type of presence here.

Flint spluttered. "That is mine. I would thank you not to—"

She rocked back the lid. A lock of hair, tied with a ribbon, rested inside the little wooden trinket. The air in the room shifted yet again. A spirit drifted nearby, longing for connection. She held the lock of hair gently in one hand and grasped her quartz crystal in the other.

She breathed deeply. "Lilacs on a fresh spring day. I smell it. Exactly as you described."

"Maud," Flint murmured.

She opened her eyes to see a tear trickle down his cheek.

"Who is—"

"Maud?" Flint reached out to the mirror, resting his fingertips on the glass. "I must be dreaming."

Another woman's face stared out of the reflective surface. Tight, curly hair ringed a round face. A soft mouth curved into a gentle smile.

He pressed against the dresser, leaning into the mirror as if he hoped to drag her from the depths. "Maud? Maud! Please, I made a mistake. I'm so sorry!"

Kimberly saw a woman standing over a desk where a younger version of Flint hunched, pen scratching across a ledger. "Jerry? It's Christmas Eve. No one expects you to work. Come to the party with me."

In the vision, Flint didn't even glance up as he totaled another column. "This needs to be done. I can't go to a party when work waits."

"But the work will be there after Christmas. And no one else is—"

"I don't care what anyone else is doing. I need to work!"

"Jerry, we talked about settling down, talked about a future together. But I feel like I'm never your priority. If you can't make time for me even at Christmas—"

"Don't you see work has to come first? What will we live on if I don't earn money? Stop picking at me. If you want to go to the party, go!"

"I am going to go, Jerry. Merry Christmas." The young woman in the vision turned back at the door, tossing over her shoulder, "Have a good life."

Flint's handkerchief was out again, this time scrubbing at his face. "I didn't mean for her to leave for good. I just wanted her to let me work."

Kimberly's voice was no longer her own again. "And how long did it take for you to realize I'd gone? Did you bother to reach out to me?"

"I wouldn't beg you to come back, if that's what you're getting at! Do you hold that against me?"

"Was the money worth it, Jerry? Worth losing everything else in your life? Being alone and miserable?"

"I made a terrible mistake. Please forgive me!"

"This is your last chance, Jerry. Don't let this one slip through your fingers."

"I'm sorry, Maud! I'm so, so sorry!" He grabbed Kimberly's arms and shook her as if trying to homogenize Maud to the surface, to make her face morph into the countenance of his lost love.

"Hey!" she heard Sterling say.

Flint shook harder. "Where she is? Where is Maud?"

Sterling and Michael separated her from his tightening grip.

She rubbed at her arms. "She's gone. And if she's contacting us from beyond, that means she's passed on. I'm so sorry."

"Of course she has. She's right. I alienated everyone, and now everyone I knew is gone." He slumped to his knees.

She turned, senses on alert, but no other spirits made their presence known. Flint's shoulders shook. Kneeling beside him, she rested a hand on his shoulder. But she didn't know what to say. She understood work coming first. But if the right time never materialized for a relationship or prioritizing her personal life . . . Was she seeing a glimpse of her future?

CHAPTER THIRTEEN

STERLING HELD the door open for Kimberly, gesturing *after you*. He'd made breakfast reservations for them at Brennan's, an iconic New Orleans establishment, where Bananas Foster was invented.

The host greeted them with a nod and a subdued smile. "Welcome to Brennan's. *Wantland Files* party?"

"Correct," Sterling affirmed.

A young woman offered each of them a jingle bell on a pink ribbon printed with the word *Brennan's*, her own necklace jingling with each step. "Merry Christmas from Brennan's."

"Pink for Christmas?" TJ asked.

"It's tradition. Each Brennan's restaurant has its own color. Ours is pink."

"Fancy." Rosie draped hers over her head.

The host led them to their tables, the group of them jingling like a sleigh ride.

Sterling pulled a chair out for her, and Kimberly dropped into it, taking note of the formal place settings and wishing she'd worn a glitzier dress. Her work wardrobe didn't include anything glamourous though.

"Allow me to direct you to the drink menu, including the

brunch mimosas. Your waiter will be here shortly." With a nod, the host left them to peruse.

"Brunch mimosas? That how they make the day drinkers feel better about themselves?" Sterling muttered.

Stan thumbed over his shoulder. "Judging by the drinks at the other tables, I'd say they have the full bar open. Guy at the table next to us appears to have a Bloody Mary, and he's not exactly nursing it."

"It's New Orleans, what do you expect?" Michael asked. "Surely you noticed all the frozen drink shops in the French Quarter. And the people weaving around in the streets, drinks in hand."

"Still hoping we can catch a little night life while we're here," Stan said. "Once the baby comes, I think my partying days will be officially behind me."

"I've never once seen you party," Michael said. "Not once in the years we've worked together."

"No, but I could if I wanted to. With a baby to worry about, I think that'll be a thing of the past."

Kimberly watched her crew look over the menus.

Sterling cleared his throat. "I wonder if maybe we could have an early Christmas gift and be allowed mimosas."

Michael looked at her. She looked at him.

At the table next to them, the man with the Bloody Mary downed the remainder of it and ordered another round for his table.

"We are in New Orleans," Sterling pressed. "None of us will get hammered, Scout's honor, and I doubt we will visit any bars while we're here. Why not?"

Michael nodded at her.

"Go ahead," she said. "But let's keep this—"

"What happens in NOLA, stays in NOLA!"

The waiter delivered the round to the table beside them, then greeted them with, "What drinks can I get you started with?"

"Mimosas for everyone except me," she replied. "I'll have hot tea. And a glass of water."

"Yes, ma'am. I'll bring those right out."

Michael rolled his eyes and intoned a high-pitched voice. "Please, sir, can I have some water? Buzzkill."

Sterling leaned close. "Surely you can have one mimosa. You're not still worried about being pregnant, are you?"

She shook her head even though the concern did in fact still nag at the back of her thoughts. "I need to stay clearheaded. You know me—buzzkill." She tried to laugh.

The waiter returned, distributed drinks, and asked, "And have we decided what we want to eat?"

She lifted a finger. "I'll have the oatmeal—"

Another round of groans rose from the table.

"Seriously?"

"Oatmeal?"

"Live a little!"

"Let her get whatever makes her happy!" Sterling said. "You guys know she doesn't want the meat or eggs or fried potatoes. How long have you worked with her?"

She squeezed his hand in gratitude, but he let go to check his phone when it lit up with a notification. And the smile that lit up his face in response didn't sit well.

"Oatmeal for Ms. Wantland," the waiter said and moved around the table.

Her thoughts went straight to Georgia Jones. The woman was everything she wasn't, and her presence had so obviously befuddled Sterling. She hadn't heard him on the phone with her, but maybe they were texting each other.

She dunked the teabag into the hot water while the others ordered. She wasn't lecturing them on how their food choices affected their bodies. Why did they feel the need to harass her for trying to be healthy?

Beside her, Sterling's thumbs flew over the screen as he

responded to a text. She wanted so badly to lean over and see if the name of the contact was Georgia.

Rosie bumped her under the table, holding her cell phone her direction. "Look at this pompous woman."

Twitter, of course, with a huge beaming photo of Georgia Jones leering under the tweet, "Georgia in Louisiana."

"Clever," she told Rosie, feeling like that woman was everywhere. She glanced back at Sterling, still engrossed in his text chat.

Hemmed in by Georgia Jones on all sides, she looked across the room, out the wall of glass doors and windows that allowed a view into the gardened courtyard. Even in December, lush greenery thrived in New Orleans's climate. A man moved through the meticulously kept gardens, trowel in hand, adding new plants to the existing ones and perhaps pulling weeds. She couldn't get a good enough look at him to see exactly what he did.

"Hey," Rosie bumped her again. "What is it? Something is wrong."

"I was just thinking this would have been my hometown. My home. Where I grew up. I could have had grandparents and aunts and uncles and cousins. If only they hadn't taken Mom to Oklahoma. Why did they do that? Why didn't they stay here?"

"You don't know that, sweetie," Michael said. "If your mom was an only child, which she appears to have been, that may not be the case."

"Besides," Rosie said, "you wouldn't be you if anything had gone differently. She met your dad in Oklahoma. If that didn't happen, we wouldn't have Kimberly Wantland."

"Dad didn't even like me. I could have had a dad who didn't reject me."

"You know that isn't true. Your dad maybe didn't understand your abilities, but now you do so much with them. You wouldn't have met Michael. Or me. No *Wantland Files* would mean our paths would never have crossed. You wouldn't have met Sterling."

She looked around the table. On the one hand, she had a great life full of these people who honestly were more than friends at this point. On the other hand, in the alternate life she envisioned she saw herself with her mother happy, living to old age, and a nebulous, faceless father who adored her, surrounded by two sets of doting grandparents and a blur of faces in a crowd of aunts, uncles, cousins—

"I don't like how pregnant this pause is," Michael said.

"No, of course, you're right. I'm so glad all of you are in my life. It's just so hard not to wonder what might have happened—"

"But it didn't," Sterling said. She was surprised he'd even been listening, as engrossed with his phone as he'd been. "There's no way to go back and change things in our pasts, so we have to deal with the present we have. Everything else is just wishful thinking and a waste of energy."

He was right, and she knew that. His somber tone communicated more than his words, though. She placed a hand on him and read his spectrum. His red chakra spun. Something concerned him. This wasn't the place to try to talk to him, so it would have to wait. And he went right back to his phone anyway.

What was he regretting? Her? The show?

"Anyway," Michael said, lifting his champagne. "How about last night? So much activity."

"Flint won't be calling us hucksters and poppycocks again," Rosie said. "Even he's a believer now."

"Not the correct usage of 'poppycock' but I think you're right."

Stan raised his glass. "To a successful first night."

They all clinked glasses. The champagne was a good idea. They looked so happy. She sipped her tea, watching the gardener again as she thought back over the previous night. What would they find during footage review? Did they actually record anything? Flint wasn't so different from her. He'd also been ostracized and grown up feeling like he didn't belong. He lost both parents at a young age. Lost his sister. Both of them had virtually no family. No spouse or children. What had happened with Maud exactly? She'd asked him—

She set her teacup on the saucer. "Maud asked him if the money was worth it."

Everyone at the table stopped talking and blinked at her.

"What, sweetie?" Michael asked.

"I was thinking about last night, and it hit me. Maud asked him if the money was worth it."

"Money?"

"Yes. Right before he started apologizing to her and asking for her forgiveness. He said he made a mistake."

"What money?" Rosie asked. "He lives like a pauper in a hotel. And it's nice enough but it isn't exactly the Waldorf. If he has money—"

"Why is he so miserly to his employees?" Stan asked.

"And to himself," Rosie said. "Maybe he had some money but lost it? Otherwise it makes no sense."

"Elise," Michael said, "did you see anything about him losing a fortune?"

Elise adjusted her glasses. "No, but I'm not in the habit of researching our homeowners' financial records. I look for anything that might suggest a reason for paranormal activity at the site."

"Considering one of the spirits brought it up, maybe we should see what we can find. And by 'we' I mean you," Michael told her.

"On it."

"But he owns the hotel," TJ said. "He can't be completely broke."

"We can discuss more at footage review," she said. "Maybe Elise will have something by then. Still, I'm not convinced losing money has anything to do with his personality. You guys didn't see what I saw. He and his sister had a really rough—"

"Everybody has a sob story," Stan said. "Not an excuse to be a mean bastard."

"My parents threw me out with nothing," Michael reminded her. "But I can still appreciate my New York flat and the finer things in life." He tipped his champagne flute. "Now if we can just convince you to 'treat yo'self' once in a while."

They didn't understand. They couldn't. And even if they recorded something useful last night, they would never feel what she felt during the session. Sterling, rather than contribute to the discussion, stared at his phone. A mimosa was starting to sound good. She sipped her tea instead.

The waiter wheeled a cart to the table by theirs. She noted the bananas on a plate and assumed their fellow diners, now quite boisterous, had ordered Bananas Foster. Her stomach growled at the thought of food, and she hoped their own would arrive soon.

After gathering ingredients, the waiter lit a small cooktop and rested a pan over the flame. He poured liquid into it and struck a match, igniting the pan into dancing flames. The guests cheered.

Beyond the flames, in the courtyard, the gardening man stood and turned to face her. He wore overalls and held—

She sucked in her breath. The man in the overalls. She grabbed the edges of her seat, holding tight to reality. This couldn't be happening. This ghost had manifested to her in Hannibal. He could not be here. Spirits remained close to the place they left their worldly bodies behind.

Through the flickering flames, the man lifted his eyes to meet her gaze and smiled broadly beneath his furrowed brow. He lifted his rusted, dirt-caked sheers.

He's coming for you.

The world around her blurred. A heartbeat thumped so

loudly it obscured all else. And then a quiet laugh echoed from a distance, building in intensity as if moving closer.

Ker-whump, ker-whump, ker-whump

The heartbeat—her heartbeat?—battered her eardrums.

Something crept closer.

And closer.

And closer.

She reached out and grabbed Sterling's hand, floundering for a hold on reality. This reality. She needed him to hold her firmly in place, anchor her, tell her she was safe.

He turned from his phone and gripped her hand in return.

With a gasp, she pulled free of the thing bearing down on her, leaving the fuzzy otherworld behind. As everyone in her crew asked what had just happened, she swore she felt a breeze ruffle her hair, as if an unseen hand had swiped at her.

CHAPTER FOURTEEN

Kimberly shook her head to clear it and looked again at the man in the overalls. But he was gone. Only a gardener, a real person, shuffled among the plants, tending to them.

She attempted to assure her crew she was fine but could tell no one believed it. Only when their food arrived did they reluctantly shift focus from her.

Throughout the meal, she flicked her eyes to the garden area. But the overall-clad spirit never reappeared. Partly relieved, but still on edge, she decided the next time the leering presence surfaced, she would face it and put an end to this. Not knowing who it was and what it wanted was worse than confronting it, she was sure.

After finishing every bite of her exquisite oatmeal, Kimberly and her crew debated the best way to go see her grandparents' final resting place. They'd walked to Brennan's since the restaurant was only a few blocks from the hotel.

"The cemetery is not within comfortable walking distance," Elise reported, checking her map app. "Not if we want to do anything else today."

"Want me to summon a Lyft?" Sterling asked.

"We could go back for the cars at the hotel," Stan suggested.

"We should ride a streetcar!" Michael decided.

"Cars would be faster," Sterling said. "Straight shot there and back, no extra stops along the way."

"We *have* to ride a streetcar while we're here," Michael insisted. "It's iconic!"

"That will take a lot longer," Kimberly said. "As much as I like the idea of walking off that incredible meal, I think we need to leave ample time for footage review."

"But *Streetcar Named Desire*? Tennessee Williams? Kimmy, as a fellow thespian I demand you back me up on this! If you don't, I'll . . . I'll tell everyone what you did at the theatre Christmas party our senior year of college!"

"Michael! You swore never to tell!"

He drew himself up as tall as he could and hit her with his deadliest expression. "Desperate times call for desperate measures."

"How is this desperate? We're talking about riding a streetcar—"

"So, our senior year of college, Kimmy had a massive crush—"

"Michael, stop! Do not say another word!"

"Now wait just a minute," Rosie said. "You cannot start a story like that and leave us hanging!"

She glared at her supposed best friend, rankled by the look on his face that meant he knew he would get his way. And he would. "Everyone else can do whatever they want, but Michael and I will be riding a streetcar to the cemetery."

He jumped up and down, clapping. "I hope it's the one named Desire!"

"There's not really a—"

He whirled on her. "I know! Let me have this!"

She raised her hands in surrender. "Okay, okay. We definitely will take the streetcar named Desire."

"We can walk to the streetcar stop in six minutes," Elise reported.

"Let's do that, then," Stan said, looking over Elise's shoulder. "Would take us as longer to walk back to the hotel to get the van. Might as well all enjoy the ride."

"Let's see. We just need to walk to Canal Street. There are streetcar stops all along that. Then we stay on Canal to City Park Avenue to the terminal stop. Easy."

"And we can walk down Bourbon Street to Canal," Stan said. "I like this plan. Still hoping to see Bourbon at night when it's really hopping, but I'll take what I can get."

They followed Elise's instructions to Bourbon Street, peering in the shop windows that lined both sides of the thoroughfare. Jazz music filled the air already, despite the early hour. And the streets weren't empty. A significant number of revelers populated the hotspot, many clutching drinks from the numerous alcohol vendors open for business.

"It's twelve o'clock somewhere, I suppose," Sterling muttered. "Want a frozen concoction to sip on the way, Kimberly?"

She knew he teased but truly was amazed by the number of locations selling frozen cocktails in more flavors than she'd ever seen in her life. Slushes and daiquiris and goodness knew what else.

They passed by a New Orleans Mardi Gras Museum. Shops full of masquerade masks and beads. Restaurants and bars. And so many happy people.

They also saw a number of people curled up, sleeping on the sidewalks. And more than once she walked past a group of smokers—and could tell they weren't smoking tobacco.

"Might get a contact high before we make it to the stop," Stan commented. "Careful, Teej. Not sure you can handle it."

"I don't need chemicals to feel good," her younger camera operator said. "Cristal liked my Insta post. I'm riding a natural high."

"News flash, kid," Sterling said. "That 'natural high' you're feeling is caused by a chemical. Dopamine, to be exact. And every time you feel good about a like, you're getting a hit of it. No different to your brain than ingesting a drug. And you want more. Next thing you know, you're addicted."

"Huh-uh." TJ's brow furrowed.

"It's true," Sterling said. "Your brain releases the drug, but the response is the same."

"Says my social media expert," Kimberly said.

"My job is to understand it and hook your viewers. And then keep them happy. I'm basically a drug dealer, vending out little hits of happiness."

"And that explains all that time on your phone?" She laughed as she said it, keeping it light. Because she knew he'd definitely been happily texting, not hard at work on social media outlets.

He frowned. "Not all of it, no."

Well. He'd been honest at least. But the fact he opted not to elaborate—

The hair on her arms stood on end. Her sixth sense tingled. She stopped to look around.

That woman trailed behind her. The same woman she'd seen at Napoleon's.

She gripped Michael's arm. "That's her. That's the woman I've seen before. The one who ran off at Napoleon House."

"Where?"

The woman stopped in her tracks and her eyes went wide. As before, she turned and disappeared into the crowd as soon as Kimberly noticed her.

Not this time. She wouldn't lose her again. She hurried after her, taking note of the woman's deep purple hat and coat—or did she wear a cloak? She didn't get a good look before the woman virtually vanished. She caught sight of a purple hat bobbing along down the street and continued her pursuit, resorting to pushing past people who stood in her way.

How did this woman keep finding her in a huge city like New Orleans? Was she following them all along and no one noticed? That couldn't possibly be. Besides, the woman set off her sixth sense. She couldn't deny the tingling sensation that preceded spotting this woman nearby. But if the woman wanted to meet her or tell her something, why did she run as soon as she was noticed?

At the next corner, a red light ground her to a halt. She looked up and down the streets of the intersection. No sign of the purple hat anywhere.

"Kimmy!" Michael caught up to her, panting. "Did you see where she went?"

She faced the rest of her crew, all eyes on her. "No. I've lost her. Still have no idea who she is or what she wants. Sorry for the detour."

THE CEMETERY they needed was part of a large conglomerate of cemeteries clustered in the same area, a short walk from the streetcar terminal. Despite his enthusiasm to ride the streetcar, Michael enjoyed the jaunt down Canal Street least of anyone. First, they'd waited at the wrong stop for fifteen minutes. Then they waited another fifteen at the correct stop, scrunched onto a tiny, covered bench with a dozen other people jostling to get under the cover.

"This has to be the least efficient way to get anywhere," he'd commented, watching the time tick by. "Are those people actually taking groceries home like this?"

"You don't get to say a word," she told him, "after blackmailing me into this. Also, you sound like a spoiled brat, so can you please just be quiet?"

She hated to admit it, but riding the streetcar was actually fun. Watching Sterling stare at his phone screen was not. He grinned at something on his phone and began typing. Who was he texting so eagerly?

She couldn't see the screen clearly but thought she saw her

name. When she leaned closer for a better look, he turned his phone away.

"You're missing some great scenery," she said. "What's distracting you?"

He shook his head, finished up whatever he was typing, and tucked the phone into a pocket. "Not anything you need to worry about."

Was this the same thing he'd talked about with Michael? Who had informed her it was Sterling's to share. Clearly something was going on that no one was telling her about. "I think I'd like to be the judge of that. What's up?"

He pulled his mouth into a no-big-deal curlicue and shrugged. "Nothing."

The way he refused to look her in the eye as he said it, combined with his chakras lighting up, blared loudly that he was not being honest with her. But he tucked an arm around her, pulled her close, and kissed the top of her head.

She snuggled in and tried again. "You can talk to me about anything. If something is wrong, I'd like to know."

He squeezed. "I'm handling it. Really. Nothing to worry about."

Her stomach squirmed. No way she could stop worrying, now that he'd confirmed he was keeping something from her.

They passed many cemeteries as they neared the end of the line. The one they needed was only a short walk from their final stop, so after descending the streetcar steps, they crossed the street, found the entrance, and wandered in.

"Mark Twain called these 'cities of the dead,'" Elise informed them.

Kimberly saw why. Walking through row after row of the concrete above-ground tombs felt much like walking through a neighborhood of tiny houses, lavishly decorated with stone statues of angels. Other plots were less elaborate, much smaller concrete blocks stacked over the ensconced remains. The air was thick with whispers, softly tugging at her as she wound through the final resting places.

"New Orleans is too close to the water level to bury their dead underground. The bodies would resurface whenever it rains. So the area developed this unique means of burial. They're running out of space though."

Elise led the way, following the row designations, much like following street signs, as they wound through the cemetery. She stopped in front of a medium-sized plot, neither enormous and elaborately decorated nor tiny and plain. A small obelisk rose above two squares, inscribed with the names Henry and Gladys LaBlanc.

She stood in silence, staring at the names that meant so much and yet so little to her. The cameras recorded, but she couldn't hold everything in check.

"How could they?" she asked. "How could they know about me but not want to meet me?"

"Maybe they didn't approve of your dad," Rosie suggested.

"Maybe that's why your mom ran off with him," Michael said.

Rosie nodded. "Exactly. They could have eloped."

"And my grandparents just moved back to New Orleans and went on with their lives like they never had a daughter? Even though they must have maintained some sort of tie and knew that I was born and existed?"

"They . . . didn't mention your father in that," Elise pointed out. "If they refused to acknowledge him . . ."

"That actually makes sense," Michael whispered.

"Plus they list your mother by her former, maiden name. And you . . . they don't mention by name."

"Maybe they have another granddaughter," Sterling suggested.

"No." Elise shook her head. "I've checked ancestry registries and traced birth certificates and pieced together family trees. Kimberly's mom was their only child. That makes Kimberly their only grandchild."

"All the more reason they should have been desperate to maintain those ties, not sever them."

Could she connect with them now? And if so, would they speak to her?

She stepped closer, standing between the two low tombs, where some of her last ancestors rested in silence, having taken secrets to their graves.

Resting one hand on the fading names inscribed on the obelisk, she clutched her quartz and breathed in the heavy, faintly briny air.

A little girl cried.

"Ronnie?" the voice of a frightened woman replied.

Nothing but a quavering sob answered.

She ran up the stairs, down the hall, into the second room on the left.

Empty.

A whimper issued from the closet.

She ran to the door, torqued the knob, and burst inside the tiny space.

A flash of bright blue—

"Do they speak to you?" a woman's voice asked.

Kimberly gasped and threw her arms out to the sides, reorienting in time and space.

The girl . . . the little girl . . . was she okay?

"Umm, who are you?" Michael asked, voice dripping with disdain. "Because you just destroyed a fantastic take."

While Michael gave the intruding woman his angry bitch face, hip to the side, hand out, demanding an apology, Kimberly bent forward, took deep breaths, and attempted to convince herself the vision meant nothing. She didn't believe herself.

Rosie moved beside her. "Here. Inhale. Deep breaths."

Orange. And lemon. All the citrus to rejuvenate and clear her mind.

The stranger spoke again. "Simple essential oils? Quaint. But I suppose they'll work if you have nothing better. Eventually. Sort of."

The woman stepped closer, but her crew closed the space between them, Stan directly in front.

"We'll ask one more time before we call the police. Who are you?"

"And what do you want?" Michael asked.

The woman peered past them at Kimberly. "You can't detect who I am and what I want?"

She sensed nothing particularly special about the woman and shook her head. "I'm sorry, no. Should I?"

"I'm here to help you. I know what you're looking for."

There it was again—*what she was looking for*. "What do you think I'm looking for?"

"Let's go back to my shop and—"

"Let me guess," Sterling said. "It's a Voodoo shop. We've already heard this sales pitch. Move along."

The woman narrowed her eyes. "Wakefield."

"And now you'll tell me you're psychic because you 'know' a readily recognizable celebrity. Sorry. Not impressed."

The woman curled a lip and turned her nose up. "Not sure why you're keeping this guy around as your little pet, Kimberly, but I assure you if you'll come with me—"

"Pet?" Sterling crossed his arms. "What's that supposed to mean?"

The woman turned away from him. "Kimberly, I sensed your presence the moment you arrived. Haven't you felt mine? Ours? We hoped you'd reach out."

Ours? "I've been focused on the investigation—"

Sterling reinserted himself. "Does everyone in New Orleans own a Voodoo shop and think they're psychic?"

The woman wouldn't even look at him. "I'm speaking with Kimberly, thank you."

"Yeah, well, I'm her partner, and I don't want to see her harassed by some fake psychic or super-stalker or whatever you are."

"Oh, yes. Her 'partner.' Kimberly, this man is the worst possible partner you could align yourself with."

The constant quick barbs were more than she could keep up with. And she didn't care for the antagonism. "Sterling is a great partner. He's brought so much to the show." He might be keeping something from her, but she didn't like the way this woman spoke to him.

"Someone as powerful as you doesn't need to slum around with a non-believer. You should be with someone who appreciates your gifts and worships the ground you walk on."

Sterling rolled his eyes. "Worships the—A little excessive, don't you think?"

"No, I don't. And the fact you do proves my point. You hold her back by reinforcing her lack of confidence." The woman held out a card identical to the one she'd been handed in the street. "There's only one legitimate Voodoo supply store in the French Quarter. Mine. In fact, it's in the name. And while not everyone in New Orleans is psychic, everyone who works at my place is. Come with me, preferably without your pet skeptic. I'll introduce you to—"

"No way," Sterling said. "You still haven't told us who the hell you are or what you want. Why would we let Kimberly go anywhere alone with you?"

Kimberly hesitated only a moment. "Please. I must ask you to be respectful of my crew, or I'm not going anywhere with you. Sterling is part of my crew. And he has a point. We don't know who you are."

The woman narrowed her eyes but smiled. "Of course. I'm Marissa. From Voodoo Legitimate. And I know why your mother had to leave New Orleans and go into hiding."

CHAPTER FIFTEEN

KIMBERLY COULDN'T RESIST the allure of learning information about her mother, even if Marissa had come on a bit strong and abrasive. She'd refused to come alone, though, as Sterling's advice was sage.

The moment Kimberly crossed the threshold of Voodoo Legitimate, the atmosphere once again soothed and relaxed her.

Marissa took a small vial from behind the counter, opened it, and dabbed some of the liquid on her thumb. Standing in front of Kimberly, she brushed the liquid onto her forehead, murmuring softly. Then she ran her thumb over Kimberly's wrists. "Here you have sanctuary. This is a psychic safe space."

"I can feel it," she said, breathing deeply of the earthy-smelling oil and luxuriating in the sense of peace. "It's exactly what I needed."

"Safe place? What does that even mean?" Sterling asked.

"In simplest terms, it means she is surrounded by others like her who welcome, accept, and understand her. We can nurture your gift, help you hone and expand it."

"Who is 'we'?" Sterling made no attempt to soften his harsh tone. This was beyond his normal skepticism. He sounded antagonistic.

Marissa glanced at him, then pointedly ignored him, returning attention to Kimberly. "Zorrie reached out to me. She shared the disconnect you've experienced. The first thing we need to do is determine the cause and repair the damage."

"That would be wonderful." She breathed a sigh of relief, tension and anxiety evaporating.

Rosie rested a hand on her. "This *is* exactly what you needed, girl. Finally."

She heard Sterling click his tongue and sigh.

"Have you truly never had any training with your gift?" Marissa asked.

"Gift!" Sterling scoffed.

She glanced at him. If he antagonized Marissa enough, the woman might withhold the information she longed for. "None. In fact, when I was little, my parents told me spirits weren't real. They told me I couldn't see or hear something that didn't exist."

"You were actively discouraged from using your gift?"

"Considering they admonished me for even mentioning it, yes, I suppose I was. But they didn't tell me not to use it. They denied it existed at all."

Marissa lifted an eyebrow. "Interesting. And your mother was Veronica LaBlanc, yes?"

"Hold up," Sterling interjected. "You said you know who she is."

"Of course we know who Kimberly Wantland is. Clearly a successful psychic. I detected your powerful presence as soon as you arrived, so I knew for sure that you weren't a charlatan. And we've long suspected you to be the rumored daughter of the LaBlanc line. But without proof, how could we be sure?"

Sterling cleared his throat. "Because you're psychic. Supposedly."

Marissa turned up her nose, as if she smelled something foul. "If not for her protection, I would cast you out without thinking twice."

"Cast me out? Seriously?" Sterling laughed. "Take your best

shot. I'm perfectly capable of holding my own, thank you very—"

Marissa's eyes stormed, appearing almost black. Air currents swirled through the room, twirling smoke from the incense into tendrils that appeared almost alive. "You have no idea. No idea what you've gotten yourself into and no idea what her concern for you protects you from. The mere fact that you are important to her, though I cannot understand why, puts such a target on your back. And you repay her with—"

Kimberly leaned forward. "A target? On Sterling? What does that mean?"

The room stilled. Marissa's eyes returned to their normal, violet color. "Really, Kimberly, how do you function around his toxic energy?"

"I don't think—He doesn't seem different from anyone—"

"Of course. You've been hidden away, cut off from the community, discouraged and derided your entire life. Toxic energy is all you've ever known. The fact your gift manifested despite attempts to quell it is testament to your sheer, raw strength. You are incredible."

This woman had to be mistaken. She must have the wrong person. No way could these words apply to her. "I'm sorry, I think you've confused me with—"

Michael rubbed his hands together. "This is story gold. An early Christmas present. I couldn't have scripted a better twist. Fabulous!"

"But Michael, I don't want to mislead my fans. What she's saying is—"

Marissa stepped closer, eyes shining, giving no indication she heard either of them, and cupped her cheek. "If you're this powerful with no training, with your gift dampened by suffo-cating negativity, think what you can become in our hands."

"What does that mean?" Sterling asked.

Ignoring the question, Marissa looked over her crew. "At least you have a little support established. With the exception of that"

—she waved at Sterling—"these people are devout believers. We can train your girl—"

"Hey!" Rosie said. "I have a name."

"We can train your Rosie while we train you, show her better ways, stronger tools, teach her to more fully empower you."

Rosie's face fell. "I thought I was doing a pretty good job."

"You do!" Kimberly told her. "No complaints at all."

Marissa addressed Rosie directly. "You do a remarkable job with what you have. No one can use knowledge they've never been given. We can give you that knowledge. Perhaps even teach you healing methods we don't often share outside our circle. For Kimberly's para-giver, we would make an exception."

Rosie wrinkled her nose. "Her what now?"

"Her para-giver, much like a caregiver. But you care for her psychic senses, her paranormal needs. We are all matched with a para-giver who connects with us in a ritual ceremony and is bonded to us for life."

"I have a title now?" Rosie asked. "I like it. Much better than 'personal assistant' or whatever I've been referred to as."

"If you'd like," Marissa said, "we could arrange a bonding ceremony for the two of you while you're here. The connection forged is—"

"Okay, sorry, I've had all I can take," Sterling said. "This is veering into cult territory, and I am not going to stand here and listen to it like it's totally normal. Michael, you don't have the slightest concern about any of this?"

"This is brilliant, Sterling. Our little Christmas episode just received a huge infusion of exciting bonus material. Let them light some candles and 'bond' Kimberly and Rosie. Who cares? People will eat it up!"

Marissa beamed, eyes bright. "But first, we should repair the damage you've incurred. The ceremony will be far more effective if your psyche is as strong as possible. I'll bring in our best healer, my personal para-giver. She can identify the disconnect and mend it. With luck she will be able to guide you to pinpoint the cause as well, to avoid future instances."

"And in the future," Rosie said, "I'll know how to heal her."

"We will do our best to train you in the time you're here. Though of course, we would prefer you stay and—"

"She's not staying here with you," Sterling insisted. "We will finish our investigation and move on to the next location."

Marissa narrowed her eyes. "That is not your decision to make. Kimberly, with your permission, I'd like to call a meeting of the entire group to introduce you to everyone. I cannot stress enough how excited they will be. We have searched for you lo these many years—"

Sterling laughed. "'Lo these many years'? No one talks like that! Is this a joke? Michael, are you in on this?"

Kimberly could read every spectrum in the room—all at once and without even touching anyone—and registered no deception, no subterfuge. Everyone in the room was open and honest. A mixture of excitement and curiosity pervaded the space. Only Sterling stood out, threatened, angry, defensive.

"I assure you this is no joke," Marissa said. "Matters this grave are not to be joked about."

"And yet we haven't even established who this group is. Who is so eager to meet her they've been searching and searching 'lo these many years' even though she's a celebrity, known across the nation, and your search should have taken about half a second?"

"We've gone international, actually," Michael interjected.

"As I said before, we suspected Kimberly to be the one we sought—the last remaining female of the LaBlanc lineage. And we"—she glared at Sterling—"are known, to those who know us, as the Paras."

"Creative," Sterling muttered.

"Your grandmother Gladys was a powerful psychic, Kimberly, as was your mother. But she possessed a unique, additional gift, possibly a mutation, we'd never seen before. Considering our gift passes through the maternal line, we believe your mother inherited the new mutation as well. She also demonstrated qualities that lead us to believe the gift grew with each generation. We suspected that if Veronica birthed a daughter, she could be more powerful than any who came before her—a leader of psychics, capable of incredible things."

"But that's . . . I'm sorry, but that just isn't possible. I'm just . . . me."

"Because you were raised to believe that!"

Sterling held up a finger. "So you're saying you knew of Kimberly but didn't know she was this fabled daughter of a psychic?"

"Correct. But now that she has confirmed her mother was Veronica LaBlanc, there can be no question. She is the one we've been searching for."

"That makes no sense. If her grandmother and mother were such powerful psychics, what did they have to fear? Why run at all, much less disappear and hide?"

Marissa's eyes glowed vivid violet, the serpentine incense smoke curling around her like a viper preparing to strike. "Because there is another. An ancient, powerful presence who seeks to possess and control the gift which passes through generations of LaBlanc women."

"Let me guess. He's a man," Sterling said.

"*Her* name is Lilith, and she will stop at nothing to bring you into her fold, Kimberly. She has the ability to cloak, and I fear she may already be searching for you, hunting you down. I'm glad I reached you first. I'll teach you to protect yourself."

"This sounds . . . wonderful. Too good to be true. Thank you."

"We have much work to do," Marissa said. "I'll reach out to the Paras and alert you to the appointed time."

"Oh, jeez." Sterling rolled his eyes.

"Speaking of work," Michael said, "we should probably go review footage and prepare for this evening."

"Before you go . . ." Marissa removed a bracelet from her

wrist and slipped it over Kimberly's. "This is black obsidian. Recently cleansed. It's been used for millennia and is associated with transformation and metamorphosis. This will help strengthen you as you develop your gift and transition into the powerful psychic you are meant to be."

The moment the string of glossy round stones rested against her skin, Kimberly sensed the difference. "I feel more at ease already!"

"That's the other effect you're feeling," Marissa said, with a pointed look at Sterling. "This stone offers powerful protection against toxic energy. It repels negativity back to the source, inhibiting it from draining you. An empath like you really needs to be on guard against energy vampires."

"Energy *vampires*?" Sterling rolled his eyes.

Rosie's gaze travelled over the store. "I see more bracelets over there. What else should I know about?"

"I know all about them!" Zorrie said, scrambling to the display of stone bracelets.

"We'll get to that," Marissa assured her. "I want to let our para-givers instruct you."

"I'm learning to be a para-giver." Zorrie's pride was evident in her tone. "Can I be at the meeting?"

"Everyone should be at the meeting," Marissa said. "I'll work on finding a time we can all gather. Until then, remain watchful, Kimberly. And protect yourself at all costs. Many creatures of the night make their home in New Orleans. The energy and magic here draw them. Some harbor dark intentions you cannot begin to fathom. And would not hesitate to act on them."

Rosie stood before a display of oils in vials. "Maybe we need some of these too."

Marissa chuckled. "You have the soul of a para-giver. No question. Your instincts are spot on. These are all hand mixed locally, infused with powerful abilities. We will teach you how to use every one of them."

"Can I anoint Kimberly before they leave?" Zorrie asked.

"Go ahead. It will help until we can schedule the meeting and heal her. Let Rosie assist."

Zorrie ran a finger over the rows of vials. "This one! To attract good energy and lift your spirits."

The young woman dabbed oil on her thumb as Marissa had and directed Rosie to do the same. "Then you can apply it like a fragrance, to the pulse points like the wrist and neck."

"Yeah, gotta repel those vampires," Sterling muttered.

Rosie followed instructions. Both women in her space, tending to her, was a bit much for Kimberly, but she allowed it.

"Now send her all the positive energy you can and infuse the oil with your will. Later you can learn some of the chants to accompany them. But you have to master control of your energy first." Zorrie closed her eyes, her lips moving as she silently chanted.

"We're allowing someone to cast spells on Kimberly now?" Sterling held his hands out to Michael, but Michael only waved him off.

"You two better be capturing every moment of this, or you're fired," Michael said, lifting his eyebrows at Stan and TJ.

They thanked Marissa and Zorrie and turned to leave.

Marissa placed a hand on her wrist, grasping the bracelet. The woman closed her eyes and murmured unintelligible words before bidding them good-bye. "There. Now you're ready. I've done what I can do for now. Until we meet again."

Kimberly was sorry to go. A chill shivered through her as she left the warmth and safety of the shop and the people inside it despite the balmy temperature outside.

CHAPTER SIXTEEN

REJUVENATED, Kimberly looked forward to meeting the other psychics. One short session with Marissa and already she felt better. For now, she couldn't wait to get back to the investigation. She knew she wasn't healed yet, but still she tingled with anticipation, as if her psychic senses were ready to go and eager for a target to focus on.

Rosie, too, seemed to be walking on air. "I've always tried to learn everything I possibly could to help support you. But after that, I feel like an illiterate buffoon. I am so freakin' excited to soak this all up."

"I know what you mean. With her training, actual training, I may finally learn to control my gift."

"It's a gift now, is it?" Sterling murmured, clearly irritated. "Never heard you refer to it that way before."

"It's always felt more like a curse."

"And this 'ancient evil' she mentioned? You really think someone is after you?"

She stopped and turned to face him, looking him directly in the eyes. "Yes. I've felt someone tracking me or hunting me. I've mentioned it and been dismissed. Maybe if you'd taken my concerns seriously—"

"I take your concerns seriously. Serious concerns. In the months we've been together, have we seen anyone following you? Even that crazy man from Oklahoma hasn't reappeared."

"Because they're attacking me psychically."

"I think it's far more probable that this woman was using classic techniques to draw out bits of information from you and then expand them into these stories. And now she's conflagrated a mild concern into a real fear."

"No, she's alerted me to a real danger. And is going to help me prepare to face it."

TJ and Stan circled them, cameras recording every bit of the disagreement.

Sterling blew out a breath and held up his hands. "Okay. I can see I'm wasting my energy, but that woman never did tell us how she knew to find you at the cemetery. I don't like people who hide things."

He set off at a faster clip, leaving them behind.

"Really?" She turned to Rosie. "Because he's hiding something from me."

When they entered the lobby of the hotel, Macy greeted them enthusiastically. "Did you have a good morning?"

"So nice. Wonderful breakfast. Saw some of the city. Met some fabulous people. And I found the home my mother grew up in."

"I'm so glad you're enjoying our city! And how about Flint's ghost? Any progress there?"

"Some. And we're about to review footage. If you want to pop in and—"

Elise looked up from her phone. "Kimberly, I have something you may want to see. I found Flint's financial history. Wasn't hard actually. His net worth is huge."

"What?" She leaned closer to get a better look at Elise's phone displaying the records.

"How is that possible?" Michael asked.

"We thought he was broke!" Rosie said.

"He and his partner, Bo, made a small fortune decades ago and invested well."

"Partner?" Michael asked. "Or *partner*? Did we ever clarify that?"

"Business partner," Kimberly said. "He mentioned his past girlfriend, Maud, would have been his wife. Except something happened."

"So maybe Bo happened?" Michael suggested.

"They were definitely close," Elise said. "Bo left everything to Flint when he died. Every penny. He never married either. No kids. No other relatives apparently."

"And Flint mentioned Bo died suddenly, which means he had something in place to determine where that money would go in case of a tragedy like that," Michael pointed out.

Kimberly considered. "Maud's spirit asked him last night if the money was worth it. Maybe there was more to it than the money."

"Exactly how much money are we talking about?" Sterling asked.

"Millions," Elise answered.

Everyone in her crew gasped.

"Why is he still running this place, then?" Rosie asked. "He's miserable. He could retire and quit working himself to death."

"This place is a tax shelter," Sterling said. "I'd bet money on it. The loss he reports on the business balances his investment income, so he doesn't owe any taxes."

"He has millions of dollars but pays no taxes?"

"Common loophole," Sterling said. "He doesn't make millions of dollars or draw a salary. So he can show a net loss."

"Unbelievable!" Stan said.

"You can't tell me you don't look for every conceivable write-off available to you," Sterling said.

"Sure. And my accountant is good at his job. But I also know I don't have millions, and I do owe taxes every year."

Rosie huffed. "Sounds about right. Only us average schmoes

pay taxes. The people who have the most find ways to weasel out of it."

Sterling gave her a look like, *come on.* "Pretty sure your income is above average."

"I doubt Macy's is!" Kimberly said. "I have the feeling she scrapes by on her salary. And clearly her benefits are not robust."

Macy startled at being brought into the conversation. "I do okay."

"You work for a millionaire! I think he could cough up more and not be any worse off." Stan worked his hands together.

"I know he's wealthy. I've been managing this hotel for a decade. I knew Bo too. His death hit Mr. Flint very hard. We're all he has. Especially around the holidays. He wouldn't even celebrate Christmas if it wasn't for us."

"Would we say he celebrates Christmas at all?" Rosie asked.

"He has that nephew," Stan reminded them. "It's his choice not to celebrate or spend time with the family he has."

"I can't leave Mr. Flint. He'd be devastated. I know he seems like an angry old crank, but he really is a nice guy under that crusty exterior."

"You sure about that?" Rosie asked.

Stan spoke up before Macy could answer. "That doesn't matter. You need to do what makes sense for you. Find a better job. Possibly even one that pays more. Flint will be fine."

"It isn't that easy. Even if I find a different job and get hired, and even if the salary is higher, most places don't offer benefits from day one. Typically, they have a ninety-day wait period before insurance starts. Abby cannot go three months without medical care. I have to keep her covered. The insurance keeps me tied to the job, too."

"What about a GoFundMe campaign to help you through the transition? Have you thought about that?"

"I only have so many hours in the day. Work and Abby's care take a lot of time. But yes, I tried that too. You know how sometimes those go viral and people make way more money than they even ask for?"

"Right. Sure."

"Yeah, not me. I'm not one of the fortunate ones."

"How much did you raise?"

"Five dollars."

No one said anything. What could they say?

Stan didn't seem to be able to let it go though. "There has to be a way. It isn't right for you to be stuck here in a dead-end job that will never allow you to move up. You're paid a pittance, have abysmal sick leave, crummy insurance that's left you with huge medical bills to contend with—"

"But she has a job!" Flint rounded the corner. "She should be grateful for that!"

"She's a hard worker. She can find another job. One where she's appreciated."

"I won't stop her then!" Flint scowled at them.

"And what would you do if she found a better job and left?" Kimberly asked.

"I'd replace her with my nephew!"

"No, we heard him turn that down. He has a job he likes."

"Someone else then! If she doesn't want to be here—"

"I'm only suggesting a raise. A small raise could make her life a lot easier. Make it easier for her to breathe instead of subsisting paycheck to paycheck. It seems only fair—"

"Life isn't fair! Some have, some don't. It will always be that way."

"Great attitude, dude. Especially at Christmas."

"Christmas! Always an excuse for freeloading." Flint turned to Macy. "Go on then! Leave. They all leave eventually." He turned around and went back the way he'd come.

"I'm not going anywhere, Mr. Flint!" Macy called after him. She shook her head and turned back to Kimberly. "He doesn't mean it. Really."

Kimberly nodded. "Well, we should get through footage review before it's time for tonight's investigation."

"Think about what I said," Stan said.

"I've thought about it more than you can imagine. He needs me, and I need the insurance. I have to stay. Good luck tonight. I hope you can help the ghost."

"Help him?"

"He seems distraught. I hate to see anything hurting. Mr. Flint or the ghost haunting him. So many hurting here."

"I'll do everything I can. I promise."

In the elevator, everyone stared ahead in silence until Rosie spoke. "Kimberly, you've granted wishes before. Maybe you can help put them in touch with Make*A*Wish and grant one for Abby."

"Gladly. But that won't pay her medical bills."

Sterling's furrowed brow indicated he was deep in thought. "Offering money can be taken as insulting. But maybe we can convince her to try GoFundMe again and then send your fans to help."

"*Our* fans," she corrected.

Sterling offered a slight smile that didn't reach his eyes. "Right. Our fans."

His spectrum lit up. Something bothered him. She wished she knew what. Her sixth sense told her they were barreling toward a huge change, and she didn't even know what was causing it.

The elevator doors opened, and they headed down the hall.

"I'll tell you what," Stan said. "After seeing the old man so scared and helpless last night, I thought he'd be different today. But he's still a jerk, still treating that stressed out single mom dealing with way more than anyone should like a—"

Kimberly could tell something more bothered him. "You're worried about your wife, aren't you?"

He whipped around to face her, his eyes glistening. "How did you know?"

"I can tell. Not a big leap. She's home alone, going through a pregnancy without you. Macy's situation surely triggered the concerns. It's not the same. Your wife has you."

"I'm not there though. I call her every day, check in as much as I can. When I do get to visit, it's a short, quick stop, over far too soon."

"We're sending you home for Christmas," Kimberly said.

"But—"

"Nope. You're going. And for an entire month. We can manage."

His head dropped, and she suspected he was hiding tears. "Thanks. I appreciate it."

"You need it. And I am not Jeremiah Flint."

CHAPTER SEVENTEEN

FOOTAGE REVIEW REVEALED NOTHING USEFUL. The crew grumbled that the time could have been spent enjoying the city, Christmas shopping, or hitting a few tourist spots. Instead, they'd had time only for a quick dinner, followed by wardrobe and makeup.

Kimberly lingered in the lobby, though she strongly suspected any activity tonight would occur in Flint's room again. The crew had fanned out to gauge activity in other parts of the hotel just in case. A more thorough check would ensure they didn't miss anything.

She snuck glances at Bram, splayed out in a chair which he spun slowly in little half circles, back and forth, back and forth. She couldn't read his spectrum. After this afternoon, when she'd read everybody in the room, she thought her ability had expanded and improved. Had it contracted again? Had Marissa's proximity impacted things? Or perhaps she'd been energized by the space itself?

Bram met her gaze.

Shoot. He'd caught her staring. She looked away but that made the moment awkward. She looked back and tried to smile but thought she managed more of a grimace than anything remotely friendly.

The young man beckoned her over.

Relieved, she crossed to the desk.

"How's it going?" he asked. "Figured out what's happening yet?"

She flushed, unsure why exactly. "No, but that's not unusual. This is only the second night."

His lips curled into a half-smile. "Happens every year. Glad a professional is finally dealing with it."

She couldn't tell if he was teasing or not. "Why do you think it happens?"

"Oh, I know why."

Taken aback, she took a moment to recover. "You must be joking."

"No."

"Then why didn't you speak up before now?"

"And interfere with fate? The continuum must progress. I'll let you figure it out. Everything happens for a reason. You were meant to come to New Orleans. I'm only here to observe."

She shivered, still unable to read his spectrum and now unable to understand him. Common sense alerted her that something was off, even without the use of her sixth sense. The continuum must progress? Whatever that meant. "If you know something—"

He turned his nearly black eyes on her. "I know everything."

Her stomach lurched, accompanied by vertigo so severe, she leaned against the counter. She felt like she was falling and yet held firmly in place—by Bram's eyes, suddenly the only thing she could see. Entranced, she wanted to lean closer to him, connect with him, become one with him—

"Kimberly?" Sterling's voice snapped her back to her real surroundings. "They need you upstairs. Flint asked for you."

Bram smirked, and she had the uncomfortable sensation he knew exactly what she'd been thinking.

She spun and followed Sterling to the elevator.

He stood absolutely still, hands on hips, staring straight ahead until they were alone in the isolated box.

"What the hell was that?"

She touched her forehead. "I'm not sure. We were talking about the investigation and then—"

"Because it looked like you were about to kiss him."

"What? No!" And yet hadn't she been leaning in, intent on exactly that? What could she say? That the guy had mesmerized her somehow? Even she didn't believe that. No way Sterling would. And yet she had absolutely no rational explanation for the bizarre feeling of being nowhere, somehow lost in time and place, that had overwhelmed her when Bram stared into her eyes.

The elevator *dinged* and the doors opened. Sterling stormed into the hallway. Her crew congregated around Flint's suite.

Flint hovered in his doorway, wringing his hands. "Where were you? He's back again."

"Who's back?" Still disoriented, she shook her head to clear it.

"Bo. I woke up and he was standing over me, rattling those damned chains."

"I told him he was dreaming," Sterling said. "But he—"

"I was not. Bo told me I haven't learned my lesson yet. What the hell does that mean? Why would I dream that? And I smell roses again. Like last night."

"You okay, girl?" Rosie asked. "You look pale."

She glanced at Sterling. He met her eyes but turned away.

"Uh-oh. What happened? You weren't even gone that long."

"Not now. It's too complicated. I felt so confident earlier. Hope I can still salvage some of that."

"Pretty soon you'll be one hundred percent again. And I'll be able to boost you up better than ever. Focus on the positive."

The black obsidian on her wrist, intended to ward off negative energy, wasn't up to the challenge Sterling's current mood presented. She'd have to do the best she could. She curled one hand around her quartz crystal and reached out, inviting connection.

The scent of roses overpowered her. "Yes, you're right. She's here again. I can feel her presence and smell roses."

"Who's here, Kimmy?" Michael asked.

"Mr. Flint's sister, Violet."

"What about Bo? Or Maud?"

She stretched her consciousness, opening her psyche as wide as she dared. "No, I don't sense any other presence. Only Violet."

Flint slammed his eyes closed. "Why do you show me these things? It's like being in a nightmare, but I can't wake up."

"What do you see, Mr. Flint? Can you describe it for us?"

"It's me, but—" He covered his eyes. "Please, no!"

"Can you share with me again?" She took Flint's hand and picked up the photos of him and Violet, closing the loop. Memories fired across her synapses. "I'm here. You're not alone. Let's see what your sister wants to show us."

A quick progression followed, a slideshow of memories—Flint's nephew Jeremy as a baby, a toddler, an adolescent, and an adult. She watched Flint accept cards and gifts, year after year, from hand-drawn construction paper decorated with crayons to heartfelt store-bought cards. His hands shook as they held each card and gift, then covered his eyes.

Violet's pain filled her too as the spirit directed her to a drawer in a nightstand where she found cards from the past decade, saved but unanswered.

"You never answered him?" she asked. "Never reciprocated or even thanked him?"

"I don't know him! What would I give him?"

"He's only a stranger because you push him away."

"Besides, he's more than happy to let me know he's well compensated by his job. What could I buy him that he can't already buy for himself?"

The slideshow ended and a familiar scene unfolded before her. She'd witnessed this—Jeremy inviting Flint to Christmas Eve dinner with him and his wife.

Violet spoke through her. "Jerry, he doesn't want your money. He wants to know you and be in your life. That's all."

Flint gave her a hard stare. "Violet? I—"

The floor dropped away from beneath her, sending a quivery tingle through her stomach. And yet she didn't fall. Flint squeezed her hand. Time and space distorted around them and reassembled into a brightly lit room, where Jeremy and several others chatted and laughed, cards in hand. Glasses of wine rested within reach on a distressed-wood coffee table. A Christmas tree, fully decked out in Mardi Gras motif ornaments, towered seven feet high in one corner of the room. Three stockings hung from the mantel of an electric fireplace—Jeremy, Nomi, and Uncle Jeremiah.

"So where's that imaginary uncle of yours, Jeremy?" One of the men slapped a card onto the table and took a drink of wine.

The woman beside Jeremy, presumably Nomi, scowled and placed a card atop his. "Shhh! That's none of your business."

"You swore he was coming this time."

Jeremy laughed. "I really thought I'd worn him down. Thought this was the year for sure."

Another man played a card and shook his head. "You are tenacious. I'll give you that. I'd have given up long ago."

Nomi played a card and patted his leg. "Jerry will never give up. As much as I hate to watch that old man hurt him, I love his deep loyalty and persistence."

"Thanks, babe."

The woman kissed his cheek. "Honestly, I think I'm the reason he won't come. Pretty sure Uncle J hates me for some reason."

Flint stiffened beside her. "Hate? I don't hate her. I think Jeremy rushed into things but—"

"Is he racist?" One of the other women played a card and downed the remainder of her wine.

Flint balled his fists. "Racist? I will thank you to hold your tongue, young lady! Why, I never—"

"Oh, no, he's not racist," Jeremy said. "Here let me refill that for you. Anyone else need to be topped off while I'm pouring?"

"You tell her, Jeremy! That's my boy," Flint said.

Jeremy poured wine for his guests, laughing softly. "He's a misanthrope, but not a racist. He hates everyone, including me I think. An equal opportunity hater."

Flint's hands fell to his side. "Equal—? Hater? I don't hate anyone! How could he think I hate him?"

Kimberly met his gaze. "Have you ever told him otherwise?"

"Why do you bother?" the woman asked. "I could not take that kind of rejection over and over."

"Seriously, dude," the man beside her said. "Give it up."

"He's my uncle," Jeremy said. "The only family I have left. I'll never give up."

The man lifted his newly replenished wine glass. "Doesn't hurt that he's a millionaire. He's gotta leave that money to someone, right?"

Flint bristled but held his tongue, leaning in as if eager to hear the reply.

"Come on!" Jeremy said. "That's really what you think of me? I make plenty of money. So does Nomi. We're perfectly comfortable. Can't have children. What would we do with his money? I wish he'd go on vacation while his health is still decent, enjoy some of that money he worked so hard to earn."

Nomi hugged him. "He'll come around, babe. I know he will."

"It's just . . . I'd like to hear about my mom, ya know? What she was like when they were little. She died when I was in college, so it's not like I didn't know her at all. But they grew up together and lived through some hard times. He could come for dinner occasionally and tell me about her. And him. I know almost nothing about my only living relative."

Kimberly sensed enormous pain well within Flint—and her own heart broke right along with his. She also knew next to nothing about her parents. While she lost her mother, Flint had lost both parents. Neither of them knew much about their history. Tears brimmed in her eyes. She noticed Flint swipe at his cheek.

"Well," Flint muttered, "maybe a dinner now and then wouldn't be so bad."

Jeremy shook his head. "Enough of that! This is Christmas Eve. Shouldn't we be merry and bright? Back to the game. I'm the judge this round, right?"

"Yep, it's all you, babe," Nomi told him. "You better pick my card!"

"No way! This round is mine!" One of the other men grinned and gulped his wine.

"Okay, you had to choose the best response for this prompt: 'I expected Santa to come down the chimney, but instead it was _______.' Let's see what you guys did." Jeremy swept the cards in the center of the table into a pile and gathered them into his hands. "Hey! What is this? This isn't a card from the game."

"Play on! Just pick the best answer!" the laughing man told him.

One of the women hid her eyes. "Mine is dumb! I had nothing good to play for this one."

Jeremy shuffled and read. "Instead it was . . . eggnog."

"Eggnog?" Flint asked beside her. "What does that mean? Eggnog down a chimney?"

"I told you I had nothing!" The woman ducked her head.

Kimberly startled, wondering momentarily if the woman had heard him.

The man beside her rubbed her back. "Sweetie, you're not supposed to say which one was yours. You'll help him narrow it down to Nomi's! And she's already ahead."

"It's a game," Kimberly told Flint. "They draw cards and then have to choose the best one they can for that round. Usually whatever they think will make the judge laugh."

"That's a great one though! Can you imagine someone pouring eggnog down the chimney?" Jeremy moved on. "Instead it was . . . SQUIRREL!"

Everyone laughed.

"Instead it was . . . a major award. Instead it was . . . neighborhood carolers."

Nomi leaned against him laughing. "Neighborhood carolers! They're so intent on singing to you that they come down the chimney!"

The laughing man weighed in again. "Well, now we know which one Nomi played. Come on, come on! Get to the last one!"

Jeremy held up the flimsy piece of paper remaining in his hand. "And our apparently homemade submission—Instead it was . . . Uncle Jeremiah."

"Me?" Flint said. "What in the—I'd never be in anyone's chimney!"

The man doubled over. "Too bad for you! You won't get anything for Christmas! Not even coal! Coal is worth something!"

Jeremy forced a smile. "Funny. Good one, Rick."

Kimberly sensed the joke hurt far more than Jeremy admitted.

"You can't deny it!" Rick laughed hardest of all the guests.

"The nerve of that man! Look at Jeremy's face! He doesn't think it's funny at all! Why I ought to—" Flint balled his fists and started across the room, but the room swirled and distorted, melting around them. "Hey! Wait! I'm not finished here! I want to give that man a piece of my—"

She lost the end of the sentence in the rush of time and space as the vortex swirled around them.

They spun back to his room, only none of her crew were

there. The bleak, empty space seemed especially dismal after the laughter and happiness of his nephew's home.

Across the room, she saw Flint, alone, a threadbare blanket over his lap and a bowl of gumbo in front of him.

"This is how you spend Christmas?" Her heart ached. Even she had Michael back before the show had brought Rosie and the rest of her crew into her life. How could this man choose to be alone when he had another option?

"Aww, I'd be a third wheel," he grumbled. "You saw—they were all couples. Besides, they don't like me."

They don't know you. She felt Violet's response more than heard it.

The desolation sucked Kimberly down. She longed for her friends. But apparently the spirits weren't finished with them yet.

Another lurch sent the world topsy-turvy again. This time they landed in a small apartment. Handmade decorations festooned the space—red and green construction-paper chains wound around the doorways and snowflakes hung from the ceiling. A construction-paper Christmas tree, sprinkled with glitter, was taped to the wall with one gift on the floor below it.

Macy and Abby sat on a worn couch, munching popcorn, huddled under blankets, watching the end of *Miracle on 34th Street*. On the television, a little girl directed Uncle Fred to stop the car and then raced inside a house.

"I wish a real Santa Claus would give us a house," Abby said. "Do you think that could happen?"

"No." Macy laughed. "Things like that only happen in the movies."

Fred swept the woman into his arms, declared his love, and kissed her.

Abby tried again. "Then maybe a man will fall crazy in love with you, and he will buy a house we can live in."

"Don't count on it, Abs. You're stuck with just me." She tickled Abby, who fell sideways.

The laughing developed into a cough.

Macy went white. "Oh no! I'm so sorry. I know better—"

The cough turned into a fit, then a wheeze, then gasps for air.

Abby clutched her chest.

Macy threw her blanket cocoon aside, sprang from the couch, and returned with a machine. She placed a plastic piece over Abby's mouth and nose. "Easy. Try to relax."

The gasps subsided, the only sound in the room the rasping of the breathing apparatus.

Macy blew out a deep breath. "You okay?"

Abby nodded.

"You scared me, baby. Sorry I tickled you. I know better."

Beside her, Flint stood quietly as cheerful music trilled from the television and the credits rolled.

Flint cleared his throat. "Kinda cold in here."

"Heat is expensive. I'm sure you remember."

Kimberly jumped. Bo had joined them. Or perhaps he'd been with them all this time.

"Of course I remember the hard times," Flint murmured.

"And yet it's warmer in this room than in your cold heart. At least love fills this home."

"Love never paid the bills," Flint said.

"Apparently neither does Macy's salary."

"At least she has a—" Flint closed his mouth.

"Yes, she has a job. And you own how many rental properties? And yet still live alone in a hotel room? How much will be enough? When will you be satisfied?"

"We built the business together! You worked as hard as I did! I'm continuing our legacy, increasing our worth!"

"My worth was measured, Jeremiah, and found severely lacking." Bo rattled his chains. *"Every link I carry is a moment of compassion I withheld. I helped only myself when I could have helped so many others. You're following the same path. Don't suffer my fate."*

Flint moved to the makeshift tree and examined the tag on the single gift. "To Abby? Nothing for Macy?"

"And who would gift her? She is alone but for Abby, works long hours. And you can see how frivolous she is with her meager salary."

"But she has a—" Flint snapped his mouth closed.

"Okay, my little dumpling," Macy said. "Off to bed so Santa can come."

Flint watched her walk Abby out of the room. "But this isn't fair. She's a hard worker. A good person. She shouldn't be dealing with this all alone. It's not fair."

"Life isn't fair. Some have, some don't."

Flint's lip actually trembled. "You turn my own words on me. But I didn't mean her. She does work hard. This isn't fair."

"Life isn't fair."

The room around them distorted. She felt the nauseating shift of time and space yet again.

"Stop!" Flint said. "I don't want to go! Will Abby be okay? Bo, don't do this—"

"When will you be satisfied? Not all worth is measured in money."

CHAPTER EIGHTEEN

KIMBERLY SAT UP IN BED, blinking in the sunlight that streamed into her room. Disoriented, she took a moment to remember where she was. The Cardinal hotel in New Orleans. Her clock read just after eight o'clock.

Her throbbing head protested her continued lack of sleep. But an unsettling mixture of fatigue and confusion worried her. What had happened last night? She'd truly felt as though she traveled to different locations and witnessed the scenes unfold, as real as any of her normal daily encounters. She would suspect mental issues or hallucinations except that Flint had fallen to the floor when they'd returned, still pleading with Bo. If Flint had experienced the same visions she had seen, didn't that suggest they had witnessed the same thing? Which meant she wasn't going crazy. And yet she still couldn't explain what had happened. She'd never encountered anything like it. Connecting with spirits and being able to "see" their memories was one thing. Moving locations was disorienting. At least, that's how it felt. Sterling insisted they hadn't left at all. So maybe this was simply another way of experiencing memories.

Her abilities to connect with spirits did not grant her telekinesis or the ability to see into the future. She'd sometimes witnessed the past, but that was simply accessing the memories of the spirits who connected with her. Last night could not have resulted from witnessing someone's past memory. Could it? Abby looked the same age. Jeremy looked the same age. She'd known, without knowing how, that she was glimpsing upcoming Christmas festivities unfolding before her. Not memories. The future.

She pushed the blankets aside and hung her legs off the side of the bed, cradling her head. Maybe she was losing her mind. She couldn't see the future. And yet how else could she explain what had happened? When Flint babbled about visions of Christmas and concern about Abby, her crew had looked to her to dispel his ramblings. And instead she'd confirmed every word. They'd all looked at her with doubt in their eyes. She couldn't blame them. She recognized how crazy she sounded. Sterling, of course, had insisted they hadn't left the room and had simply stood quietly for a few moments before Flint dropped to his knees.

A few moments? How could that be? She'd felt like they'd been gone an hour or more, shifting from one home to another.

She shook her head. Maybe sheer exhaustion distorted her perception. Her body ached, and her mind screamed for sleep. How did Bram do it? He described switching to a nocturnal schedule as if it were as simple as flipping a switch to turn off a light. Not for her it wasn't. She'd been at this for years. And still couldn't fully acclimate. She simply couldn't sleep all day. Then again, Bram had demonstrated another ability last night that left her dumbfounded. She'd never heard of a psychic who could daze someone as he'd shown he could.

What else did celebrity psychic Kimberly Wantland remain ignorant of that normal, everyday psychics had mastered?

Considering she was the one with the target on her back, at least according to Marissa, she needed to correct her lack of knowledge quickly.

For that matter, Marissa had warned Sterling he was also a

target because he was important to Kimberly. But who targeted them? Lilith, the powerful psychic? But why? She wasn't the only psychic in the world. Marissa hadn't fully explained the threat or why her grandparents had fled New Orleans, taking her mother into hiding. She needed to pinpoint the danger and learn to defend against it.

She hoisted herself to her feet and made a cup of coffee. The caffeine would do little to improve her mood but hopefully it would help clear her brain fog a bit.

After a hot shower, she dressed and joined everyone in Michael's suite for footage review. Someone had arranged for a nice breakfast spread, including a big container of coffee.

"Hey, girl," Rosie greeted her. "Feeling any better this morning?"

She filled a cup with coffee and added a bit of milk. "Not really. First cup of coffee made no dent in the exhaustion."

Sterling sat at the table, involved with his phone. He barely glanced up to greet her. He was exhausting on an entirely different level.

"I brought up oatmeal for you," Rosie said. "But if you want something else, they have breakfast down in the dining room. We just thought we'd eat while we review footage."

Michael yawned. "I wanted to finish this morning to leave the afternoon for sightseeing. But now I think I just want to sleep all afternoon."

"Sucks to travel like this," Stan said. "We go all these great places and then barely get to see them." He dropped his head into his hands. "I may be getting too old for this, guys."

Kimberly knew the baby on the way made this even more difficult for him. Why was her life unravelling all at once? Everything had seemed great just a few weeks ago.

"We may all be getting too old for this." She drank deeply from her coffee.

"Hey! Stop talking that like that!" Michael scowled at her.

"You're just tired. Drink more coffee, and let's see what we can find in the recordings."

"What's to find?" Sterling asked. "They stood in one spot and claimed to 'see things.'"

Was this for the show? She couldn't tell where skeptic Sterling ended and everyday Sterling began. But he gave her no reassuring smile, no gentle confirmation his attitude was all for the cameras.

"I saw more than the cameras could possibly capture," she said. "I can't explain how, but I'm confident Flint and I witnessed upcoming Christmas Eve celebrations. We began at his nephew's house and ended at Macy's place."

Her prediction proved correct. Nothing on their recordings added to her personal experiences. At least she still added significant value. She swallowed the last of her third cup of coffee and stretched, noting Sterling grinning at his phone. Again. He'd remained distracted all morning. And those grins of his had nothing to do with her.

She checked her phone every time it lit up with a social media notification—why had she allowed Sterling to turn those on?—but nothing from Marissa.

"I don't think we're going to find anything useful from this," Michael finally admitted, then stretched into a wide yawn. "Let's break for lunch and try to get some rest."

Sterling stood. "I think I'll do my own thing for lunch today."

"Wait. What?"

"Yeah. No big deal. Just want to clear my head. Run a couple errands."

"What errands?"

He shrugged and shook his head. "Nothing, really."

If it was nothing, why did he feel compelled to hide it from her? And why did his spectrum radiate guilt?

She tried to follow him, but Rosie grabbed her wrist. "Don't, girl. You look desperate."

"But he—"

"Trust me on this. Let him go do his own thing."

"Guess I'll go to my room then," she muttered.

"Wanna grab some gumbo?" Michael asked.

"Nah. Go ahead." With her stomach churning, food was the last thing she wanted.

Her phone lit up and vibrated, this time with a message from Marissa.

I'm at the store today. Drop by anytime. You're always welcome.

"We could do something if you want," Rosie suggested.

"Actually, I think I'll go back to Voodoo Legitimate. I felt so good while I was there."

"So did I! I'd love to go with you! Just us girls."

"That sounds great!"

In the lobby, TJ chatted with Cristal. She nodded at her obviously twitterpated young camera operator.

"I could bring food back here if you can't leave," TJ said.

Cristal bit her lip and turned to Macy. "Is it okay if—"

"Oh, go on," Macy told her. "Take your lunch break now. I'll go later."

Cristal squealed and scampered out the door with TJ.

Kimberly hesitated at the desk. She'd witnessed an intimate, personal moment in Macy's life. And Macy had no idea she and Flint had lurked in the shadows, observing . . . her next Christmas? She shook her head. That was discombobulating. But, noting Macy's pale complexion, particularly the dark, sunken bags under her eyes, she had to check in. "Are you okay? You seem—"

"Exhausted? Yes. Abby had a bad night. She probably ought to see her specialist, but I just can't afford an office visit copay or potential new medications until payday. Specialty medications are classified top tier and carry the highest out-of-pocket copays. Ironic since most people who need them would die without them."

Kimberly covered the woman's hand and squeezed. "I so wish I could whisk you away for a spa day right now—"

"Oh, no, I couldn't—"

"I know. You can't leave. But you deserve it more than anyone I know. Can we at least bring you lunch?"

"I brought food."

"Dinner then? What's Abby's favorite place to eat?"

"Well, we don't go out to eat much. But she does love Fat Boys Pizza."

"We'll bring back dinner for you to take home. How about that?"

Macy shifted on her feet and stared at the desk. "That would make Abby very happy."

"Done. See you later."

The sun shone and the streets were mostly quiet. A perfect day for a walk.

"We'll get pizza for them, but let's watch for someplace more upscale and bring back something really nice for Macy."

"I love it!" Rosie said. "I'll check out restaurants while we walk."

"I just wish we could do more."

"Sterling's right about one thing. Macy would not accept money from us to help pay her bills. I'm starting to wonder if she'll even accept a wish from Make*A*Wish."

Kimberly thought about the construction-paper Christmas tree with the single gift beneath it. "She will. If it's for Abby, she'll agree. Maybe . . . maybe we could bring some Christmas presents for Abby."

"There you go! And for Macy too!"

"Absolutely. Let's do it."

When they arrived at Voodoo Legitimate, Zorrie jumped from her seat. "I hoped you'd come during my shift!"

Marissa emerged from the back. "Perfect timing. I heard from my para-giver. She's free on Sunday, as are quite a few of our group members. The store is closed Sundays. So why don't we plan on holding the ritual then?"

"I can't guarantee when our investigation will be over. Does it need to be at night?"

Marissa cracked a smile. "No. Not at all. A daytime ritual is equally powerful. For that matter, Sunday is a holy day for many, which will charge the spirit realm with energy. We can tap into that. It's perfect."

"Fantastic. That worked out so well."

"Everyone is so excited to meet you. Most of them would have canceled other plans to accommodate your schedule. The chance to meet you is too irresistible."

"I cannot wrap my brain around that. But I'm happy to meet them. And am anxious for the healing ceremony."

"I'll be a real healer!" Rosie said. "Bonded for life to my best friend!"

Marissa laughed. "We will train you. Of course, training takes time and practice. But we have to start to make progress. I'll confirm the meeting. Will two o'clock work or need it earlier?"

"We'll make it work."

"How is the investigation going?" Marissa asked.

"I'm making progress, I think. I had an unusual encounter last night."

"Unusual how?"

"I think I was seeing glimpses into the future. But that's never happened before. I've had spirits connect and share glimpses of the past, but those are from their memories. How could I see something that hasn't yet happened?"

Marissa cocked her head and lifted an eyebrow. "You've never tried to see the future before? Not even the near future?"

"How could I?"

"Fascinating. Psychics can see anything—past, present, future. All we have to do is find a willing spirit and ask. You've only seen into the past because that's all you've asked about. Or perhaps the spirits you've encountered were only willing to share the past. You've been primarily involved in simple domestic hauntings which tend to be the result of a spirit fixated on its history. But some spirits see along all the planes. That is basic metaphysics. You truly don't know this?"

Kimberly shook her head, wondering what Sterling and his physics degree would think of this theory.

Marissa smirked. "You are truly uneducated and untrained. It would be funny if it wasn't so sad."

"Funny?"

"Perhaps ironic is a better word than funny. One of the most powerful psychics in the world has no idea how to harness her power."

"I still don't understand why you keep saying—"

Rosie frowned at her phone. "What the actual hell?"

"What's wrong?" Kimberly asked.

Rosie turned her phone to display a picture on Instagram of Sterling sitting at a bar with Georgia.

"He said he was running errands!"

Marissa's mouth curled into a smile. "That's the Carousel Bar. Most people go there for fun. Not business."

"But he said—"

"He's most certainly on an errand, but I doubt it's related to work." Rosie scowled. "I've heard of this place. I wanted to go. It looks like a carousel and turns while you drink."

"Slowly, I hope," Kimberly said.

"Well, yeah. I suddenly want a drink very badly. You know where this place is, Marissa?"

"Yes, but why in the world would you race off after him?"

"He committed to Kimberly and her show. I want to confront him—"

"I don't want to confront him, Rosie. You just told me to let him go do his thing or I'd look desperate."

"That's when I thought he was really running errands."

Kimberly massaged her temples. "This is exactly why I resisted a relationship. If he—"

Marissa spoke up again. "He's not right for you. You're a

legend in the psychic community. Why would you even consider slumming with someone who doesn't believe? "

"Slumming? I mean, Sterling is a nice guy. I don't think I'm slumming."

"I disagree."

"Besides, I think he does have some abilities. He doesn't know or maybe doesn't want to admit it, but—"

"You haven't had the opportunity to be around others like you. I get it. You're desperate to see a sixth sense in someone else, desperate to believe he's like you. But he needs to be with his own kind—"

"Own kind?" Rosie asked.

"Just like you should be with your own kind."

"You don't know Sterling. He's not the same when we're alone. He's really nice to me."

"Is he? Or is he simply pretending, trying to win your trust and get close to you? Insinuate himself in your life and then spin it to benefit himself. You mentioned you've been feeling off. Of course you have. You have a skeptic draining you every moment of the day. You need someone who supports you. And now you'll have that."

"He's good to me. Tell her Rosie."

Rosie glanced at her phone and shook her head. "I don't know anymore, girl. I thought he would be good for you but . . ."

"What does your gut tell you right now?" Marissa asked. "He snuck off to meet someone else at a bar and didn't even tell you. Forget him. I'm going to introduce you to others like you, who will appreciate your special gift. We need to stick together."

Rosie stared at her phone. "I still vote go confront him."

"I could take you to the home your mother lived in," Marissa said.

Kimberly brought up Instagram on her own phone. "I've seen it already. Rosie, where did you see that picture?"

Marissa spoke before Rosie could answer. "You've been there? You went?"

Rosie glanced at her phone. "It's in Georgia's story, girl. Not Sterling's post."

She glanced at Marissa. "Yes. Elise found it for me. We went this morning. A story? What?"

Marissa gripped her arm. "Did you go inside? Could you feel a connection?"

Weird. The woman seemed oddly excited about her old house. She wasn't ready to admit what she'd seen and experienced there. Not even to Marissa. "How do I find a story?"

Marissa covered her phone screen. "Enough of that. Forget about Sterling. We need to connect you to your roots. Come. I'll show you around."

CHAPTER NINETEEN

THE VIBRANT, colorful streets of New Orleans pulsed to a different beat, in complete contrast to Kimberly's hometown of Albuquerque. The ambience, the colors, the crowds and music. Entirely different smells filled the air—a salty sea breeze tang combined with the enticing odor of rich, decadent foods. She loved Albuquerque—that was home—but imagined how different her life would be if she'd grown up here instead.

A celebrity with the paranormal community? New Orleans' energy thrummed on a different wavelength. And maintained a spiritual community not only accepting but supportive of those often considered fringe crackpots. Things would be so different if she'd grown up with a support network, encouraged to develop and use her gift.

She had so many questions and needed so much training and only had a few days to—

A sharp, stabbing pain shot through her head. Her knees nearly buckled. She gasped for air, fingers pressed to her temples.

Marissa smiled. "I hoped you'd be affected. I thought you would be, but we never know until we know. But of course you are."

"Why are you happy about this?" Rosie asked, then bent over Kimberly's hunched frame. "What's happening?

"I . . . don't know." She could barely speak. "What is causing this?"

"Terrible evil," Marissa said. "I normally avoid this street entirely. The negative energy overwhelms psychics."

Kimberly lifted her head long enough to read the sign on the building beside them before excruciating pain ricocheted through her skull again. "The Pharmacy Museum?"

"Yes, that's the source. Can you tell why?"

She didn't want to know, much less connect with it. But Marissa's eyes shone with such excitement, she wanted to please the woman. And perhaps impress her.

Rosie tried to intervene. "I'm not sure she should—"

She grabbed Rosie's hand. "I can do this."

After several deep breaths, she extended her psyche, reaching into the building mentally.

The grisly images that filled her mind, worse than any horror movie she'd ever watched, turned her stomach. A scalpel, restraints, a metal table covered in blood, screams of agony, bodies dropped from an upper window to a waiting wagon below then dumped into the river. When a man approached a screaming woman tied to the table, and Kimberly realized where the scene was headed, she clamped down hard on her psyche, disconnecting from the vivid, sickening scenes unfolding.

"Horrible, isn't it?" Marissa asked.

Beads of sweat collected on her brow and trickled down her temple as she nodded, trying to catch her breath.

Rosie bent beside her hunched figure. "Aren't you supposed to be helping her? She isn't even healed yet. And I'm not trained to offer support when she's like this."

"She disconnected. And I'm here. I would have intervened if she needed it." Marissa squatted in front of her and ran a finger over her cheek. "You are extraordinary."

"But what did I see? What . . . happened here?"

Marissa stood and helped Kimberly to her feet. "This is the first established apothecary, built and managed by the man who went on to become the first licensed pharmacist in the country, Louis Dufilho. But after that, the family sold the business to Dr. Dupas, a physician who appears not to have taken his oath to do no harm seriously. Rumors of his practice include tying down patients and performing surgery on them unnecessarily and with no anesthesia. Women in particular were favored victims. Once tied down and helpless, the good doctor could do whatever he wanted to them. And he regularly did."

Nausea gripped her stomach. "I saw that. Until I couldn't watch anymore."

Marissa took her by the elbow and led them away from the museum. "I know it's unpleasant. But you need to fully understand the danger you will be exposed to. Monsters and demons, yes, but even the spirits of truly evil people can assault you. That building is soaked in the blood of its victims and retains all the violence and terror they experienced. The pharmacist remains there too, trying to retain his bloodthirsty habits. But also fearful of crossing over and paying for the crimes he committed while alive."

"Still not sure why you felt the need to expose her to that," Rosie muttered.

"I needed to make sure she could handle it. There's someplace worse. Someplace connected to you directly. To your family."

She gripped Marissa's arm. "My family? Something about my mother?"

"The women in your family are powerful psychics."

"Yes, you mentioned that."

"I'm taking you to a place rooted in your family history. As much as Marie Laveau did to highlight the good surrounding alternative religious practices, not everyone accepted Voodoo, witchcraft, and psychics."

She knew that all too well. "They still don't."

"As your pompous Sterling proves."

She kept her mouth closed. Not the time to argue. She might vomit, considering the nausea still roiling in her stomach.

Marissa looked at her sideways before continuing. "Some, like our murderous doctor back there, have no misgivings about inflicting pain and suffering on others. True sociopaths. Others enjoy inflicting suffering but feel the need to justify their actions. Thus, they hurt those they believe deserve it. People they believe to be less than themselves. Slaves, for example, who were deemed expendable and replaceable. Witches, obviously, since the practice was twisted into a demented religious cult by those who don't understand it. Strong, powerful women, healers, spinsters who managed to succeed without a man were all labeled witches and thus fair game for punishment in the eyes of crazed fanatics. And then psychics, who some liken to witches, but reserve the greatest disdain for."

"I've experienced that. Been called a witch," she said.

"Not that long ago," Rosie confirmed. "That religious zealot who harassed you in Guthrie. He threatened you."

Marissa's head snapped around. "What happened in Guthrie? Why were you there?"

She stopped. The woman's gaze bore into her. What in the world? "We had an investigation there. Why? Have you been?"

Marissa looked suddenly confused and lifted one hand to her forehead. "I . . . no, I'm sure I haven't been there. I don't know why that name struck such a chord. How odd. Anyway, back to—"

Crushing pain and debilitating nausea dropped Kimberly to her knees. The negative energy of the apothecary was nothing but a mild headache compared to the migraine-inducing, soul-sucking toxicity currently wreaking havoc on her system.

"Torture," she managed through gritted teeth.

Rosie dropped beside her. "Something is torturing her!"

Marissa squatted in front of her and caressed her cheek. "No.

She senses the torture others endured here. This is the LaLaurie mansion.”

Rosie stood, peering across the street. “Wait a second. I’ve heard that name. Something I heard or saw . . . *American Horror Story*!”

“Season three.” Marissa tucked a lock of Kimberly’s hair behind her ear.

“But those are just stories,” Rosie said. “Right?”

“Stories, yes. Embellished, sure. But rooted in truth.”

“You knew this and brought her here anyway? You have some strange methods, and I’m not sure I approve.” Rosie grasped Kimberly’s shoulders and tried to hoist her to her feet. “Let’s get you out of here.”

Certain she’d vomit in the street, Kimberly shook her head. She couldn’t move.

“Kimberly doesn’t want to leave,” Marissa said. “See.”

“I doubt that,” Rosie insisted. “Why would you do this to her?”

“She needed to feel it for herself. To know what happened to her great-great-grandmother.” Marissa encircled her wrist—the one with the obsidian bracelet, which didn’t seem to be working well—with her thumb and middle finger, drew a symbol on the back of her hand, and whispered barely audible words.

She recovered her equilibrium and stood. “Thank you. That’s at least tolerable now.”

“Once you’re healed, and I instruct you in basic training, you’ll be able to manage this sort of thing on your own.”

“What a relief that will be.”

“Now that she can stand upright again, can you explain why you brought her here?” Rosie asked. “Something about her great-great-grandmother?”

“She was a victim of Delphine LaLaurie, or Madame LaLaurie as she was also known. The woman grew wealthy by inheriting her numerous husbands’ fortunes. Husbands who died under mysterious circumstances. Her third husband, a much younger doctor, and she were members of New Orleans elite society, their wealth and status upholding her position as socialite. And yet, on April tenth, 1834, their mansion caught fire, summoning the public in an effort to rescue the inhabitants of the home and the adjoining slave quarters, which the LaLauries refused to surrender the keys to. People broke in, determined to rescue trapped residents—and discovered a gruesome scene of torture and carnage. Servants were bound in unnatural positions, tied up, stretched—all twisted into grisly shapes, starved to skin and bone, and barely alive. But alive. Besides the servant's quarters, the LaLauries used the attic as a torture chamber as well, which the horrified public discovered. Eventually the authorities discovered that the cook, kept chained in the kitchen and routinely whipped for sneaking food to the torture victims, set the fire, deciding death was preferable to her hideous living conditions."

"What does this have to do with Kimberly?"

"Her great-great-grandmother worked in the household and was freed from the attic. One of the few who survived. Madame LaLaurie had overheard some of the other servants gossiping about her abilities to channel spirits and tortured her, demanding she bring forth the spirits of her deceased husbands to swear she hadn't murdered them. Desperate, she was ruthless."

"I felt it," Kimberly whispered. "I know exactly what she did to her."

"Why would you do this to Kimberly?" Rosie demanded.

"I needed her to know what we're up against. The sheer magnitude and intensity of the suffering concentrated in this location attracted attention of powerful, malignant entities who feed off the negative energy."

"Lilith," Kimberly said.

"Exactly. Where you and I avoid the onslaught of suffering that brings us to our knees, others, like Lilith, thrive on it."

"Who is she exactly?" Rosie asked.

"An ancient one. I don't know more than that. No one knows exactly how old she is, but some of us believe she was alive while Madame LaLaurie was torturing her servants. In fact, I believe I have proof."

"That isn't possible," Rosie said.

Marissa turned her phone, showing them a faded, sepia-toned photo.

One of the pictured women jumped out at Kimberly. Her heart skipped a beat. "That's her. That's the woman I've seen following me."

"It can't be her," Rosie said. "That photo would have to be—"

"Nearly two hundred years old."

"So Kimberly has seen someone who closely resembles this woman but—"

"Seems like Sterling has gotten inside your head." Marissa lifted an eyebrow at Kimberly. "We have evidence of other sightings. Quite a few actually. Kimberly isn't the only one who has seen her recently. And I know her quite intimately. I'm embarrassed to admit I was once affiliated with her. I counted myself as one of her followers, the Psys, along with many other Paras. We broke away when we reached a disagreement we couldn't resolve."

"Paras and Psys? Are you talking about groups of psychics?"

"Yes. And some of us don't agree with how to best use our gifts to help others. I need you to understand, Kimberly. Lilith is extremely powerful. I'm pleased to see how strong you are with the limited guidance you've received. Lilith has had far more time to develop her powers. She's aware of the unusual gift the women in your family possess. She'll stop at nothing to bring you under her control. She wants us Paras back in her fold as well. She has tried to bring us back since we splintered off."

"Do you think I can resist her?" Kimberly asked. "I feel almost helpless. How will I ever learn fast enough?"

"Of course you can. And you have us to help protect you from her. Once you're healed, I'll teach you some exercises to build and strengthen your gift." Marissa stopped and stared straight in her eyes. "I'm serious when I say how impressed I am that you're as strong as you are. No guidance or training. In fact, you were apparently scolded and discouraged from using it."

"I did feel like it grew stronger as I hit adolescence. I thought, I don't know, that maturity or maybe having more electronics and batteries around helped the ghosts appear more frequently?"

"Fascinating. No, we develop our abilities as an athlete or a bodybuilder would—by training and exercising. The more we use the gift, the stronger it becomes and the more we master it."

They'd arrived back at Voodoo Legitimate. Zorrie waved at them from where she stood, assisting a customer. Once the customer paid and left, the young woman hurried to them.

"The phone has been ringing since you left! Everyone confirmed they'll be here! Everyone!"

Marissa turned a satisfied smile on them. "You see? No one would miss the chance to meet you. To be present at your welcoming ceremony is the greatest honor."

"Healing ritual," Rosie corrected her. "And bonding us together."

Marissa blinked. "Yes. What did I say?"

"Welcoming ritual."

"So sorry. Healing ritual. And to better assist with that, can you pinpoint exactly when you noticed this disconnect?"

Kimberly thought. "Sometimes when I overexert myself, I feel drained—"

"I've seen you appear to pass out on your show. Is that genuine or theatrical?"

Marissa suggested she played for the camera? She expected better understanding from a fellow psychic. "No, I really do black out sometimes. Doesn't everyone?"

"Absolutely not." Marissa lifted an eyebrow. "That could be attributed to your lack of training I suppose."

Rosie looked thoughtful. "The problem started in Hannibal."

"That's right. I couldn't control my abilities. I fazed in and out, sometimes couldn't see spirits at all. Once I saw a spirit but didn't realize. Thought she was a real person."

"And what happened there?" Marissa asked.

"Nothing remarkable."

"Something unusual must have triggered this. Where were you before Hannibal?"

"That was the Guthrie investigation."

Marissa's eyes went wide. "That must be it then. I must have sensed the connection when you mentioned it. After all, I've never heard of Guthrie, Oklahoma before today. What happened there?"

"It was a rough investigation but nothing out of the ordinary."

The woman narrowed her eyes. "Don't withhold critical information."

"I'm not. Rosie, can you think of anything?"

"Nothing strange."

Marissa looked like she didn't believe them. "Try to remember. The more we know, the better we will be able to heal you."

"Of course. That's what I want. We don't have any reason to keep anything from you."

Marissa collected Kimberly's hands between her own and muttered softly. "There. I've put a protection charm over you. You should be okay until we meet again. Sleep well tonight. Tomorrow your life will change forever."

CHAPTER TWENTY

On the way back to the hotel, Kimberly relished the calm disposition that had settled over her, a feeling she could handle anything that came her way.

"I feel so good," she said, eyeing an antique store window. "Even after the difficult experiences today. Every time we hang out at Voodoo Legitimate, I feel calmer and yet also energized."

"I love it! This is exactly what you've always needed." Rosie beamed at her.

"Imagine if I'd grown up here. If I'd had support, family, a network of other psychics."

"Well, I don't love that," Rosie said. "We probably never would have met. You would have been assigned a completely different para giver. I hate that thought."

"You're right. I'm sorry. I need to stop thinking that way. I can't imagine a life without you and Michael and the others. Without the show. Bram told me everything has to unfold the way it's intended to. He's right."

"What exactly happened with him?" Rosie asked. "Sterling seemed pretty mad about something."

"It was nothing. Weird, but not anything."

"I don't like this, girl. I thought you and Sterling were a done deal. Now you've got some Goth guy making a play for you, and Sterling is at a bar with an old friend?"

"Bram was not making a play. And Sterling is . . . I don't know. But I'm sure there's an explanation. Let's grab food for Macy and Abby."

While perusing the menu at Olde Nola Cookery, Kimberly's stomach growled so loudly Rosie heard it.

"I'm surprised you have any appetite at all after that psychic beating you took today," Rosie said.

"I'm surprised too. Maybe Marissa helped. Anyway, let's eat. We didn't have lunch yet and who knows when Sterling will resurface—" Kimberly couldn't bring herself to finish the thought, knowing he was with another woman. Suspicion squirmed in her stomach until she lost her appetite. "Maybe I don't want food."

Just as the maître d asked if it was just the two of them today, Rosie said, "Actually, we've changed our mind. We will be back."

"Why are we leaving?" Kimberly asked.

"Because we are a three-minute walk from the Hotel Monteleone."

"And?"

"That's where the Carousel Bar is."

She knew where this was headed. "Let's just sit down and order. I'm not really into confrontation—"

"Fortunately for you, I am. Come on."

Before she knew what was happening, Rosie dragged her out the door with a promise to return for food.

"This will be just like the time I walked in on Jimmy and some tarted-up redhead," Rosie said. "He told me he was going to the library to study for his GED. Well, that was the most suspicious thing he could have said."

"I don't think this is exactly the same as—"

"Maybe not exactly. More like the time I followed Kyle and discovered he had another girlfriend across town and—"

"I think this is the place," Kimberly said, ready to change the subject away from cheating boyfriends.

They stood in front of an exquisite, towering building of white stone, the front decorated with ornate embellishments. Flags flew beside the name of the hotel, which was written in script. A doorman opened the gold-framed door for them and gestured them inside.

The lobby was as magnificent as the front of the hotel. Marble flooring, a glittering chandelier, and a grandfather clock added to the regal atmosphere. The polished floors and glass of the chandelier reflected sunlight so that the entire room seemed to glow softly.

"I wish Elise was here to give us the history and details of the building," Kimberly whispered to Rosie. "Are those gold?"

"Brass, ma'am," a gentleman in a suit answered with a smile.

"Thank you," Rosie answered. "Can you direct us to the bar?"

"The Carousel Bar is down that hallway, ma'am."

Kimberly wanted to stand still and take in the sumptuous lobby, but Rosie grabbed her arm and dragged her toward the hallway.

"They may not still be here," Kimberly pointed out, reluctant to face Sterling like this.

"If they are, we can find out what he's doing. And if they're not, you may not want to know what they're doing."

At the entrance to the bar, she stopped. "Rosie, wait. I don't know if I can do this."

"If it's innocent, it's all cleared up and you don't have to wonder anymore."

"I suppose so." She squared her shoulders, heart thumping, sure she'd be more relieved if she didn't have to face him.

They rounded the corner and entered the bar. And there he sat, Georgia by his side. Hours later and here he still sat. Something crumpled inside her.

"I don't think I—"

"We're doing this." Rosie grabbed her arm as if sensing she was about to bolt. "Look, two vacant seats right next to them."

"Great."

Sterling leaned away when they sat before he glanced over and nodded a perfunctory greeting followed by a double-take. "Oh. Hey. What are you guys doing here?"

"Just sightseeing," Rosie said. "Crazy we bumped into you." Under her breath she muttered, "Busted."

"Kimberly doesn't drink though so I—" He followed her gaze, which rested on three empty glasses sitting in front of him.

"*You* have been though." She lifted an eyebrow.

"What, these? No, we just got here." He lifted a finger at the bartender, who watched with a crinkled brow. "Could you clear these away, please?"

Like the bartender, Georgia cocked an eyebrow and shook her head.

Rosie leaned forward. "Oh hi, Georgia. Didn't see you down there."

Georgia tossed back the remainder of a drink before the bartender cleared the glasses. "Hi, there."

"What brings you two here?" Rosie asked the same moment Sterling asked the same question.

Georgia watched Sterling squirm, then rolled her eyes.

The bartender returned. "What can I get you two? Errr, everyone?"

"I have to work tonight, so I'll just have a virgin daiquiri," Sterling said.

"Oh, for the—" Georgia stopped when Sterling gave her a look. "Diet soda for me, whatever brand you have."

Kimberly's senses tingled with the brittle anxiety that crackled through the space. Who did Sterling think he was fooling with this ridiculous charade? Here was another way the two of them weren't a good match. He could go out and grab drinks with someone like Georgia. And clearly, he missed that. "Sterling, I—"

"You two are out doing some sightseeing, huh?" Sterling asked.

Rosie leaned forward to talk past her. "Yep. What are you two up to?"

"Same. I mean, I was sightseeing and ran into Georgia here."

Rosie squinted. "Just happened to run into her?"

"You said you had some errands to run," Kimberly reminded him.

"Right. I ran them, noticed this historic building and popped in, and here sat Georgia—"

"I don't see the point of playing coy," Georgia said. "Obviously we arranged to meet here. I'm interviewing Sterling, and he wants—"

"The publicity," Sterling said. "The publicity for the show will be fantastic. And won't cost a thing."

The bartender slid their drinks in front of them.

Georgia flattened her lips, then shrugged. "I don't consider a relationship successful if you feel the need to keep secrets. Or the need to check up on each other. But that's none of my business." She picked up her soda and took a drink.

Kimberly deflated. This woman was absolutely right.

"I'm sorry we interrupted your interview," she told Georgia. "Please continue. We will enjoy our drinks and then be on our way."

Sterling sighed. "This is more than an interview. Georgia . . . well, she suggested me for director of a new show she's developing, and I've been offered the job."

"Oh." She fought to maintain a neutral expression but heard the shock in her tone.

"But he has a job," Rosie said, when Kimberly couldn't manage more words. "A good job that he likes."

Georgia sipped her soda. "This would be much more in alignment with his interests. Not exactly *SpookBusters* but at least it will be back in his wheelhouse. And he'd be the director, not a sidelined cohost."

Sidelined cohost? Was that how he felt? She lifted her gaze to meet his and could see in his eyes how conflicted he was, even before she read his spectrum and found him clouded by sorrow.

"We'd work together on consumer protection pieces, debunking urban myths, that sort of thing. With appearances in an ongoing guest spot on a national news syndicate as well. He'd be a fool to turn it down."

"I . . . told her I'd think about it," Sterling admitted. He rested a hand on hers. "This isn't a reflection on you or your show. I wasn't expecting . . ."

Your show. No longer *our* show. "Yeah, no, that's great."

"We could still see each other when our schedules allow."

"Mmm-hmm." She'd seen how that worked for Rosie and Lorenzo. Or rather how it didn't work.

She lifted her virgin Hurricane to her lips but quickly returned it to the cocktail napkin. Her hand shook so hard the drink nearly sloshed over the rim. The thought of him leaving sent a shock wave through her system, which left a cold waste-land in its wake. If this opportunity was as good for him as Georgia claimed, she could not stand in his way.

Never mind that this new job meant he'd be working closely with no-nonsense, model-gorgeous Georgia. How long until he remembered he'd dated models before joining her show? Until he realized Georgia managed to combine the face, figure, and elegance of a model but also the brains of a PhD? Brains she used to investigate and debunk, just like Sterling preferred to do. How long until he realized Kimberly and her psychic abilities could not gel with his beliefs?

She blinked and swallowed hard, attempting to dislodge the lump in her throat. Lifting her glass into the air, she forced her lips into a smile. "Congratulations."

His features relaxed as if his anxiety melted away. "Thank you. I haven't accepted yet, though, so—"

"He will," Georgia said. "He'd be a—"

"Fool not to. Yeah, you mentioned that." Rosie's brow

furrowed deeply enough she could have planted seeds in the grooves.

"It's a lot." Sterling's eyes searched hers.

She nodded and squeezed his hand. The decision had to be his.

When Rosie nudged her, eyes wide, and gestured at Sterling, she shook her head. She couldn't bring herself to pressure him to pass on a job that he wanted and that would make him happy.

<hr>

KIMBERLY AND ROSIE returned to the Olde Nola Cookery and sat down for a late lunch/early dinner of some of the best seafood pasta she'd ever eaten in her life. She couldn't help but think Sterling would have loved it but was trying to push thoughts of him out of her mind and simply enjoy herself. She needed to adapt back to a life that didn't include Sterling with her every day. A little ache burned in her heart. She'd miss him.

Rosie sat back before finishing her food. "I can't eat another bite. I wonder if Marissa has any infused oils that help you lose five pounds fast."

Or one to convince Sterling to stay? Marissa would be all too pleased to learn Sterling was going his own way. "We can eat less next week and exercise more to work it off."

"I don't know, girl. That approach seems less and less effective the older I get."

"Diet should be more about health than weight. We eat well most of the time. That's what matters most." She considered Sterling's regular attempts to persuade her to lighten up and eat something unhealthy. She'd miss that too. Though it would allow her to return to her strict dietary choices with no temptation. Somehow, that didn't seem as important anymore. She'd gladly weigh a few extra pounds if it meant enjoying time with Sterling.

"*You* eat well most of the time. I'll start tomorrow. Like I do every day. Meanwhile, let's get this wrapped to go."

They flagged down the waiter, paid, gathered their leftovers and the to-go order for Macy, and headed for the hotel.

"At least we can walk off some of the calories," Rosie commented. "That has to help, right?"

They walked in silence until Rosie nudged her. "So, Sterling. I didn't expect that."

"I knew something was bothering him but never dreamed it was this."

"How do you feel about it?"

Tears pricked her eyes, but she refused to cry. "He needs to do what's right for him."

"That's not what I asked."

She stopped and turned to face her best friend. "I imagine how you felt when Lorenzo decided to stay in Eureka Springs."

Rosie ran a hand over her back. "Yeah. It sucks, I know. But we'll manage."

Though no part of her felt okay, she smiled her gratitude. "I know. Just like we managed before he elbowed his way into my life."

Kimberly caught sight of a purple coat and nearly dropped the bag of food she was carrying. "Rosie, that's her! That's Lilith!"

The woman saw she'd been spotted, turned, and ran.

Rosie spun in place. "Where?"

"She's running away again! Right there! In the purple coat!"

"I see a purple coat, but I didn't see her face. Not even a glimpse."

"Why does she keep doing this? I'd almost rather confront her than be constantly worried I'm being followed."

"You know there's no way that can be the same woman from Marissa's photo, right?"

"I know it sounds crazy, but this woman looks exactly like her. I think it's her."

"It may be a woman named Lilith, but she can't be two hundred years old. There has to be another explanation."

They picked up the pace and walked in silence. Kimberly knew how outlandish the idea was that someone could be over a hundred years old and look in her mid-thirties. And yet, she knew what she'd seen.

She remained alert the last couple of blocks. How long had Lilith tailed them before she'd noticed? And what might have happened if she hadn't?

Stepping back into the safety of the Cardinal Hotel, she breathed a sigh of relief. Then noticed Macy was gathering her things and appeared to be readying to leave. She glanced at the time. 5:15.

"I didn't realize how late it was. The day got away from me," she said, handing over the food to Macy. "Thank goodness we weren't any later or I would have missed you."

Macy accepted the food but looked away. "Thank you for this. I hate that you bought food for us, but I really appreciate it."

"My pleasure!" She checked the desk but only Cristal stood behind it. "Shouldn't Bram be here?"

"I've never actually met Bram," Macy said. "Cristal hangs around until he arrives so I can get home to Abby."

"He never appears until it's dark outside." Cristal shrugged. "Anytime now, he'll show up. Gets dark early this time of year."

"Thank you again," Macy said. "I hate to grab and run, but—"

"Go! Go home to your daughter!"

After Macy left, Cristal said, "I'm glad she's never met Bram. I think he'd creep her out."

Rosie lifted an eyebrow. "Why do you say that?"

"Hasn't he done that sketchy thing to you guys?"

Kimberly sucked in a breath.

"What was that for?' Rosie asked. "Is that why Sterling is upset with you? What did he do?"

"Has he mesmerized you too?" she asked Cristal.

"Mesmerized. Yeah, that's a good word for it. A couple of times."

She turned to Rosie. "See? It wasn't my imagination. But it was nothing. Not what Sterling thinks—"

"What was nothing?" a low male voice whispered in her ear.

She jumped and turned to discover Bram directly behind her. "When did you—How—"

That front door had *not* opened. No way had he come inside without setting off the jingle bells adorning the door.

He never appears until it's dark outside.

The sun had set. She looked to Cristal to see if the young woman was equally confounded by the sudden appearance.

Cristal shrugged and reached for her purse. "No issues to pass along. Have a quiet night."

Apparently, Bram's behavior did not concern Cristal. The door pealed her departure twice—when it opened and as it banged closed.

Bram stared directly at Kimberly, his hard black eyes shining. "Oh, it won't be quiet. Not tonight."

He took his place behind the desk. She followed him.

"Do you live in the hotel?"

He flicked his eyes at her as he signed into the desktop. "I do not."

"Then how did you get inside and appear out of nowhere?" She whirled and pointed. "That door didn't open but you suddenly—"

"The hotel offers more than one mode of entry."

The smirk on his face along with the obvious solution closed her mouth. Thank goodness Sterling wasn't here to witness this ludicrous exchange.

"Come on, girl." Rosie pulled her arm. "Let's go get you ready for the camera."

But the door jingled happily again, and an exhausted-looking Sterling entered the hotel.

He looked pointedly from her to Bram. His jaw tightened. "Of course. You're with him."

"Just now getting back?" she asked. And all that time Georgia was no doubt telling him how great his new job would be.

He rubbed a hand down his face. "Yeah. Sorry that took so long. We had . . . a lot to talk about."

"Oh. And what did you decide?" She swallowed hard, not sure she wanted to know.

Sterling looked away. "I'm still thinking about things. And Georgia is helping me out with another issue. We really were dealing with something important to the show."

"Wait. Important to the show? What could Georgia possibly be helping with that impacts my show?"

Sterling checked the time. "Is it really after five already?"

Bram grinned. "Indeed. Night has fallen. Where did the day go?"

Sterling scowled. "None of your business."

"Rhetorical question." Bram leaned forward and propped his chin on one hand. He looked ready for a tub of popcorn to accompany the unfolding drama.

"It is *our* business," Rosie said. "But we already know how you spent the day."

Sterling turned to her, the most hangdog expression she'd ever seen on his face.

"Rosie, stop," she said. Pressuring him into a decision or making him feel guilty about making the right choice would only result in resentment in the long run.

Rosie gave him "the look" and then pulled Kimberly toward the elevator. "Time for makeup. Sorry."

"Wait. What are you guys doing for dinner?"

"We've eaten," Rosie called over her shoulder as she pressed the button to summon the lift.

Sterling's face fell, tugging at her heart. Her stomach churned at the idea of losing him. The seafood pasta heaved, and she was glad she'd eaten when she did. Her emotions were such a mess, she couldn't stomach food now.

He watched them leave. "I'm sorry," he mouthed. As the elevator doors closed. He said, "Let's talk later."

Tears sprang to her eyes. She swiped at them all the way to the fourth floor. Luckily, no one else joined them on the ride up.

Once inside Rosie's suite, her best friend guided her to the makeup vanity and pressed a tissue into her hand. "Blot that away. Get it out of your system. We need to meet the others before the investigation starts tonight. And we don't know for sure that he's going to take the job. So let's not—"

"Then what was that look on his face? Complete and utter guilt."

"Yeah. 'Let's talk later' doesn't usually presage anything good."

"Presage? Nice."

"I've been reading a lot of romance books lately."

"Does it help?"

"Improve my vocabulary? Sure. Replace Lorenzo? Not so much. But I enjoy them."

"Maybe I should try one. I seem fated to be alone."

"You two were fine in Hannibal. More than fine. I was jealous. He won't leave the show now. He can't."

"He's obviously interested in the job offer. Is it more money? Or does he want to focus again on his interests? Whatever it is, Georgia isn't helping."

"She's smokin' hot for sure."

"And an old friend. And a skeptic like him. They have more in common than he and I have."

"He's crazy for you, though. He didn't jump at the offer, which means being with you means a lot to him."

"I understand his dilemma. If I was on a show that focused on disproving paranormal activity, I think I'd get tired of being the voice of dissent. Well . . ." She blotted her eyes. "Time to focus on work."

"It's going to be okay. Whatever happens, it will all be okay."

She blew her nose and forced her face into a bright smile. Whether she believed that or not, she had to keep going. "Yep."

Rosie grabbed the eyeliner and got busy hiding that she'd been crying. "What are you doing for Christmas? Going home?"

"And bump Angela out of the house for a couple of weeks? Nah. No one there for me anyway. What about you? Going to stay with your parents?"

"I am! Mom is thrilled."

"And Lorenzo?"

Rosie sighed. "Isn't ready to meet the parents. But didn't seem too thrilled I didn't accept his invitation to spend the holidays with him. Maybe New Year's Eve, but I already promised my mom Christmas."

"That's rough. No one is fighting over my Christmas. I think I'll stay here in New Orleans, then head straight to the next investigation."

"What about Sterling? Close your eyes." Rosie swiped eyeshadow on her lids.

"He hasn't said a word about Christmas."

"Not a good sign. Suck in your cheeks." She brushed blush over her cheekbones.

"Let's face it. He's—"

A knock at the door interrupted.

"Maybe that's him, coming for his makeup."

But the open door revealed Michael, not Sterling. "Flint is downstairs raising a huge fuss. He says he's not going to bed tonight."

Great. Just what they needed. "I guess I'm ready."

Rosie pushed her back into the seat and powdered her face. "Now you're ready."

When Kimberly arrived in the lobby, Flint stood, resolute, behind the desk. TJ's handheld recorded the exchange. Stan followed from the elevator, focused on her.

Flint shook his head. "I don't care. I'm running the desk tonight."

Bram appeared vaguely amused and lifted one eyebrow. "You're the boss, but I'm here to work my scheduled shift and don't agree to loss of hours and, thus, reduced pay because you're suffering from insomnia."

"I'm not going to bed tonight!" Flint railed.

Bram shrugged. "I'm not your mom. I don't care if you do or don't. But I'm not going home. I'm working my shift as scheduled."

Flint balled his fists and appeared ready to throw an all-out, toddler-style fit. "You have to do as I say! This is my hotel!"

Bram laughed. "Except labor laws exist. Welcome to the twenty-first century." The pale, dark-haired young man turned his black eyes on her. "Told you it wouldn't be quiet tonight."

Kimberly approached the desk and the spluttering man behind it and used her most soothing voice. "Now, Mr. Flint. Wouldn't it be better if we finish the investigation tonight and—"

"There's no such thing as ghosts!"

She looked to Sterling.

"Don't look at me. I agree with him."

Except he'd been coming around, beginning to acknowledge the possibility. "Thanks to Georgia and her new job."

"What does that mean?"

It means I feel like I'm losing you. All the dreams about working side by side, a paranormal investigation team. She'd let herself hope, let herself start to believe it was possible, and this was the result. Why did they have to bump into that woman? In the whole entire world, she happened to be in exactly the same Voodoo shop in New Orleans that they wandered into? "I'm sure you know better than I do what that means."

"Look, I'm still by your side and completely support your show."

"Except you were calling it our show. I think we can see where this is headed."

"This investigation is *gold*," Michael nearly sang.

Kimberly wondered how thrilled he'd be if he knew Sterling was teetering on the brink of leaving the show.

"Tis the Season" played through the sound system. *Yes, tis the season, for disappointment and reminders of everything you don't have in your life.*

Bram smirked. "And to think it's normally dead around here all night."

She noted the emphasis he placed on "dead" but before she could respond, Sterling spoke.

"Welcome to *Wantland* life."

She sucked in a breath as if sucker punched. He blamed this on her? "What's that supposed to mean?"

"All drama, all the time," Sterling said.

"Says the man who forced his way onto my show stirring up drama and controversy. You literally started the hashtag *Wantland* drama."

He shrugged and turned away.

She wanted to drag him to another room and talk about this. But the timing was terrible. She needed to move the investigation forward. She tried another approach. "Mr. Flint, the sooner we resolve this haunting, the sooner we all leave. Won't you feel better once you know what the spirits are trying to tell you? They'll leave you alone and you can—"

"Nonsense. No such thing as spirits. I either dreamed it all or imagined it. You people can do as you please, but I'm working tonight with Brad."

"It's Bram. If we're going to be working together, maybe you should know my name."

Flint's face twisted into a scowl. "What kind of name is that?"

"My name." Bram rolled his eyes.

"But Mr. Flint, I really don't think we'll be able to make any progress without you. The spirits clearly want to communicate with you."

The older man shrugged. "I'll be here at the desk if they want to talk to me."

She turned to Michael and Rosie. "Looks like I'm all made up with nowhere to go."

Michael pursed his lips. "Well, I don't want to call the whole night. Okay, everyone, let's spread out with a focus on the fifth floor. See if we detect any activity. Maybe we will get lucky and make a connection. Walkie check, please."

While her crew confirmed equipment was functioning properly, with fully charged batteries, she pulled Elise to the side.

"You found my mother's birth certificate—"

"I did! Would you like to see it?" Elise retrieved her phone.

"Yes. But I wanted to ask how far back you can trace the female lineage. Could you possibly identify my great-great-grandmother?"

Though she'd sought privacy, her crew could clearly tell something was up. They crept closer while appearing distracted by other things.

Rosie didn't bother pretending. "Maybe she can learn the identities of the victims of the fire. Or if that was nothing but a ghost story."

"If what was a ghost story?" Sterling asked.

She turned and discovered they'd all gathered around her. She sighed. "Guys, if I wanted to share, I would have—"

"Oh, no, no, no," Michael said. "That confirms it. You have something. Let's hear it!"

"I don't know if it's something," she said. "That's why I was trying to *quietly* request some research. I want to find out if a story we heard today about a fire is true."

She recapped the story. If Flint wasn't going to cooperate, she doubted they'd gather much for the show tonight anyway.

Sterling spoke first. "If the fire was that big and affected that many people, there should be records to—"

"Oh, it's true," Bram said. Of course he'd been listening. "The LaLaurie Mansion is a historical landmark and its history infamous. Madame LaLaurie escaped punishment though. She and her much-younger doctor husband fled to France and never returned. So if you're hoping to connect to her spirit, you'll need to plan an international investigation."

"Love that idea!" Michael clasped his hands. "Kimmy, you're brilliant. Have the show fund a European trip to—"

"I don't want anything to do with her."

Rosie rested a hand on her shoulder. "Now, let's not be too hasty. A European vacation, I mean, business trip sounds good to me too."

"I'm trying to determine if someone in my family lived in the house and survived the fire. And if so—"

Bram's eyes glowed. "And if the house of horrors somehow contributed to your psychic heritage?"

"What do you know about it?" she asked.

"Plenty. And you'll have ample records to sift through. The case was quite sensational. Plenty of eyewitness accounts."

"If you're familiar with it, why don't you simply share what you know and save some time for me?"

"Because it's your story to unravel. It will mean much more if you learn it yourself. I'll let you confirm Marissa's story. If you can."

She stared at him. "How did you know I heard this from Marissa?"

Sterling swung to face her. "You were with Marissa again?"

She nearly reminded him who he'd been with and why but didn't want to blurt that out in front of everyone. They'd find out soon enough the crew was losing the newest addition to their team. "Why do you care?"

"I don't like her."

Yeah, well, I don't like Georgia, but here we are. "What reason do you have to dislike her?"

"She called me your pet, for starters. But I don't trust her. She hedged around a lot of direct questions. Wouldn't answer. Something seems off."

"Smart man," Bram said.

"Thank—" Sterling seemed to realize who he spoke to and thought better of it. "I don't like you either."

"Sterling!" Kimberly said. "Now you're just being rude."

But rather than take offense, Bram laughed before narrowing his eyes at her. "You'd do well to follow his lead. New Orleans is home to many who would harm you, Kimberly Wantland."

The strange disorientation overcame her again. She swayed on her feet.

Sterling caught her by the arm and steadied her. "You said you'd eaten."

She lifted a hand to her forehead, woozy. "I did. He's—"

Her cell phone rang. *Angela.* Something was wrong. She could feel it. "I need to take this."

"Kimberly?" Angela's voice trembled, a note of anxiety evident that she'd never heard from the woman before. "I think someone is in the house."

"In the house? Get out now!"

Her house sitter whispered, as if afraid she'd be overheard. "Not a . . . living person. But I hear a man's voice. From the attic. He says I should tell you . . ."

She waited for the message but heard nothing but breathing. "Tell me what?"

"It said, 'He's coming for you.' Do you know what that means? Who is he? What does he want?"

The whispered warning and subsequent questions echoed through her mind. She'd heard that warning before. Where—

Her stomach sank as she remembered the man in the overalls with his rusty garden tools. He'd said the same thing.

She turned when the bells on the door jingled. The door remained closed.

But leering at her through the glass was the man in the overalls.

He lifted a rusted trowel and winked at her.

"What does it mean, he's coming for you?" Angela asked again.

The man moved his lips with Angela's warning. *He's coming for you.*

She could barely draw enough breath to speak. "Get out of the house, Angela. Get out now."

He's coming for you.

She dropped her phone.

Everything went black.

CHAPTER TWENTY-ONE

"Yes, I'm sure I'm okay," Kimberly assured her crew for the umpteenth time. "Other than confirmation that someone is watching me and closing in on me."

Sterling rubbed her back. "That's due to Marissa filling your head with this nonsense."

Michael clicked his tongue. "I don't know. I've never known Kimmy to overreact or imagine things that aren't there."

"No. Something is harassing Angela. And sending messages to me. Warnings. I need to see if Angela left the house. I'd never forgive myself if she were to be hurt." She reached for her phone.

Bram had left the desk and joined her crew, who had gathered around her in a little half-circle. For once, his normally amused eyes looked serious, his crooked grin gone.

Angela had texted apologies over and over but confirmed she was packing her things and moving for the time being. She responded.

Please don't apologize. Go someplace safe and don't return. I'll be there to investigate soon.

"Who would be sending you a warning like that?" Rosie asked. "Who's coming for you?"

"I don't know, but I saw that man in the overalls again. I'm so glad the healing session is tomorrow. I can't shake the feeling I'm going to need—"

"What healing session? What are you talking about?" Bram's voice held a note of anxiety.

She stared at him. What was this sudden mood shift about? And why did he care about her healing session?

Sterling filled in Bram when she did not. "That obnoxious woman, Marissa, has promised to 'heal' Kimberly."

"Okay, I get that you don't like her but obnoxious seems a bit—"

"When?" Bram asked. "When is she healing you?"

She tried to read his spectrum but couldn't. In fact, she sensed nothing at all from the man. Nothing. Between that, the sudden change in behavior, and his apparent ability to mesmerize people, she didn't trust the guy at all and saw no reason to share anything with him.

Once again, Sterling spoke for her. "If they've set a time, they must have done it today while I wasn't with her. Why? Do you know something about the woman?"

Bram stared at her. When she met his gaze, she felt the irresistible allure pulling at her, drawing her in, clouding her mind. She could tell Bram anything. She should tell him, she thought, drifting weightlessly into the—

She slammed her eyes closed and shook her head. "Stop that!"

Bram went back to his place behind the counter. "I'm not supposed to interfere."

"You're supposed to be working!" Flint said. "You kids sure do screw around a lot."

"Kids?" Rosie said. "We're none of us exactly young anymore."

"Excuse me," Michael said. "Speak for yourself. Young at heart counts."

"You have no idea what old is." Bram drummed his fingers on the counter before snatching up his phone and typing furiously.

"He doesn't look any older than me," TJ said. "That is one weird dude."

"Agreed," Sterling said. "What did he do that you yelled at him to stop?"

She cradled her head. "You wouldn't believe me if I told you. This night is a disaster and it's only begun."

"Plenty of time to bring things around then, right?" Michael asked.

"We can try. But I have a feeling we won't get anywhere with Flint preoccupied and refusing to cooperate."

"So we hang around him down here," Michael said. "Macy reported a spirit near the lobby. Maybe they'll come to wherever Flint is."

"Maybe." She couldn't fault Michael's energy and enthusiasm. But something told her tonight would be a bust.

<hr>

BY MIDNIGHT, the rest of the crew agreed with her. Nothing was happening. Flint, despite normally going to bed in the early evening, somehow managed to not fall asleep on his feet. The fifth floor and the lobby both remained quiet, not so much as a rustle to indicate paranormal activity.

"I'm calling it," Michael said. "We can leave some sta-cams and review them in the morning. Maybe those will catch something."

Stan erected a tripod and mounted a camera on it facing the desk.

"Absolutely not," Bram said. "I do not consent to my likeness being recorded or potentially used on a television program."

"We won't use this unless a spirit makes an appearance," Stan assured him. "And Kimberly says the room is cold. You should be good—"

"I refuse to be recorded. Do not turn that camera on."

"And I thought the old man was cranky," Sterling whispered to her.

Stan looked at Michael who looked at her.

She shrugged. "Nothing is going to happen. If he won't let us record, let's just go to bed."

Michael ran a hand down his face. "I'm getting too old for this."

"What happened to young at heart?" Sterling elbowed him.

"That was hours ago. I need some sleep."

Kimberly also felt bone tired. "Getting a few hours extra sleep won't hurt any of us. And they know where to find us if something does happen."

They bid each other goodnight and went their separate ways.

Sterling hopped into the elevator with her. "What's up with the healing thing? I think I need to be there."

"It's only for Rosie and me. Although, I know Michael intends to record some of it for the show if we can get permission. I forgot to ask Marissa about that."

"I don't like you going there alone. At all."

"You can come if you want to." The doors opened and she yawned widely. "Well, goodnight."

She crossed the hall and unlocked her door, but Sterling didn't continue to his room.

"Can I come in?" he asked.

As badly as she'd hoped for this two nights ago, now the idea made her uncomfortable. If he took another job and left her show, she had a hard time seeing how they would manage to stay together. And if they were going to end this, spending more nights with him would make the inevitable break-up all the more difficult. Her heart twisted. She didn't want him to go. Not now, not ever. "I don't know. I don't think—"

He tucked a strand of hair behind her ear and leaned closer. His orange chakra spun, humming for her. In her mind, she knew she needed to protect herself, to prepare for the eventual heartbreak, but her body felt differently. Her chakras resonated in response to his nearness.

She caught her breath and leaned away. "Sterling, if you're going to leave, I think we need to work on putting some distance—"

He looped his arms around her waist and pulled her to him. Warmth radiated against her as he leaned close. "Let's not talk about that right now. Let's go inside."

She took several steps backward, into the room, allowing him to mirror her movement, following her in. He guided her to the bed, and her body ached for his reassuring touch. How did this man continue to excite her in ways no one else could? But as his lips melded with hers and she rode a wave on a sensual sea, more engulfing even than Bram's hypnotic stare, the pragmatic voice in the back of her mind reminded her he would probably leave soon.

She extricated herself from the warmth and comfort of his arms. "I can't. Not if you're about to leave the show."

He cupped her cheek in his hand. "It was only a meeting. Not a done deal."

She covered his hand with hers. His scent, masculine and musky, had always stimulated her senses. But now she equated it with security. He would take that with him if he left. Could she admit how much she wanted him to stay? Not if it would pressure him into declining an opportunity that he should take. She forced a smile. "You were there all afternoon. That sounds like more than just a meeting about an offer."

He glanced away. "There was more to it than that."

His spectrum told her what his words didn't. "You're upset about something. What is it?"

"Let's talk about something else. Or not talk at all." He leaned closer.

She countered, keeping some space between them, and forced eye contact. "I think we need to talk about it."

His shoulders slumped. "I was trying to avoid discussing it.

I'm actually the one who asked for the meeting today. Georgia is . . . helping me with something."

Her brow furrowed. "Helping with—Does it have to do with whatever you were talking to Michael about before the introduction?"

"Yeah."

"Well, what is it?"

He raked his fingers through his hair. "I really don't want to discuss it with you."

Oh. Well. She leaned back and narrowed her eyes. "But you discussed it with Georgia?"

He nodded, his mouth a tiny line, anxiety oozing off of him.

"Does this mysterious topic of discussion have to do with me?"

He sighed heavily. Nodded again.

"And you could discuss it with Georgia but not with me?"

"I planned to tell you. I *will* tell you. I just wanted to resolve it first. Then Georgia asked if she could interview me, then she sprung the job offer." He dropped his arms. "It all happened so fast."

"I just don't understand why you can't talk to me about it. If it's bothering you—"

"I thought I could keep it quiet until it was resolved. Can you let me handle it? Please?"

"But maybe I could help resolve it."

"I don't want to upset you with it. Can you trust me to deal with this?"

She thought she could trust him. He'd never done anything to lead her to distrust him. But the fact he refused to share with her something he had shared with another woman didn't sit well. Add the concern he might be leaving her show to go work with that other woman . . . Well, no matter the level of trust, that stirred up some emotions she didn't want to work through while she was exhausted and probably not at her best.

"This is a lot, Sterling." She gathered his hands in hers. "One o'clock in the morning is not the time to sift through it all. Especially not the way I'm feeling right now."

He squeezed her hands and stood. "Yeah. I get that. Let's talk tomorrow, after we've rested."

Closing the door on him left her feeling empty. She wanted his arms around her, wanted to fall asleep to the gentle rhythm of his chest rising and falling with each breath, with her head tucked against his shoulder.

Exhaustion pulled at her as she went through the motions of washing up for bed and climbing into the cold sheets.

She thought of her empty house back in Albuquerque. Where had Angela gone? She hoped finding someplace safe hadn't been too difficult for the woman. She couldn't let anyone into the house until she got inside and checked out the disturbance. What waited for her there? She'd long suspected a demon resided in the house. If so, what roused it now after being dormant for so many years?

Her dad had always frowned at her anytime she mentioned spirits or the belief that something remained in the house. She remembered vividly the crease between his eyebrows that grew deeper over the years, mostly, she suspected, as a result from all the frowning she caused. He'd never accepted her or approved of her. Why couldn't she have been a normal person, someone her father could have been proud of?

Or why hadn't Mom chosen a husband like herself? From what everyone in New Orleans told her, the psychic abilities of the women in her family were legend, not a secret. At least, not until she came along. Was that Dad's influence? Did Mom embarrass him? If that was the case, why did they get married in the first place?

She knew he'd been embarrassed of her. He'd never hidden that. Once again, she couldn't stop herself from imagining a life with a father who was proud of her, who supported her gift. If she'd grown up here, surrounded by an entire community of psychics, how different would her life be now?

Marissa hinted that she'd be welcome to stay with them, to move into a position of leadership within the group. She couldn't even imagine being appreciated and admired instead of ridiculed and ostracized. Being encouraged and taught instead of instructed to hide her abilities. Maybe she should consider moving here. Why should she go back to Albuquerque? No one waited for her there. Sterling had been looking at houses there but that would end if he took this new job with Georgia and stayed here. If he stayed here, maybe she should too. Would she want that?

She'd allowed herself to think they could be happy together, but maybe that was all fantasy. If he accepted the show and returned to his skeptic roots, maybe he would be embarrassed of her and want her to hide her gift or at least not talk about it. Staying here with Marissa and the Paras would make that impossible. She'd want to increase her knowledge and abilities, not hide them. As her mom had chosen to do. Why would Mom—

A soft susurrus in the room interrupted her thoughts.

She lay still, ears strained. Had she imagined it?

Another rustling. She sat up and scanned the room.

A shadow shifted in the corner, the movement reflected by the mirror. She whipped her head, trying to get a good look at whatever invaded her space.

Bram's face stared back at her from the mirror.

Surely that couldn't be what she saw. She blinked and shook her head. The reflection didn't disappear.

She threw the blankets aside and hopped to her feet. His intense gaze pierced her, willing her closer. She moved forward until she stood directly in front of the mirror.

"Tomorrow," the reflection said.

"Tomorrow," she repeated, her lips moving as if on their own.

"What time?" he asked.

"What time?" *What?* she wondered through the fog clouding her brain.

"What time is the ritual? Where is it?"

The need to respond pulled at her. Her lips moved to answer. But something in her psyche fought back. *Don't tell*.

"What time?" Bram's reflection pushed harder.

She opened her mouth to tell him.

Don't tell!

Intense pain stabbed her brain. She clutched her head, closing her eyes as nausea threatened to upend her dinner.

When she opened her eyes, the reflection no longer stared back at her.

Had she imagined it? She definitely wasn't imagining the lingering throb pounding her temples. She staggered back to bed.

The scent of violets and roses perfumed the air, thickening until she could barely breathe, the cloying scent filling her nose. She flung the comforter over her head but couldn't escape the sickeningly sweet floral essences.

Chains clanged in the corner of the room.

Oh boy. "Try something else. This doesn't work on me."

The clanging grew louder, more insistent.

"Fliiint."

"Yep. I know. He didn't cooperate tonight."

Feminine voices whispered, pinging around the room in an onslaught of whispers.

"Don't give up on him."

"He's out of time."

She sighed and sat up again. "You're pestering the wrong person. Go harass him. Tell him he *must* cooperate."

The room fell silent.

The scent of flowers cleared.

Really? That worked? She shrugged and laid back down. Marissa had suggested a good night's sleep. Snuggling back into the little cocoon of warmth she'd generated, she intended to get one.

Tomorrow, her life would change forever. She was ready for it.

CHAPTER TWENTY-TWO

SHE SLEPT until eight o'clock and woke without a headache for the first time in years. Seven hours of sleep in one stretch. Luxurious.

The memory of Bram mesmerizing her from the mirror seemed distant—and ludicrous, even to her. She'd intended to confront him this morning but the sunshine streaming in through her windows suggested he'd be long gone. If that "creature of the night" didn't show up before nightfall, he'd surely be gone before dawn.

Showered, dressed, and ready for coffee, she met the others in the lobby. The entire crew looked more rested than she'd seen them in a long while. Excitement crackled in the air as they chatted and readied equipment.

Macy smiled and waved from the front desk.

"Morning, Kimmy!" Michael had donned a bright red sweater with a Christmas tree motif, complete with little blinking lights. "What? No ugly Christmas sweater for you?"

She squinted and held up a hand to shield her eyes. "I don't want to give our viewers epileptic seizures."

Rosie rested her chin on a fist. "You should be more festive for tonight though. I'll find something Christmas-y but classy."

"Maybe one of us can be in green and one in red," Sterling suggested as he sidled close and pressed a cup of hot coffee into her hand.

"Green for me," she said. He also appeared far more rested and had a little of the old Sterling sparkle back in his eyes. "And thanks for the coffee."

"My pleasure." He nudged her with an elbow. "Don't give up on me, okay?"

She nearly choked on her first gulp of coffee. He echoed the sentiment of the spirits last night, which she'd assumed implored her not to give up on Flint. The spirits peppered her with fragmented bits and whispered pieces but left her to puzzle it all together. Sometimes lacking important pieces.

"I never intended to," she told him. But she wasn't the one thinking about leaving the show.

"We'll talk later. I'll explain. I promise."

"Please. Whatever it is you're dealing with, I'll feel better knowing."

He lifted his eyebrows. "I'm not so sure. But I don't want your imagination running away with you." He took her hand as they left the hotel.

The walk to Voodoo Legitimate couldn't have been nicer. Clear skies. Warm temperature. Quiet streets. A perfect day for her to begin her training—her new life, supported and empowered.

They gathered around the still-locked door. Kimberly knocked.

Marissa opened it, beaming. But her delighted features melted into a scowl. "What are all these people doing here?"

Michael held out his hand in greeting. "Here to record the momentous occasion for posterity. And the show. Will bring a great element to Kimmy's story."

Marissa shook her head furiously. "I didn't realize I needed to stipulate, but they can't be here. Especially him." She glared at

Sterling then turned back to Michael. "Also, that sweater is hideous. It's not helping your case."

"They won't disturb us. I promise," Kimberly said. "They go with me everywhere—"

Marissa held up a hand. "This isn't up for debate. You and your Rosie. That's it. No recording. And absolutely no negative energy from a skeptic."

She turned to look at the others.

Marissa crossed her arms. "Why are you looking at them? This shouldn't even be a question for you. Do you want to be healed or don't you?"

She did. So badly. But the looks on the faces of her friends hurt. Asking them to leave and not participate seemed unnatural. They did everything together and had for years. Not only that, but this affected them too. Whatever had damaged her caused problems for the entire show. Without her abilities, she couldn't resolve their investigations. She'd be disappointed if she walked away from this opportunity, but she would disappoint her friends if she asked them to leave. Neither choice pleased everyone.

"We go where she goes," Sterling said. "Frankly the very fact you insist on having her here alone raises a red flag—"

"These rituals are sacred and not for public consumption. Would you expect to walk into a church or temple and film sacred rites? Of course not. You should extend the same courtesy to us."

"Fair enough. But we would at least be welcomed into the space. We don't have to record anything."

"This is a private gathering. Members only. Some of them don't want to be seen whether you record or don't. You were not invited to participate."

She looked at all their disappointed faces again. "Well, I guess we should—"

Marissa scowled. "You must be joking. Come inside. They're all grown-ups. They can find something to do for a few hours."

Rosie's brow twisted. "I was looking forward to being your bonded para-giver."

Kimberly nodded. "And I really need to be healed. I don't think we have a choice."

Michael tossed his hands in the air as if in surrender and let them drop. "I don't love it. I was envisioning our ratings going through the roof with this. But I'm not going to hold you back. You go, girl. Take your gift to the next level."

Sterling stood straighter. "You cannot possibly agree to this."

Michael shrugged. "She needs it. I wanted some footage for the show but that's not going to happen."

"I'm not comfortable leaving her alone—"

Marissa rolled her eyes. "She's a grown woman and doesn't need a man telling her what she can and can't do."

"That's not—She definitely doesn't need a total stranger directing her activities. We're expressing concern, not dictating what she can do."

"Everyone else seems fine with it." Marissa shrugged. "I'm not arguing this anymore. I have other things I could be doing."

Sterling drew her to the side, away from everyone else. "I don't like this. At all. That woman sets off all kinds of red flags for me."

She could sense his deep concern and appreciated that he had her back. This genuinely worried him. She smiled. "She's going to heal my psychic abilities and help me master them. What could happen? Do you even believe she can? As far as you're concerned, I spend a couple of hours here and nothing changes, right?"

He looked away, shaking his head. "I don't know. Something seems off."

"I'll be fine. But thank you. I really do appreciate the concern."

"Text me as soon as you're finished here. I won't be far. As soon as you reach out, I'll be right back." He squeezed her hand.

He stood with the others as she and Rosie turned to the

door. Marissa held it open for them, the scent of incense and oils beckoning. A soft chant filled the air as well.

"We've already begun a welcoming ritual," Marissa said as she closed and locked the door. "To make the space as comfortable for you as possible."

"I feel it." A sense of calm suffused her nerves, warmth flowing through her limbs.

Marissa led them to a door at the back of the building marked EMPLOYEES ONLY. She opened it to reveal Zorrie smiling—and more women gathered in one place than she'd ever seen, all of them murmuring softly in the dim light, holding candles, and all of them staring at her raptly.

Shelves of books, jars, candles, and boxes lined the walls. Some of the jars appeared to hold things she'd rather not identify. Bunches of plants and clusters of flowers hung from the ceiling. Smoke curled from sticks of incense and more candles than she could count. She breathed deeply of the soothing scent.

The women pressed around her, reaching out to shake her hand or touch her shoulders. She'd dealt with enthusiastic fans for a few years now, but even her most impassioned fan didn't gaze at her with the wild look that filled the eyes surrounding her.

The circle of women opened. Marissa guided her to the center, where a blanket waited, surrounded with candles.

"Sit down upon the blanket," Marissa instructed her.

Stepping carefully over the open flames, she situated herself on the rectangle of cloth.

The chant ended. Zorrie brought her a cup, steam rising from the rim.

"This tea will help you relax," Marissa said, as Zorrie held out the cup.

"What should I do?" Rosie asked.

Marissa blanched. "Please refrain from speaking. Wait there in the circle until called upon."

Okay. So maybe the healing session was first, and the

bonding ritual would follow? Rosie shrugged in response to the raised eyebrows she sent her way, as if to brush it off as no big deal. But she knew being relegated to the sidelines couldn't feel good. This wasn't what she expected.

"Drink," Marissa repeated.

She sipped the tea, detecting some herbs familiar to her from the decoctions Rosie routinely prepared, as well as some flavors she couldn't place. The peppery odor assaulted her sinuses. Several drinks later, a gentle buzz filled her entire body. Her skin tingled and her heart thudded. The room was entirely too warm. She tugged at her blouse, waving the heavily perfumed air, hoping for relief.

The Paras knelt and resumed chanting. Marissa lowered herself behind Kimberly and waved her hands over her body. "Breathe deeply."

Breathing deeply as instructed, she struggled not to choke on the pungent odor of the scented oil. Fingers pressed against her temples. Marissa spoke softly as the other participants droned on.

The voices around her grew fuzzy and then faint. Her enervated body seemed to levitate above the floor. Or perhaps melt into it. Her hands went clammy. She fought to keep her heavy eyelids open.

She thought Rosie called out to her, but the warm, thick air weighed upon her, drawing her toward darkness. Her body went limp.

Many hands rested on her, pulling at her, or maybe pushing her down. Was this part of the healing therapy? Her indigo chakra thrummed, as if her lighthouse beacon shone full force. Her head pounded. She wanted to open her eyes, to tell Marissa she'd changed her mind. Nausea rolled through her stomach. This didn't feel restorative at all.

The darkness shifted, blue light beckoning from a distance. Voices whispered from the shadows as she drifted closer to the light. On some level, she recognized her eyes remained closed.

She saw with her psychic third eye. A gnawing sense of unease churned in her stomach, yet her body remained inert while a guiding presence reassured her.

Go toward the light. Healing waits for you in the light. Your destiny waits for you in the light.

Marissa's voice. In her head? Was she expanding her abilities? How was she doing this? Her head pounded. She thought she heard other voices, muffled whispers, as if from a great distance. But Marissa's voice repeated again, clear and distinct in her mind.

Go toward the light. He waits for you in the light.

She drifted closer to the light, to healing.

As she stood before the dazzling light, surrounded by orbs, an alarm went off in the recesses of her mind. Did she say *healing* waited in the light or *he* waited in the light?

She threw her hands to the side, grasping for anything to slow her forward momentum, but she continued as if on a conveyor belt. Hands pressed against her back and arms, urging her on. Her feet glided toward the bright blue chasm yawning before her. How could she dig in and stop when her feet didn't touch anything?

Something waited for her on the other side. She felt him suddenly, could sense him gleefully rubbing his hands together, ready to pounce the moment she crossed over.

That was what was happening. She was leaving her body behind, her spirit propelled toward the Nightshade. She fought to stop herself, struggling to flail her arms and legs, to open her eyes. She couldn't cross like this, out of control and with no one waiting to ensure her safe return to the living.

But she also couldn't break free of whatever Marissa had done to her.

She saw him, whoever he was. Evil manifested into a being. He took delight in suffering and smacked his maw in anticipation of joining with her. If this spirit had ever been human, she could not detect it now.

Still, she drifted toward him, unable to stop. He leered at her. *We've been waiting for you, Kimberly.*

Laughter, hideous laughter that set her teeth on edge, filled her ears. Who were they and what did they want? Why would they have been waiting on her? Whatever the reason, it wasn't good.

Never in her life had she feared a spirit as she did now. Pulse pounding, blood whooshing in her ears, she knew this was her end. No more investigations. She wouldn't even complete this one and felt renewed annoyance at Flint for squandering the opportunity. How many opportunities had she squandered? And now she could never fix it.

Lavender and freesia flooded the air around her. Her mother's scent. The thought her mother was nearby gave her new energy. But no matter how hard she squinted into the light, she didn't see anything resembling the silhouette of her mother. Nor did she hear her voice as she thought perhaps she had a few times over the years, whenever she was close to the Nightshade. Nothing but the terrible cackling greeted her.

Until screaming, distant but frantic, took the place of the laughter. She sensed scrambling but had no idea what was happening.

A yank pulled her backwards, away from the light, which receded until it disappeared. She flew backwards through darkness, disoriented as time and space distorted again.

She opened her eyes, back in her body. And saw Lilith standing over her.

CHAPTER TWENTY-THREE

Kimberly's sluggish body didn't respond quickly, but her brain moved even more slowly, attempting to process the scene in front of her.

Marissa and the Paras clustered to one side of the room. Lilith bent low over her.

She met the woman's eyes but saw no malice in them. Nothing about the woman's countenance matched what Marissa had told her. Lilith grabbed the obsidian bracelet and yanked it from her wrist. A weight lifted from her.

Lilith rose and stepped over her, standing between her and the Paras, and told Rosie, "Take her and go. Get her outside and away from here."

Rosie grabbed her under the arms, hoisting her to her feet. "Come on, girl. These women are crazy."

Her best friend didn't know the half of it. Then again, she had no idea what they'd done to Rosie while they'd attempted to send her into the Nightshade.

The moment she staggered out of Voodoo Legitimate, she reached for her phone and managed to tell Rosie, "Sterling. I need Sterling."

Before she could choose his contact information with her

shaking fingers, he rounded the corner. He took one look at her and ran to her side.

"I knew it," he said, as he pulled her into his arms. "I knew this was a bad idea. What did she do to you?"

All she could do was shake her head. Even if she'd been able to manage words, she had no idea what the woman had done, how she'd assumed such complete control over her.

"Where's everyone else?" Rosie asked.

"They headed over to Bourbon Street. I wanted to stay close."

"If those women come after us—"

The door opened. Only Lilith emerged. Kimberly's heart skipped a beat as the woman approached.

"That's the woman I've seen following me," she told Sterling. "And Marissa told me she's the reason my grandparents fled with my mother."

Sterling held her close with one arm and held out his other. "Close enough. What do you want with us?"

Lilith glided closer. "Only to usher Kimberly to safety. You must get her away from here before the Paras regroup. I can hold them off but briefly."

"Who are you?" Sterling asked.

"No time. Return to the hotel immediately."

"How do you know where we're—"

"I've been watching you since you arrived, hoping you wouldn't require assistance. I knew better. I should have warned you not to come to New Orleans. I promised your mother—"

The door opened, revealing a wild-eyed Marissa.

"Go!" Lilith called.

Rosie grabbed her arm. "Look, girl, all I know is Marissa wouldn't let me near you and you weren't responding. I was pretty scared and then this woman burst in and terrified Marissa and got us out of there. I vote we do as she says."

"Good enough for me!" Sterling dragged her away.

The sun and fresh air cleared her mind. She heard Rosie call Michael and fill him in as best she could.

Just as they reached the hotel, Lilith caught up to them. "They won't follow you. For now. Let's get you to your room."

"Michael says go to his room, so we can all gather, and they can hear what happened. I have his second key."

Inside the suite, Rosie started the tea kettle.

Sterling sat beside Kimberly, rubbing her back gently as she attempted to make sense of what had happened.

Lilith smiled, watching him soothe her. "You've found your flame."

She couldn't connect the word to anything that made sense and thought she'd misunderstood. "My what?"

The woman gestured to Sterling. "Your twin flame. Your father was your mother's flame. I'm glad to see you've found yours as well. You'll need him."

Sterling peered at Lilith, eyebrows drawn together. "You mean a soulmate?"

"Like a soulmate, but a stronger bond. A soulmate is someone very similar to you, someone with the same likes and interests with whom you connect deeply. But a twin flame is far more intense and connected, as if one soul were rent in two and resides inside separate beings. Once reunited, the fire burns powerfully."

"I care deeply for Sterling. I'm not so sure he's my twin anything though. Psychics and skeptics don't mix. My parents proved that. My father was—"

"That isn't true at all. That's Marissa and the Paras filling your mind with their divisive thinking. They want to control and use people. Your father adored your mother and would have done anything for her. Twin flames experience tumultuous and intense relationships, but that's because they are catalysts for spiritual change in one another, igniting the other to become the best version of themselves they can be."

She blinked. That wasn't how she remembered it. This

woman claimed to know quite a bit about her mother when she didn't realize how unalike her parents had been. "I never saw my parents behave as if they ignited one another."

"You were young. No child wants to think of their parents that way."

"My father was embarrassed of my mother. And me."

"I know for a fact he wasn't. Twin flames are the yin to each other's yang, sometimes referred to as mirror souls. Strong where the other is weak. The two challenge yet heal one another. Your twin flame forces you to face your deepest fears and most secret insecurities. But in the end, both emerge stronger and more powerful than they could ever be alone. When you first met Sterling, did you feel inexplicably drawn to him?"

She dropped her gaze, afraid her eyes would betray her. Because as much as he had infuriated her in the beginning, she could never deny the initial attraction, even if she didn't want to admit it.

He leaned forward, stroking the inner skin of her forearm. "I don't mind acknowledging how I felt. She blew me away. I'll admit I showed up ready to disprove your abilities and knock you down a peg or two. But one look at you and I—" He sighed. "I felt like we were meant to be together."

She met his eyes, recognizing the vulnerability in their dark depths. "I felt something too," she whispered.

Lilith nodded. "The first sign of encountering your twin flame."

Sterling's gaze never wavered. "And you do force me to consider things I never believed possible before. But somehow, when we explore the ideas together, it isn't so scary."

"I recognized you as an anchor," she said. "But I'd never heard of a twin flame."

Lilith placed her hands over theirs. "You will need each other more than ever very soon."

She tore her gaze from him. "Would a flame be embarrassed of their twin?"

Sterling sat up straight. "What are you talking about?"

"It's okay. I get it. Expecting you to stay with me when you have the chance to work in your preferred field is too much to ask of anyone. I wouldn't want to stop using my gift either. I get it."

He looked genuinely confused. "You get what?"

"That you want to leave the show and stay here in New Orleans. For the job with Georgia."

Lilith cocked her head. "You're not staying with her? Do you realize how rare it is to find your twin flame?"

Kimberly dove ahead, speaking the words she'd struggled with, knowing separation from him would be worse than anything else. Except rejection. But she had to take the chance. "I could stay here. In New Orleans. Well, not now. I have to finish the season. But everyone knows the show won't last forever." How often had she been reminded of that lately? "Marissa invited me to stay, but obviously I can't work with her after what just happened. I think I could figure out something though."

"Sorry. I'm lost. Why would you stay here?"

"To be with you. So you can take the job Georgia offered."

Sterling leaned close, his eyes softening. "You'd do that? You've really considered relocating to be with me?"

She nodded. "Is that too much? I mean, I've been trying to be quiet about the job, so I wouldn't add any pressure."

"You were so quiet I thought maybe you didn't care. Maybe you wanted me to take it so you could have your show back."

She shook her head furiously. "Absolutely no. I would miss you so much."

He pulled her into his arms. "I didn't see this coming."

Lilith smiled gently. "I'm not surprised. Once they burn together, twin flames cannot stand to be separated from one another."

Sterling leaned back and forced eye contact. "But I couldn't ask that of you. Investigating . . . that's what you do."

"But you're not getting to pursue what you want to do. And

Georgia can give you that. Maybe you'd be happier with her. Or someone like her." As much as it hurt to voice her concerns, it also lifted a weight off.

"Stop. I really and truly don't feel that way about Georgia. It isn't . . . I'm being harassed online. Someone is trying to blackmail me. Georgia has contacts. Knows people who investigate regularly. Yes, we had a drink and caught up. But primarily she put me in touch with someone to track down this scumball. In return I promised her an interview."

"Why didn't you tell me?"

"Because the guy is threatening you. Apparently, he sent you some direct messages on Twitter or Facebook—"

"I never read those."

"He found that out when you didn't respond. So then he came to me as your media specialist. He's Photoshopped some images of you that . . . well, let's just say I know you don't want them released. They're trash. And not you, obviously. But the graphics work is so good, most people will believe it's you. I knew you couldn't handle that. But I'm not about to pay this creep either."

"I'm so sorry. I—"

"I'm handling it. I wanted to save you the worry."

"I don't know what to say. Except you'd probably never deal with this kind of garbage if you take Georgia's job."

"I've thought about it. A lot. And what good is a job if I don't have someone to go home to at night? As long as you want me, I'm not going anywhere. You think one creep can run me off? Not a chance."

She launched herself at him, squeezing him as hard as she could. "I'm so relieved to hear that."

Sterling hugged her in return. "I mean it. And hearing that you'd be willing to relocate for me blows me away. I'm finishing this season of the show no matter what. If Georgia's job offer is still open at that point, then we can consider all our options.

And make a decision together after we determine where we want to be."

Relief coursed through her. "That sounds good."

"You see?" Lilith asked. "Twin flames."

Kimberly believed it. Despite their differences, and for reasons she didn't fully comprehend, she and Sterling seemed to belong together. "But we will have to be careful. Marissa warned me you'd be a target because you're important to me."

Lilith shook her head. "Marissa did not allude to online stalkers. Mal will know how to hurt you most deeply and will use whatever means possible. Now that you've found your twin flame, you're more vulnerable than ever. In this, Marissa is correct. She should know better than anyone, as Mal's servant."

"Mal?" Kimberly asked.

"The reason your mother ran and hid. Mal was after her and was trying to get to her through your father. And now he's after you. And your flame."

Sterling shrugged it off. "Ghosts don't scare me."

"Mal isn't a ghost. He's a demon, pure evil. And you *should* fear him. Kimberly, we've worked hard to protect you for so long—"

"Who—"

"But we were foolish to think leaving you ignorant of the danger would protect you. Whatever you do, you must not open the Nightshade. Mal will find you."

The door opened and Michael and the others spilled into the room.

"What in the world happened? We leave you alone for thirty minutes—" His head whipped around. "Who is this woman?"

"This is Lilith. I'm not entirely sure who exactly she is. But she's the woman who's been following me."

Rosie brought a mug of tea. "And she showed up out of nowhere to rescue all of us."

"What the heck happened?"

"Marissa drugged Kimberly, I think," Rosie said. "I don't think they ever intended to heal her or bind us together."

"They are followers of Mal," Lilith said. "That ritual was intended to offer you up to him, to sacrifice you."

"But why me?" Kimberly asked. "Marissa had an entire room full of psychics to choose from. I'm not that powerful. I've had no training, which Marissa made quite clear, plus my abilities are damaged."

"The promise of healing left you vulnerable to Marissa's influence. That's my fault. I should have approached you sooner. Your mother and I—"

"How did you know my mother? You mentioned my father too, but I know I'd remember meeting you."

"I knew your mother when she lived here. And we remained in touch after she fled. I knew when she met your father. I knew where they settled. I knew when you were born. Your mother, grandmother, and I spoke regularly, trying to decide how best to protect you, to keep you hidden from Mal."

Michael held both hands out. "Somebody start from the beginning and explain what the heck is happening. And you two —" He pointed at Stan and TJ. "If those cameras stop rolling, you're both fired."

Her camera operators scrambled for extra batteries. Rosie prepared more tea. They settled around the table, eyes on Lilith.

CHAPTER TWENTY-FOUR

"Marissa misrepresented your history," the platinum blonde woman began, "and deliberately took you to locations I wouldn't want to follow. She knows that any dwellings imbued with heavy toxic negativity—"

"Hurt us," Kimberly finished. "I felt it. She said you wouldn't avoid such places because you feed off the negative energy."

"No, I am sickened by such negativity, exactly as you were. Possibly I feel it worse. Tell me, did Marissa seem affected?"

"I was so weakened I didn't—"

"No," Rosie said. "She was fine. Looked delighted even."

"Of course she did. She's the one who feeds off such horrific energy. Plus, she knew that would weaken you, make it easier to hand you over to Mal."

"Kimberly truly did have a relative in that house," Elise said. "That wasn't a lie. I found the records."

Lilith nodded. "Evil begets evil. Mal was drawn to the house due to the great suffering Madame LaLaurie wrought there. Then Mal's influence drove her to more heinous acts, which fed Mal's appetites, which propelled Madame LaLaurie on."

"Until the fire exposed her inhuman behavior."

"Yes. She saw certain people as less than human and harbored no guilt for the pain she inflicted on them. The cook, however, could no longer bear the tortured screams and set a fire that burned the place down. Death became preferable to that life. Her intended self-sacrifice freed them all, one way or the other."

"Your great-great-grandmother survived, Ms. Wantland," Elise said.

"More than survived," Lilith said. "She believed she'd endured for a reason and spent the rest of her life casting out devils, healing the sick, helping people with nowhere else to turn, determined to make the most of her gift."

"Helping people with nowhere else to turn. That's . . ."

"Yes," Lilith agreed when Kimberly couldn't find the words. "She would be so proud of you for continuing the family legacy."

Kimberly didn't expect the tears that filled her eyes and blinked them away. "What happened to her?"

"She married a man who adored her and lived a long and happy life. As did her daughter. And hers, your grandmother."

She stared into her mug, dregs swirling through the amber liquid. "But my mother didn't. Why?"

"Somewhere along the way, science took over. People stopped believing in demons and devils—"

Sterling sat forward, hands clenched on the table. "Hey, I'll take antibiotics over shaking chicken bones or applying leeches any day."

"No arguments from me," Lilith said. "Modern medicine and research help all of us live much longer, healthier lives. I'm well aware that had I lived centuries ago, the odds of surviving to my current age would be close to zero."

Remembering the photo Marissa had shown her, Kimberly wondered exactly how old this woman was. And if she was as old as Marissa had implied, no amount of modern anything could explain that longevity. Something else would have to be in play here.

"Okaaay," Sterling said. "Then how does science explain what happened to Kimberly's mom? I fail to see a connection."

"When we stopped believing in evil, we stopped fighting it. Not all of us, but the vast majority. Mal thrived in that vacuum. Tell me, Sterling, do you pray?"

He shifted, uncrossing and recrossing his legs. "Here we go again. Yes. So?"

"To whom?"

"Well, to God, of course."

"Did you know that Marie Laveau identified as Roman Catholic?"

He squirmed in his seat. "The Voodoo queen we keep hearing about?"

Lilith nodded. "She attended daily mass, tithed, maintained close relationships with the priests of her parish. She visited the poor, tended the sick. She embodied the teachings of Christ."

Lilith spoke as if of a friend, as if she shared actual memories of someone from her past. But Marie Laveau had lived during the 1800s. That was simply impossible. And yet that photograph swam to the surface of Kimberly's thoughts again.

Sterling frowned. "I'm not sure what you're—"

"The priests gave her their blessing to perform rituals on church grounds at midnight, whenever she needed to. They enjoyed close friendship. No one criticized her for blending the two practices, for seeing the benefits inherent in both."

"Are you suggesting I should practice Voodoo?"

"Not necessarily. But perhaps allow yourself to be a bit more openminded. You admit you pray to God, your Roman Catholic God. But when I tell you a demon is targeting Kimberly, you find the idea ludicrous. How can you accept one and not the other? Marie Laveau, and the priests who knew her well, understood that both exist. Good and evil vie for human souls. Certain Catholic priests are trained to perform exorcisms. Your own religious hierarchy acknowledges the existence, the need to sometimes fight evil, yet you continue to adamantly deny it?"

Sterling brought a hand down. "Why are you singling me out? The vast majority of people these days—"

"Because you are Kimberly's twin flame. But you don't believe. You don't believe that evil stalks her. And you must. She will need your full faith, your full protection—"

"I always protect her—"

"And your full belief. If you don't believe she is in danger, you will drop your guard. You won't be constantly vigilant. And you must be. He grows stronger, feeding off the followers Marissa brings to her fold. As Kimberly has grown into her full powers, she also grows stronger, making her more easily tracked by those who mean to harm her."

Sterling dragged a hand down his face. "Okay. Let's say I acknowledge this demon, this dark power. Why? Why her? Why is he targeting Kimberly?"

Lilith's brow furrowed. "You haven't figured that out?"

Sterling looked at everyone seated around the table, finally resting his gaze on Kimberly. Everyone looked to her, tipped heads and raised eyebrows all asking the same question: What were they supposed to have figured out?

"Kimmy?" Michael asked. "Are you keeping something from us? From me? I've known you forever."

"I . . ." Something told her it all tied together with her mother, who fell down in the kitchen despite being perfectly healthy and never got back up. But what was the connection?

"You truly do not know?" Lilith asked.

Sterling shrugged. "Supposedly all those women at the Voodoo shop are psychics. And they apparently think Mal is pretty amazing. So why not join with them? Why is he after Kimberly?"

Lilith looked directly at Kimberly. "Many psychics, yes. But few are Shadewalkers."

Shadewalker?

"This relates to the Nightshade?" she asked.

"Exactly so. And your ability to cross over to it. Did you not know that is a rare gift?"

She shook her head. "I assumed every psychic can do anything I can do."

Lilith laughed lightly. "Oh my, no."

The laughter highlighted yet another gap of ignorance in her knowledge and caused an embarrassed flush that warmed her cheeks.

Sterling shrugged. "That still doesn't really explain—"

"He envies us life. To live, to breathe, to eat, to love, to touch. These are all denied him. He senses memories of these things in the spirits who walk the Nightshade, those who cannot let go, who continue to long for their previous existences, who refuse to move on. Jealousy consumes him. He believes if a Shadewalker brings him back to the living world, a rebirth of sorts, he can experience life."

"Again, why Kimberly? You said, 'few' are Shadewalkers, not that she's the only one."

"True. I myself am a Shadewalker. I can cross the Veil. But Kimberly . . ." Lilith turned her piercing blue eyes on her, a question burning in them. Could she figure it out on her own?

She remembered crossing into the Nightshade to rescue Faith, kidnapped from the living world and held in the spirit realm. And Hannah—she'd returned the girl's spirit to her final resting place, where her mother waited for her so the two could cross over together. "I can bring them back."

Lilith smiled. "You can bring them back. The women of your family have all been blessed with the psychic gift as well as the ability to Shadewalk. But somewhere along the way, you developed a new ability. Your mother was a Key, and now you are as well. You possess the ability to unlock passage between realms and transport others. You are the only Key we're currently aware of. Which is why Mal is determined to control you."

CHAPTER TWENTY-FIVE

KIMBERLY'S HEAD SWAM. Sterling held up his hands, as if struggling to piece together a puzzle. She knew exactly how he felt.

"Every time I think I'm starting to get a handle on this, you confuse me again," Sterling said. "Bring spirits back from . . . what? I thought you helped lost spirits here, those who didn't make the transition to heaven or whatever you call it."

"She does do that," Lilith replied. "Communicating with spirits who haven't left this plane of existence is what Kimberly does for this show. And she assists in translocation for spirits who make their peace with death and are ready to cross over. Many people refer to those lost spirits as hauntings. But there is far more to it than that."

"So we have this world and the next, plus something else? Not just our world and then heaven or hell? Is that what you're saying?"

Lilith smiled as if at a child. "Your concept is extremely simplified. Common perception, strongly held convictions, but overly simplified. A spirit unfettered from its body is able to transmogrify, to adapt to most any environment. That frees us to cross time, space, other planes of existence. However, our modern minds are hindered by the simplified beliefs in the after-life. We don't think to consider all the possibilities."

"And how does the Nightshade factor in? If we can go anywhere, do anything, at any time—"

"Most spirits remain close to their place of death, or at least close to where they lived. They want to get back to that life. The Nightshade is nearest to us, a spirit realm separated by only a thin veil from our own reality. Sometimes spirits cross without realizing it."

"I've been experiencing difficulties myself, getting pulled into the Nightshade without trying. I don't even want to, but suddenly I'm there."

"I'm not surprised," Lilith said. "That's Mal forcing you into his realm so he can control you. Mal wishes to release devastation on the world. He may wish to experience life, but he's not motivated by anything good. He's still a demon at heart and is completely self-concerned. He will not be content to enter the world and enjoy all the good things it has to offer. He intends to unleash everyone else too, every tortured soul, every restless spirit to walk the Earth again."

"Then the Nightshade is like Purgatory?" Sterling asked.

Lilith sighed. "If that helps you envision it, then yes. It's entirely more complicated than that, but the comparison works well enough for your purposes."

"My purposes?"

"We need you to believe. If we can incorporate this into your established beliefs of good and evil, of Heaven and Hell and Purgatory in between, then so be it. Kimberly needs you."

Sterling scowled. "So I'm too simple-minded to grasp the finer nuances—"

Kimberly rested a hand over his. "It isn't just you, and no one thinks you're simpleminded. I don't fully understand either. I've never heard any of this or considered what exactly seeing spirits meant . . ."

The day her mother had died, Kimberly had seen her. Her

mother had smiled and reached for her. At the time, she'd been terrified of the manifestation. All these years, she'd thought her mother wanted to hug her, to tell her good-bye, and guilt had dogged her ever since, because she'd been too afraid. But now—

Her breath caught in her throat, and she grasped the table as the world began to spin.

Lilith stood, extending a hand. "Kimberly, don't—"

"My mother . . . was right there. She reached for me. I could have brought her back! She wanted me to bring her back!"

She couldn't breathe. The table shook. The air around her crackled, shifting to a grainy, gray-blue hue.

Lilith's voice broke through the static din filling her ears. "Kimberly, stop! You must not cross into the Nightshade! Mal will find you and come for you!"

She smelled lemon, then lavender. Hands massaged her back and shoulders. Quiet voices soothed. The room rematerialized, solid and living.

"I could have brought her back," she repeated.

Lilith shook her head. "Your abilities had not yet developed and matured. I assure you, you could not. You were not ready."

"Speaking of ready," Rosie said. "Marissa promised to heal Kimberly."

"Those who do not love, who envy others and desire only power and control, are not capable of healing others. Marissa detected your weakness inflicted by Mal but lied when she claimed she could heal you. She only intended to hand you over to the demon."

"But how did he damage me in the first place?"

"You must have crossed into the Nightshade in your full corporeal form. Perhaps you didn't realize you'd crossed. Or—"

Faith. "No," Kimberly said. "I know exactly when that happened. A spirit pulled a little girl into the Nightshade during one of my investigations. I crossed to bring her back."

"That was Mal's opportunity," Lilith said. "Perhaps he was working with the spirit."

Rosie shook her head. "If Kimberly can't be healed, how can she protect herself against—"

"I didn't say she can't be healed, only that Marissa could not heal her. Rosie, come."

Lilith got up and stood behind Kimberly, gesturing for Rosie to stand in front of her.

"What's happening?" Michael asked.

Sterling stood. "I think Kimberly has been through quite enough today."

"She has been through more than anyone should endure, I agree," Lilith said. "But as Rosie pointed out, she is vulnerable to future attacks, and her psychic injury compounds that vulnerability. Kimberly, if you consent, I can repair the damage done to you."

She didn't have to think twice. "Yes. Definitely yes."

Sterling sighed. She met his gaze and nodded, assuring him this was a good thing. Even from a distance, she could sense his concern. His red chakra spun wildly.

Michael watched like a man savoring a Christmas gift before opening it. "If those cameras aren't rolling—"

"We're recording!" Stan yelled.

"Come on, Michael." TJ sounded disgusted. "I'm not a noob anymore. We know what we're doing."

"And I'm taking notes!" Elise's pencil scratched furiously across her pad of paper.

What notes could she be taking? Kimberly didn't spend time on that, eager to know what Lilith could do to help her. "What do I do?"

"You simply relax," Lilith said. "Rosie, place your hands over her sternum."

"We gotcha, girl."

Once Rosie situated herself, Lilith rested her palms flat against her back. "There it is. He attacked your heart chakra. Of course. If the heart isn't in the right place, nothing comes into alignment. Rosie, brace yourself."

Michael stood. "Hold up! Why does Rosie need to brace herself?"

"I promise no harm will come to Kimberly," Lilith said. "I understand Marissa shattered your trust, but I am truly here to help."

Rosie gulped and shuffled her feet, planting them firmly, then whispered, "What do I do?"

"Pour all the love for your friend into her heart. She's hurting and needs your support."

Rosie nodded and gulped. "Got it."

Kimberly stared into Rosie's eyes, terrified of whatever—

A jolt of lightning struck her from behind, shooting up and down her spine. Her vision blurred and she tasted metal. Her psychic energy stirred and stretched, expanding to the point she was sure she'd burst and shoot forth rays of light. If someone told her she glowed, she'd believe them.

She wanted to scream but seemed unable to produce a sound. Or maybe she was screaming. She couldn't tell. She could no longer hear or see anything clearly. A blue haze surrounded her, along with the whispers of a thousand voices.

For a moment, she saw eternity—felt forever stretching on beyond the horizon, sensed the presence of those who had come before her, those who remained, and those who were yet to come. And not simply beings exactly like herself. She detected animals brushing past and even beings she didn't recognize, similar to but unlike herself.

The enormity of it all overwhelmed her, but she settled into the connection, allowing it to suffuse her system.

The electric pulses subsided. Like a stretched rubber band, her psychic energy snapped back into place, her chakras clicking into alignment—like the feeling she experienced after an adjustment at the chiropractor, sore but better. Everything out of place had been returned to proper order.

She opened her eyes and blinked, relating herself to the environment, opening and closing her fists.

Rosie lifted her hands to her mouth. "Are you okay?"

Her skin tingled. Energy buzzed through her veins. She jumped to her feet, restless, and crossed to a mirror. The same face, unilluminated, stared back at her. "I don't look any different."

"Your metamorphosis was entirely internal," Lilith said.

Metamorphosis. Who was she now?

She turned back to the mirror. Her eyes didn't blaze, skin didn't shine. She'd half expected to glow green like an irradiated comic book hero. She looked completely the same.

But something was different. The cogs of her psyche spun in tandem, whirring away like a well-oiled machine.

"I feel good."

Lilith nodded. "Every time you use your ability, you will improve, building your psychic strength like a weightlifter builds muscle. Experience will take you much further than training."

"That's great! I'm so happy for you, Kimberly," Rosie said. "Too bad about the bonding."

Lilith tilted her head. "Bonding?"

"Marissa said she would bond us in a ritual. That I would be Kimberly's bonded para-giver."

"There are no givers in the Paras. And Marissa didn't include you for a bonding ritual. She wanted you present to sever the bond the two of you share, to further weaken Kimberly. But she couldn't. The bond of your friendship is too strong. Kimberly, even without guidance, you somehow found your twin flame and the perfect friend."

Michael cleared his throat. Loudly. "Ummm, hello? What are we?"

"Friends." Lilith emphasized the plural. "No. Family. The perfect family for Kimberly."

A rustling drew Kimberly's attention. She turned to see Bo drift across the room, moaning and dragging his chains. A cold draft lifted the ends of her hair, swirling them about.

Sterling held up a hand, clearly searching for the cause of her dancing tendrils.

"It's Bo," she said. "I can see him. In the light. How can I see him during the day?"

Lilith smiled. "I think you'll notice a number of changes. You'll adapt. Never fear your strength, Kimberly. Use it."

CHAPTER TWENTY-SIX

KIMBERLY'S BRAIN buzzed as if she'd downed too many espresso shots. She could detect activity previously unavailable to her—the constant undercurrent of the Nightshade running parallel to but separated from the world of the living.

Since Lilith had realigned her chakras and jumpstarted her psychic energy, she'd been itching to connect with a spirit. The new awareness combined with the warning not to enter the Nightshade under any circumstances left her restless. She'd wandered the French Quarter aimlessly, jazz bands filling the air with Christmas carols on every corner, soaking up the shadows and glimpses of wispy spirits walking the streets. Many of these retraced their steps from life, caught in an endless loop. But some made eye contact with eyes that widened at her recognition. Whispers trailed her everywhere. She should have asked Lilith how to tune them out. The constant static created low-level anxiety as she could hear them but not reach out to assist. She'd only ever focused on establishing connections, not blocking them.

She was ready for this evening's investigation, ready to wrap this up and move on.

Flint grumbled while her crew prepared for what she hoped would be the final night of the investigation.

"Well?" he demanded. "What's everyone waiting for? Let's get moving. A man needs peace and quiet to sleep and you—"

"Hold up," Stan said. "Last night you didn't care one bit about sleep."

"In fact," Michael said, "you insisted you don't need any."

"Yeah, well . . ."

Kimberly knew, could feel, what he thought but didn't say. "The spirits have been more insistent, haven't they?"

"I still don't believe in ghosts," Flint muttered.

"They know you don't believe in a lot of things," she told him. "But they continue to hope. I can't explain it other than they care about you."

"Hope for what? I'm fine!" Flint insisted.

Air currents swirled around her, teasing the edge of her hem.

"Movement on the FLIR," TJ said. "Isolated around Kimberly. Varying shades of blue."

A floral scent greeted her, followed by the musty odor of a crypt, accompanied by rattling chains.

"They've joined us," she announced.

"What do they want?" Flint demanded.

"Definitely sounds like you don't believe in ghosts," Sterling said, rolling his eyes.

"Why do you plague me, spirits?" Flint cried.

She moved closer and grabbed his wrist, ready for the barrage of memories. This time she felt ready.

TJ moved closer with the FLIR. "Disturbance is isolated to Ms. Wantland's immediate vicinity."

"Let me see that." Sterling checked the camera screen then joined her next to Flint. He ran a hand through the space surrounding each of them. "I can confirm, though not explain, colder air enveloping Kimberly and Mr. Flint."

She nodded to the trembling man beside her. "We're ready."

I love you, Jeremiah.

Take care of Jeremy.

The smell of flowers disappeared as quickly as it had arrived.

This is your last chance, Flint. And mine.

With a final clank of chains, the musty odor cleared the room.

They were gone. All of them.

"Wait! What do we do?" she asked. "What does he need to do?"

This would not do. They needed to come back and tell her how to resolve this haunting. She opened her sixth sense, ready to demand they return—

And received an icy blast that left her gasping.

From the corner of the room, darkness sucked away all light, all warmth, and spread like an oil slick over the surfaces of the room—walls, ceiling, and floor all disappeared, leaving them in a black void.

From the darkness, a hooded figure emerged and drifted toward them.

Flint clutched at her hand. "This cannot be real. This cannot be real."

Whatever approached them had no interest in connecting with her. She sent out her psychic beacon but was rebuffed. He swatted away her attempt as if brushing at a pesky fly. It appeared to have no interest in her. Or in speaking.

Suddenly reminded of a famous Christmas story, she wondered if Charles Dickens had been a creative genius after all —or a clairvoyant haunted by images he couldn't explain.

The hooded figure stood directly in front of Flint and stooped low. She still could not see a face but heard an otherworldly clicking sound echoing deep within. It lifted a bony finger and pointed at a door that appeared across the dark space.

"Spirit, please, no," Flint spluttered. "I'll be nice. I'll be—"

It pointed again. Emphatically.

"I'm here," she told Flint and squeezed his hand. "We'll be okay."

They stepped through the door—and into the hotel lobby. The somber quiet of the space echoed with the ticking of a clock.

Macy sat behind the desk as usual but dressed all in black. She dabbed at puffy red eyes with a tissue.

"Well, this isn't . . . I thought he was sending me to hell." Flint started across the room.

The phone rang. Macy lifted the handset. "Front desk."

Her monotone voice carried none of the lilting sweetness Kimberly had grown accustomed to from the woman.

Flint stopped. "She sounds a bit . . . off."

Macy listened, then said, "Who cares?" and hung up the phone.

"That's not— What's gotten into her?"

Before he could move, another Flint rounded the corner and spoke. "Now, Macy, you know you can't speak to our guests like that."

"You know I don't care." The woman didn't even look at him. She didn't sound angry. Just emotionless.

"Come, now. You've worked here a long time and I'd hate to—"

"See me go? Say the word, I'll leave."

"Now, now. Let's not be hasty. I don't want that, but I do think I've been more than patient—"

"Maybe I wasn't clear. I don't care. I stayed for Abby. Understand? Not you. Well, that isn't true. I cared about you and believed if I worked hard enough and did everything you asked of me that eventually you'd appreciate me. But I can see nothing is ever enough for you. You had me over a barrel when Abby was here. Now that she's gone—" Macy choked and clutched at her chest.

Beside Kimberly, Flint stiffened.

Macy composed herself and drew a deep breath. "It's clear you'll never be satisfied. You'll never appreciate me, never promote me, never have a nice thing to say about me. And now that she's gone, I have no reason to stay. So, I repeat, say the word, and I'm gone."

"This is worse than hell." Flint whirled to the hooded specter who stood mutely beside them. "What happened to Macy? This can't be right. This isn't real, is it? Tell me you're not showing me the future."

The figure lifted its bony finger and pointed to the door again.

"No! I refuse to go anywhere until you tell me what will happen to her little girl! I want to know she'll be okay."

Kimberly thought she heard his voice catch.

The figure pointed again.

"Tell me this isn't real! She's only a little girl!"

Smoke swirled around them, erasing the scene and reforming into another.

They stood in a cemetery, surrounded by monuments and above-ground tombs, a city of the dead filled with rows of cement houses. Jeremy and Nomi stood by a tiny plot, marked by a simple stone.

"No." Flint backed away. "I've seen this story. I know how it ends. I don't want this."

The hooded figure appeared behind them and pointed.

"Don't make me look!" Flint said, attempting to back farther away.

Her heart twisted for him. No one wanted to face their own mortality.

When Flint refused to move, the black-clad figure—Death itself?—placed a bony hand on each of their backs and propelled them forward. They slid until directly behind Flint's nephew and niece-in-law.

Nomi sniffed and blotted her face. "It isn't fair. He's surrounded by monuments and all he gets is this little plot and tiny plaque? And the two of us."

Jeremy draped an arm around her shoulders and squeezed. "Everyone else preceded him in death. Who else would come?

This is the best I could manage. For now. Maybe once his assets are sorted out and released, we can replace it with something bigger. But with a baby on the way—"

Flint shook his head. "A baby? They were told they can't have children."

Nomi rested her hands on her abdomen. "I know. I can't believe he won't get to meet our little one. I thought for sure that would win him over. We didn't even get to tell him."

Flint turned to the specter. "How are they having a baby? When? When will this happen?"

Unsurprisingly, no response.

Jeremy sniffed. "I never thought dying of a broken heart was a real thing, but he just withered away after Macy left. It devastated him. Wish he'd realized sooner how much she meant to him."

Flint's hands balled into fists. "Macy can't leave!"

Nomi clicked her tongue. "For someone whose entire sense of self was tied up in his business, I'm stunned he didn't have something in place to protect his assets in the event of his death. He didn't even have a will."

"I guess he considered it something he could do later. Then it was too late. Now the government will probably take most of it."

Flint clutched his head. "No!"

Whatever else Jeremy went on to say was drowned out by Flint's protestations.

The man dropped to his knees in front of Death. "Take me back! Please, give me another chance! I'll make this right! I'll make it right! I'll make it—"

Pitch black enveloped her. Flint's bedroom rematerialized around them.

"I'll make it right! I'll make it right!" Flint continued, his eyes pinched shut.

She tugged the hand he maintained a death-grip on and pulled him to his feet. "We're back."

"Actually, you never left," Sterling said.

Flint peeked one eye open, then sighed in relief and threw his arms around her.

"Hey!" She braced herself for the usual flood of emotional input. For the first time in her life, an uninvited hug didn't short-circuit her energy. She hugged back.

"You saved me!" he declared.

"No, I was mostly along for the ride. I didn't do much at all. You've been granted a second chance." She took him by the shoulders. "I hope you realize what a gift you've been given."

"Gift? It's a miracle! A Christmas miracle!" He moved about the room, shaking hands and kissing cheeks.

Elise spluttered and wiped her cheek. "Boundaries, please."

"Oh, forgive me, dear. I'm afraid I can't stop myself." He wiped tears from his eyes.

Michael's face scrunched in confusion. "Kimmy, what is wrong with him?"

"Well, he—"

"Wrong with me? Not a thing. Why, I haven't felt this good since . . . you know, I can't remember ever feeling this good. I have a chance to do better and I'm going to. And it feels wonderful, just thinking about it. Oh, I can't wait to see their faces this Christmas! Might as well pour eggnog down their chimneys! 'You won't even get coal' indeed! We'll see if Santa out-gifts ol' Uncle Jeremiah this year! Yes, sir! No one is dying any time soon either!"

Michael curled a lip at her. "Eggnog down chimneys? Is he having a stroke? What is he talking about?"

"It's a long story. I'll tell you during footage review."

Flint fell to his knees. "Thank you, spirits! Thank you. From now on, I'm a new man! I promise. You'll see."

"Sure," Sterling said. "And all thanks to spirits."

"That seems awfully quick," TJ agreed.

"Can't teach an old dog new tricks," Stan said.

"I, for one, will believe it when I see it," Michael added his two cents' worth.

"He did just kiss me," Elise pointed out.

Rosie looked at her. "Kimberly? You're awfully quiet. What's your opinion?"

She rested a hand on his back and read his spectrum. And detected a definite shift. His heart chakra spun vividly with concern and kindness where once it had sputtered.

"I think you're all going to be surprised."

CHAPTER TWENTY-SEVEN

Bed had never looked so good or enticed so much. Of course, Kimberly thought the same thing every time exhaustion sapped her this completely. On the other hand, she'd never experienced anything close to the healing session with Lilith. Combined with Marissa and her followers' attempted sacrifice and Flint's transformative experiences, she'd had quite a day.

After a super quick rinse in the shower and perfunctory application of moisturizer, she paced the room. Nothing beat going to bed without setting an alarm, knowing she'd be able to sleep as late as she needed to—except knowing Sterling would soon be at her door. Her stomach quivered with a thrill of excitement that she'd soon be nestled in his arms and enjoying the nurturing rest only possible while enveloped in his embrace.

She sat on the edge of the bed and watched the numbers on the clock, afraid to lie down lest she doze before his soft knock announced his arrival. Minute after minute clicked by. Much longer than he should take. Sterling had asked her to give him a moment to shower, then kissed her and promised to hurry back. He should have returned by the time she'd shimmied into her silky pajamas.

A burst of energy jolted her to her feet. Something was

wrong. Nothing seemed imminently amiss and yet her fight-or-flight instinct screamed at her to get up, to help. This was presumably another instance of a new aspect of her abilities she'd need to adapt to.

She listened, straining not only her ears in the quiet of the sleepy hotel but also her sixth sense. Her ears told her nothing—

Then she heard a thump followed by a muffled gasp. Quiet struggling. Then more silence.

That's when her sixth sense stepped in to help. Someone had been silenced yet mentally screamed for help.

Sterling.

He called for her. She heard him, though not with her ears.

No longer plagued with fatigue, she raced to her suitcase and scrambled into clothing. She had to check on him. Maybe she'd bump into him in the hallway, and he would be fine and they'd have a laugh about the whole thing. He would tease her about "hearing things" but would be so happy she'd come to rescue him that they'd tumble into the bed, making up for the time in separate rooms this week. Yes, that's what would happen.

So why didn't she believe herself?

A new wave of anxiety hit hard. She grabbed her phone to text him.

"He won't answer."

She nearly dropped her phone. Bram stared at her from the mirror. And this time she knew she wasn't dreaming.

"What's wrong?" she asked.

"Marissa took him," he answered. "I'm trying to reach Lilith so she can intervene. No matter what happens—"

"I have to help him!"

In the mirror, Bram leaned forward as if he might come right into the room. "No! You must stay here. Marissa is trying to lure you out, wants another chance to hand you over to Mal."

"I'll be down in a moment!" She shoved her feet into loafers and dashed out the door.

She pressed the button to summon the elevator—and was

overcome with the urge to take Rosie. She hurried down the hall to her friend's room and raised a fist. Before she could knock, however, Rosie's door opened.

Her friend was still dressed, thank goodness. "Hey, girl. Did you call me?"

"Not out loud. I do need you though."

"No worries. I was talking to Lorenzo. Didn't even put on pajamas yet. What's up?"

She grabbed Rosie by the wrist and tugged her to the elevator, sharing the little bit of information she had on the ride down.

Rosie shook her head. "Let me get this straight. We're going to charge down the streets of New Orleans in the middle of the night and take on a group of angry psychics who kidnapped Sterling?"

"That sums it up."

"I'm in!"

The elevator doors opened, revealing Bram blocking their path and shaking his head. "You cannot go. This is precisely what Marissa wants you to do."

"I won't leave him," Kimberly said. "This isn't his fight. Either come help or stand aside."

"I can't risk being caught outside after dawn. It's too close to daybreak. Lilith is on her way—"

"Good. She can help. But I'm only a few blocks away. And he's mine. My twin flame. He called for me, and I won't leave him to those psychopaths."

"I'll be there too," Rosie said. "I owe Marissa for what she did to us earlier."

"I can't let you go," Bram insisted.

Kimberly started to argue, but Rosie stepped forward. "Trust me, little guy, we can take you down."

Bram's determination seemed to wither in the face of Rosie's. He moved aside. But he wasn't happy about it. "If she hands you over to Mal and all hell literally breaks loose, they will never forgive me."

"If anything happens to Sterling, I could never forgive myself. But trust me. The only hell about to break loose is the one I intend to unleash on Marissa."

Under the light of a full moon and the glow of neon signs, she and Rosie nearly sprinted to Marissa's shop.

"They won't hurt him, will they?" She finally voiced the concern propelling her steps ever more quickly.

"Nah. Like Bram said, she's after you. Still, I wouldn't trust her at all. If she tries to make a deal, I suggest you tell her no."

They discovered the door to Voodoo Legitimate unlocked and cracked open, though the building was completely dark.

For the first time all night, she hesitated. She didn't think Marissa intended to offer any deals. "This supports Bram's theory that this is a trap."

Rosie shrugged. "Did we ever doubt that?"

"True." She pushed the door open further, peering inside.

Nothing seemed to wait for her except darkness and silence.

The moment she crossed the threshold of the building, pain shot through her head. She bent forward, pressing against her temples.

Rosie leaned over her. "What is it? Is it Marissa?"

She nodded. "Her. And all her followers. Attacking psychically."

"Don't worry, girl!" Rosie raced around the room, dimly illuminated by ambient light from the street, pulling tinctures and herbs from the shelves. "Your para-giver picked up a few things this week."

"Using Marissa's own teachings against her? I love it."

Rosie returned and sprinkled a circle of something around her. The relief was immediate.

"Much better. Is that salt?"

"Yes, but treated. Here, give me your wrists." Rosie squeezed several droppers over her wrists and rubbed the oils into her skin. The infusions sent warmth coursing through her veins.

"You learned all this in a week?"

"I'm a quick study. One last thing." Rosie slid bracelets over her hands, covering her wrists with a rainbow of hues. "Each of these stones offers unique protection. Think of them like armor."

She breathed deeply, fully recovered. "Amazing. How did you learn all of this in a few days?"

"Zorrie shared some of it. She doesn't seem to be a true Para yet, only aspiring. Marissa discouraged her from teaching me, but I think she couldn't help showing off a bit. After that, I did some research online myself. Some of it skews a little dark. But mostly it's in line with the practices we already follow. Just more."

"You're the best." She stepped outside the salt ring and immediately detected the attempted onslaught against her. But they couldn't affect her. The shields Rosie anointed her with held against their attacks.

Her psychic energy rallied, strength swirling through her and charging her sixth sense.

A smile spread across her face. She liked this.

But she didn't like the mental SOS pulsing at her like a distress beacon. Sterling. His red chakra spun out of control. She sensed he was bound and gagged—and scared. Who wouldn't be?

Curling her hands into fists, she strode toward the door to the back room. No one had to tell her that's where they held him. *She knew*.

As much as she liked the idea of kicking in the door, something less dramatic might better serve her purposes. She clutched the quartz pendulum hanging from the chakra necklace that Sterling—her twin flame—had given her. Breathing deeply, she tapped into her psychic energy.

And detected Marissa. Plus her followers. She could sense every one of them.

Using hand gestures, she attempted to communicate to Rosie how many waited to face off against the two of them.

"I know you're there," Marissa said from the other side of the door. "We knew the moment you crossed our threshold. Do you really think you can detect me but remain hidden?"

"You know why I'm here then."

"Of course. I have this ridiculous man you inexplicably care so much about."

The door opened, revealing Sterling exactly as she'd pictured him, tied to a chair, surrounded by Marissa's minions who all held black candles.

Kimberly raised her hands, mostly in defense, but also to issue a warning. "Since you know everything, you're also aware what I'm willing to do. And that I'm not leaving without him."

"You're not leaving at all."

Kimberly balled her fists. "Wanna bet?"

Marissa laughed. "Lilith got her lily-white hands on you I see. And you're thoroughly enjoying that little taste of power, aren't you? Too bad it will be so short-lived. Nothing compares to Mal. You want this little toad? Come take him."

Sterling grunted until Marissa nodded and one of her lackeys removed his gag.

"Kimberly, don't! Get someplace safe and call the police!"

Marissa sneered. "Excellent plan. They'll enjoy hearing about this little skirmish in the psychic wars."

"I don't know squat about this 'war,' but kidnapping is illegal."

"One of my top-ranking Paras is monitoring the switchboards tonight. She'll route the call appropriately."

Sterling struggled with his bindings. "Don't fall for this, Kimberly! Just call the police."

Marissa smirked. The sheer arrogance set her blood boiling.

She stepped into the room and faced off against Marissa. "Sorry, Sterling. This is between us."

Marissa's eyes slanted downward. The woman finally stopped smiling. "Last chance to do things the easy way. You won't like what happens next."

"I've always been difficult."

"Don't do this!" Sterling said before an acolyte stuffed the gag back into his mouth.

She gripped her quartz just as Marissa slammed against her psychic energy full force.

"I was being nice before." Marissa spoke through clenched teeth, but Kimberly sensed her opponent hadn't yet begun to push her limits.

Fortunately, her heightened energy level from Lilith's healing session earlier still fortified her defenses. Not only could she hold the attack at bay, but she also contemplated something she'd never before attempted—fighting back.

She'd always considered herself a force for good, reaching out to both the living and the dead who found themselves outcast or lost. Friend to the lonely, support in the face of ostracism, love in a world of hate. She'd never lashed out or struck a blow.

Maybe, like the cook in the LaLaurie mansion, she needed to fight evil. And if that meant casualties, so be it.

She raised her hands, prepared to send Marissa's attack back at her, intensified with her own energy.

"You think you can take me on? An untrained psychic like yourself? You have no idea what we can do!"

She didn't know. But this woman crossed a line bringing Sterling into this. Whatever happened, she would get him out of here. She focused her energy and pushed with everything she had. Marissa stumbled backward.

Kimberly wasn't sure which of them looked more startled.

The woman regained her balance and dropped into a fighting stance. "Rude! Now you've made me mad."

"You started this." Another blast from Marissa knocked the breath out of her. She staggered but stayed on her feet.

Sterling struggled in his chair, muffled cries indicating his desire to help. Rosie stood by, like a trainer watching her charge. She knew they'd do anything for her—but she had to do this alone.

Or maybe Sterling's grunts were to warn her. She glanced at him and noticed Marissa's minions had shifted, moved closer.

"Get back!" she told them.

Marissa grinned and waved them away. "Doesn't matter. She's not going anywhere."

Kimberly sent another psychic attack at Marissa. The woman didn't even flinch. Her energy was waning already.

Marissa struck. The blow doubled her over. Her head throbbed, radiating pain down her spine. Her psychic energy sputtered.

Marissa prowled like a tigress circling prey. "Cute, in a way. You think you stand a chance when your mother, one of the most powerful psychics in the world, couldn't stop us."

She suddenly sensed Marissa knew more than she'd shared. "Us? What do you know about that?"

"Know about it?" The woman laughed. "I tracked her down. I was there that day, nearby your house. I opened the portal for Mal. Right beside your mother. She stepped into it before even realizing it was there. Mal—"

She didn't hear words after that, only an angry ringing as fury ignited her spectrum. Marissa wasn't simply aware of what had happened to her mother—she'd been complicit in the plans. Responsible for her mother's death. No longer fully aware of what she was doing, she pushed again and again, throwing one psychic blast after another. How dare this woman pretend to befriend her.

Marissa held her palms out, in defense or to attack she wasn't sure. She didn't feel a thing as she pressed on, hammering the woman. Energy pulsed through her, stronger than a jolt of adrenaline.

A cry filled her ears as she closed in on the murderer in front of her. Only when she stood over Marissa's prone body did she realize she produced the sound. Tears streamed down her face.

Staring down at the woman, she panted deep breaths. "You

took my mother from me. And for what? What has he promised you?"

Marissa's eyes gleamed. "Everything. You can't begin to imagine. If we'd been successful, you and your mother would be together now, working with us to create the beautiful world Mal wants for all of us. Take my hand. Let me show you just a little taste of what Mal can do—"

"If you'd left us alone my mother and I would be together!" She lifted both hands, ready to silence this woman forever.

Rosie's hand curled around her wrist. "Don't do anything you'll regret."

She hadn't noticed Rosie approaching. She shook her head to clear it, sweaty from the exertion. Her hands nearly glowed in front of her. What was she doing? No matter what this woman had done to her, she couldn't reciprocate. Revenge wouldn't bring her mother back. Rosie was right. This wasn't her. At all. She only wanted Sterling and to get the hell out of this place.

She turned to the Paras, who now looked shaken and uncertain. "Get away from him."

They hesitated a moment too long. Anger flared through her limbs. She pushed—and they all stepped back as one.

"Holy shit, Kimberly," Rosie said. "Telekinesis? What was that?"

This wasn't the time to request an owner's manual or contemplate her recent upgrades. Where was Lilith? She wasn't sure how much longer she could hold out on her own. Or refrain from seeking revenge now that she knew the whole truth about Marissa. Her former confidence was wearing off along with her energy level. Exhaustion weighed her down and sadness hovered on the edge, ready to pounce. She couldn't think about her mother and what could have been. Not now.

"We can figure it out later," she told Rosie. "Untie Sterling and let's get out of here."

Marissa stirred, raising onto her elbows. "You can run. But there's nowhere you can hide that we won't find you. Willingly or not, you will help Mal in his plans to remake this world into the image of—"

"You can tell Mal I will never bring him across the Veil. Never."

"Tell him yourself."

A blue fissure cracked the edge of reality, ozone burning through the air, as a portal to the Nightshade opened.

CHAPTER TWENTY-EIGHT

THE PORTAL WIDENED. A pulling sensation tugged at Kimberly, as though something drew her toward the blue light.

A dark shadow appeared in the opening—a silhouette she remembered vividly from her childhood night terrors. The memories remained some of the clearest of her life, despite the decades that had passed. He'd stood over her bed night after night as she squeezed her eyes shut and repeated what her dad told her anytime she complained of the scary man in her room:

There's no one there. There's no one there. There's no one there.

The mantra never made him disappear though. And now here he was, the evil entity Lilith warned her about, that Marissa had attempted to sacrifice her to—the same menacing presence that had plagued her since she was a little girl.

And had taken her mother from her.

She knew it. She'd suspected for a long time that her mother's death was more than the medical mystery that confounded doctors and destroyed her dad. Destroyed her family.

Like those nights all those years ago, she faced off with him, both of them motionless. She'd been scared to move then, paralyzed by fear. He apparently had been stuck, waiting for her powers to mature.

Marissa struggled to her feet. "You weren't strong enough as a child. When your mother didn't survive his attempt to cross, he had to wait for you. But then you left home. Not until you started using your abilities to connect with spirits were we able to locate you again. And now you've come to us."

"Kimberly, let's go." Sterling stood, rubbing his wrists, now freed from their bindings. He turned to Marissa. "Let us walk out of here, and I won't press charges."

Marissa laughed. "She won't leave. Not now. Mal enthralls all."

"He took my mother from me. He will never—"

"But he can give her back."

The scene in front of her dissolved, then reformed into the kitchen of her home in Albuquerque. In the vision, she stood beside her mother, chopping vegetables. Mom stirred a pot on the stove—whatever she cooked smelled incredible. Her mouth watered.

"I remember that dish. Some kind of pasta she made. I'd forgotten all about it. I can't believe I forgot."

What else had she forgotten but didn't know because she'd forgotten? She stepped closer, unable to shift her gaze from her mother. Exactly the way she remembered her.

Marissa whispered. "Isn't it wonderful? I've seen Mal's world too. Let Mal cross, and it will be like your mother never left. Whatever you see, that will become your reality."

Entranced, she watched scenes shift again and again, as her mother helped with homework, took her shopping, taught her recipes. They watched *Bewitched* on the classic TV station, waggling their noses at each other. Mom scooped her into her lap and explained they weren't witches, not exactly, but that the ungifted sometimes confused psychics with witches. Mom told her neither faction should be feared—

The images and sounds of the vision distorted. Her mother's voice, anxious and concerned, filled her ears, drowning out the garbled scene in her mind. "Fear black witches and demons, baby girl!"

She shook her head, attempting to clear it. Something was off. Not right. But just as she tried to focus on her mom's face, the scene changed.

She sat in a chair in front of a mirror as her mom styled her hair and makeup for prom. She stared in the mirror, drinking in her mom's features. Everything was perfect. Her dress was amazing, her hair curled perfectly. Her mom teared up and said she couldn't believe how grown up Kimberly was—

I didn't go to prom.

The quiet voice in her head barely finished the thought before everything changed again.

This time, she entered her bedroom and discovered her mom sitting on her bed, arms outstretched for a hug.

Relief coursed through her. This was the afternoon when her mother had died, suddenly and inexplicably, and Kimberly had seen her spirit, smiling and inviting a final hug. She'd been too scared as a child, had turned and run away. Now she had the opportunity to get this right. She could hug her mom and say good-bye. She leaned forward.

Hands restrained her by the arms, pulling her back.

Lilith. "None of this is real, Kimberly. Whatever you see, it isn't real."

"It could be real!" Marissa snarled. "She could make it real!"

Kimberly blinked rapidly, clearing her mind of the vision-filled fog cast over her. She'd been unaware of walking forward, unaware of everything except the soothing images and gentle happiness she'd felt. But she stood only a hair's breadth from the portal, leaning into it. She stumbled backward.

Mal had tricked her. And despite her new-found strength, it had nearly worked. She stepped back and stood beside Lilith. "I will never help you or Mal or any of the Paras."

Marissa struggled to her feet. "Oh, you'll join us. One way or the other."

"I said I'll never—"

Mal reached to the side and yanked a spirit into view.

Her mother.

"Mom!"

This wasn't a vision. This time her mother stood before her, mere feet away, close enough to reach out and grab. She'd waited for this opportunity for so long. For over a decade, every time she'd glimpsed the afterlife, she'd longed for a chance to connect with her mother. And here she was.

Her mom attempted to speak, but she couldn't hear the words. If she leaned just a bit closer—

Lilith's grip once again held her back.

"He has Mom!" She shook her arm, but Lilith held fast. "We have to help her!"

"We have to leave, Kimberly. Your mom wants you to go."

She struggled again. "No! She's right there. I can reach her! I can bring her back, away from—"

Lilith must have asked for help because Sterling and Rosie stepped forward to restrain her.

Sterling sounded alarmed. "Whatever is happening right now, we need to leave before this mob of women decides to tie me up again."

Rosie's soothing voice tried next. "Come on, girl. We came for Sterling. Remember? Let's get out of here."

"But my mom needs help! All these years I worried she was trapped and needed me. And she is!"

"Mal is using all your most intimate thoughts against you. The memories you longed for didn't work, so now he's found your greatest fear. Block him out!"

Marissa drifted closer. "She's there. Right there. Close enough to reach. All this time she's been Mal's prisoner, and only you can rescue her."

Kimberly yanked one arm free and reached for the portal. "Mom!"

Lilith raised her voice. "If you break the plane, Mal will cross! No one wants that, including your mother."

"I didn't tell her good-bye. I didn't—"

"Look at her clearly, Kimberly. See through Mal's false images. She's telling you she's okay."

Focusing as hard as she could, she breathed deeply and gripped her quartz. Her mom came into clear focus. Mal remained present, but Kimberly could see her mother shaking her head and holding out her hands, gesturing to stop.

"I want her to know I love her so much."

Lilith pulled her into a fierce hug. "She knows. Someday you'll be together again. But not today."

Her mother smiled, kissed her fingers, then waved.

"I love you too!"

Mal appeared to roar in anger. The fissure snapped closed.

Marissa stomped a foot. "No! You're keeping all of us from the wonderful world where our dreams come true!"

Lilith shook her head. "Lies and fantasies, Marissa. I've been telling you for decades. I hope eventually you'll understand that real life, with all its pain and challenges and suffering, is better than a dream. So mote it be."

"So mote it be," the acolytes repeated in unison.

"No!" Marissa yelled. "No mote it be!"

"I don't know what that means," Rosie said, "but can we go now?"

"You're not going anywhere!" Marissa yelled. "Paras, stop them!"

The cloaked women surrounded them, blocking their escape route.

Sterling grabbed Kimberly, pushing her behind him.

Rosie stood beside her. "I don't think we're getting any sleep tonight."

"I'm not sure we're getting out of here alive," Sterling said.

Lilith spread her arms out to shield them. "You can't stop us, and you know it."

"You've been away too long," Marissa said. "We've only grown more powerful in your absence."

"So have I. Plus I have Kimberly. You're no match against a Key."

"A Key who won't use her power is useless! Shadewalking is wasted on you!" Marissa stared past everyone else and locked eyes with Kimberly. "You could be so much more."

Kimberly felt a nudge against her psyche. Marissa was trying to get inside her head, as Mal had done. She concentrated, blocking the woman out.

The group stood behind Marissa, watching intently.

"We outnumber you," Marissa said. "You won't be able to hold us all off."

The intensity of the attack increased as the other Paras joined Marissa.

Jab after jab prodded against her mind. Some of them eventually broke through her defenses, sending sharp, shooting pains ricocheting around her brain.

Marissa nodded and the Paras closed in.

"Ideas?" Sterling asked, turning side to side.

"Kimberly, can you do that telekinesis thing again?" Rosie asked.

Marissa and her followers pressed closer. One of them lunged for Sterling and another for Rosie. They stepped back but were running out of space to retreat. Her hands crackled with energy and her skin tingled. She held up her hands to ward them off. Nothing happened.

"What do I do?" she asked Lilith.

Lilith remained absolutely calm. "You'll know."

"I don't know!"

"She needs you, Sterling."

"Me? What the hell can I do? I'm not even psychic. Get away from me, you psychos!"

The acolytes reached for him, but he evaded their grasps.

"You're her twin flame," Lilith said.

"Look, lady, that's sweet, but we could use some help about now."

Marissa smiled. "I told you you'd never leave. The power of Mal flows through me."

She met Kimberly's gaze.

Pain so extreme she thought her head would split open sent Kimberly to her knees, cradling her head.

"Kimberly!" Sterling elbowed several women and rushed to her side.

"Now would be a good time, Sterling," Lilith told him.

"A good time to what? I don't—"

Marissa reached down and grabbed her wrist. The woman's touch burned. Kimberly cried out again.

Then she felt it.

Sterling's hand on her back, against her spine, sending energy pulsing into her spectrum. Her chakras fired, charging her psychic energy.

She yanked free of Marissa and stood.

The other women stepped back.

"What are you doing?" Marissa asked. "Get them!"

Kimberly stood tall and threw her hands out as energy flowed through her, crackling over her skin, and illuminated the entire room. Marissa and her followers were thrown back, then stood huddled on the other side of the room, clutching their heads.

She grabbed Sterling and Rosie and took off for the door. Marissa continued to hurl threats as they fled, but Kimberly didn't stop until they were blocks away, the crisp night air filling her lungs as she paused and gasped for breath.

"I told you you'd know what to do," Lilith told Sterling.

"You got lucky. That's all. Coincidence I reached for her."

"Not a coincidence. A twin flame always knows what the other needs."

Kimberly turned to Sterling. "Are you okay? Other than, you know, being kidnapped and all that. They didn't hurt you?"

He scooped her into a hug that nearly cracked ribs. "I'm okay. Thank you for coming to get me."

"Of course. You're my twin flame."

"Yes, I am." He cradled her face in his hands and caressed her cheeks, then pressed a kiss to her lips. "Don't ever forget that."

CHAPTER TWENTY-NINE

IF SOMEONE HAD TOLD Kimberly one year ago that she'd be sitting on Sterling's lap on Christmas morning, she would have laughed it off as the most ridiculous thing she'd ever heard. But perhaps from now on she'd attempt glimpses into the future. She simply needed a willing spirit.

She and Sterling were the only two of the crew who'd opted to stay in New Orleans. Everyone else had gone to be with family or loved ones. Sterling had offered to take her anywhere she wanted to go.

"A mountain cabin, snow outside, snuggled beside a fire," he'd suggested.

"I only want to be where you are," she'd told him. "And I'd love to stay put and breathe instead of run off somewhere."

Besides, Macy and Abby had started to feel a bit like family in the time they'd been here. And she had a surprise gift for them herself.

The lights on the tree glimmered, "Silver Bells" played over the lobby speakers, and Sterling rubbed her back, periodically murmuring, "All I want for Christmas is you." The only thing missing was a crackling fire, but the sixty-five-degree weather was not conducive. Regardless, it was the best Christmas she could remember in a very long time.

He kissed her temple. "I didn't realize how hot being rescued would be."

"You liked that?" she asked, her insides quivering like a bowl full of jelly.

"You were amazing. Standing there like my own personal Wonder Woman. I know things happened that I couldn't see, but when I had my hand on your back . . ."

"Did you share my energy?"

"I have no idea. I can't explain it. But I saw a blue light and swear I saw something moving inside it. And you . . . You were glowing."

"I've never done that before," she admitted. "Something changes when we connect."

"This skeptic is confused."

She raised up to look him directly in the eye. "I know this is difficult for you. I'll try not to share my energy with you unless it's an emergency and I need—"

"Are you kidding? I'll share your energy anytime." He pulled her close again and nuzzled against her. "In fact, I wouldn't mind 'sharing some energy' now. We could adjourn to my room—"

His phone pinged, alerting him to a new message. She saw Georgia's name on the cell phone screen.

She scowled. "Her again? Tell her you're taken."

"She knows. And believe me, it isn't like that. At all. If this is what I think it is, I want you to see too."

He opened the contents of the message—a video—and played it. A muscular man banged on a door. The mousey young man who opened it appeared confused.

"Can I help you?" the young man asked.

"Yes, and you'll help yourself too. You will stop harassing Kimberly Wantland and attempting to blackmail her crew effective today. Otherwise, I will personally deliver an asskicking every day until you do. Are you going to delete that trash, or shall we commence with asskicking number one?"

"Language!" Macy called from behind the counter.

"Sorry!" Sterling said.

Another message from Georgia followed, confirming the faked photos had been deleted.

Kimberly sighed and relaxed against Sterling's chest. "While I don't normally condone violence, I admit the look on that little guy's face was pretty gratifying. And I'm glad to have you back to normal."

"Me too." All his muscles seemed to relax at once.

"I hope in the future you'll share issues with me, no matter how bad they might be."

"I'll try to. This one was tough. I really didn't want to deal with the fallout from deep-faked images of you with that little weasel."

"They were with that guy? Ewww. That means he had pictures of him with a woman. Gross."

"I don't care how many women he's with as long as none of them is you." He nuzzled her neck. "I believe we were discussing sharing some energy—"

The door jangled, and Flint stomped in, scowling features as sour as ever.

Sterling sighed. "I thought you said this guy would be different now."

She gripped her quartz and read his spectrum from across the lobby. Something was off.

He trudged across the room. "Macy!"

"Yes, Mr. Flint?"

"I suppose you've been complaining about having to work on Christmas?"

"Oh, no. Not at all!"

"Hmph! Most people would simply be glad they had—"

Abby's oxygen tank hissed and clicked.

Flint's head whipped around. "She's here again, isn't she?"

Macy's face fell. "Oh, Mr. Flint. It's Christmas."

"Exactly as I suspected."

Sterling stirred. "Are you kidding me right now? I'm going to throw that man out of his own hotel—"

Kimberly rested a hand on his chest. "Give him a minute."

Flint leaned toward the counter. "Come on. I know you're back there."

Abby's face peeped over the edge of the counter, plastic cannula in her nose. "Hi, Mr. Flint."

"Hmph! Come on out here, then."

Abby complied. Macy watched with worried eyes. Sterling remained tense and ready to spring.

"And what did Santa bring you this year, young lady?"

Abby blinked her brown eyes and beamed. "New shoes!"

"New shoes, eh? Let's see them."

Abby stuck out a foot and rocked it side to side, allowing the light to catch the pink sparkles.

Flint grunted and nodded. "Those are lovely. Very pretty. Do you know what those shoes need?"

Abby's brow furrowed, then she shook her head.

"A new closet to keep them in."

In the silence that descended on the room, the only sound was "Joy to the World" from the speakers.

Macy tipped her head and lifted an eyebrow. "A new closet?"

Flint withdrew a picture from his jacket pocket and handed it to Abby. "Well, and a house to go with it."

Abby took the photograph. "Is this a real house?"

"Real and empty. Lonely for a family." He looked to Macy.

The woman pressed her hands to her chest and shook her head. "What are you saying?"

"I'm saying I hope you and your daughter will move into this empty house of mine. We'll fix it up however you'd like."

"I couldn't possibly afford—"

"Did I ask you for money?"

"I couldn't possibly accept—"

"My gift? Why not? Santa brought the girl a house to live in. He just dropped it off with me to make sure you got it."

Abby wheezed, her oxygen tank clicking. "Can we, Mommy?"

Kimberly whispered in Sterling's ear. "Convinced yet?"

"I'm more than impressed. What brought this on?"

"Reminders from some old friends." She paused. "And a pretty harsh warning."

Sterling cocked his head. "Has he really been redeemed if he's ultimately acting in his own self-interest? Are good deeds altruistic, that is, inherently good, if they serve to gain—"

She pressed her fingers to his lips. "I know I said I didn't want anything for Christmas, but I changed my mind."

"On Christmas morning?" He laughed. "It's a little late."

"You can gift me this. No philosophical discussions of morality and/or religion. Let me enjoy this win."

He tapped his cup of black coffee against her marshmallow-topped gingerbread latte. "Deal."

"Is it just like the movie, Mom?" Abby asked. "Are we going to live in a house now?"

"It definitely feels like a miracle," Macy said, dabbing at the tears welling in her eyes. "Mr. Flint, I—"

"Good. That settles Abby's gift. On to yours."

"Oh, no, you've been much too generous already!"

"Ms. Macy, if I've learned anything these past few days, it's that we aren't promised tomorrow, and we can't take anything with us when we go. Why, anything could've happened to me the last few nights. Anything could happen in the near future—" He choked up and rested a hand on Abby's head as her oxygen tank rasped again.

Macy placed a hand on his. "We love you, Mr. Flint. And no one is going anywhere so enough of that talk."

"Yes, enough of that." He swiped at his eyes, reached into his jacket pocket, and withdrew an envelope. "This is your Christmas gift. You'll find all your back Christmas bonuses along with this year's bonus."

"Mr. Flint—"

"That should be more than plenty to pay off any outstanding medical bills. You'll also find a contract naming you my partner and inheritor of the hotel when my time comes. Your new position, of course, comes with a significant increase in salary."

Tears raced down Macy's cheeks. "I don't . . . I can't . . ."

"I want you to think of yourself as the daughter I never had." Flint clasped one of her hands between his own. "That makes your little one my granddaughter. So from now on, you bring her medical bills to me for payment. And she'll only see the best doctors, cost be damned."

"This is too much!" Macy threw her arms around Flint. "You must join us for Christmas dinner tonight!"

"I must regrettably ask for a raincheck. I'll be dining with my nephew and his wife this evening." Flint rubbed his hands together. "I can't wait to see their faces when they see my gift. 'Lump of coal,' indeed. Plus I'm setting up a trust fund for any future children of theirs. And they don't even know they're going to have a baby some day!"

Abby threw her arms around his legs. "You really are Santa, Mr. Flint!"

He squatted before her, brushing tears from his own eyes. "And it feels so good. How about you call me Grandpa Flint?"

"Okay, Grandpa Flint." Abby's respirator kicked into overdrive.

"I would scoop you up and dance you around, but we don't want to overexcite you."

"I'll dance with you!" Macy pulled Mr. Flint to the center of the lobby.

As the two of them swayed to "Jingle Bell Rock" the relief and joy flooding the room from all three of them filled Kimberly with happiness. To the point of tears.

Sterling hugged her. "What are you crying about? This is a happy moment."

"I know. I'm so happy it's spilling out my eyes." She pulled Sterling to his feet. "Dance with me."

"First things first." Sterling held his hands up, palms facing out. "Nothing in my hands. Nothing up my sleeves." He held his arms out for inspection.

"I don't want chocolate for breakfast. Just come dance—"

He circled his arms about her waist, hands behind her back but not touching. So close she felt his warmth and smelled his intoxicating masculine scent.

She leaned closer. "Are we standing beneath mistletoe?"

"Like I need mistletoe as an excuse to kiss you. No!"

With a flourish, he stepped back—and held a red-foil-wrapped package topped with a gold-foil bow in front of her.

Abby giggled and clapped. "How did you do that?"

Sterling bowed. "Thank you. Thank you."

Kimberly's jaw dropped. "How *did* you do that?"

His eyes gleamed. "More importantly, what's inside?"

She looked behind her. "Seriously. I'm not standing in front of a table. Where did that come from?"

"How the tables have turned. I don't understand ghostly phenomenon, you don't understand illusions. Just open it. Please."

She couldn't deny him anything when he looked at her that way. She took the box and sat.

Abby crept close to watch, but soon little fingers pulled at the wrapping.

"Abby! That's not your present!" Macy chided. "Let Ms. Wantland open it."

Kimberly waved away the concern. "Actually, I have a gift for you to open. It's under the tree and has your name on it. Want to go get it?"

Macy stopped dancing. "Another gift? I couldn't—"

"It's already done." She smiled at the woman. "I think you'll like it, although it may pale in comparison to Mr. Flint's."

Abby returned with the small box and tore off the paper. The girl held up the piece of paper inside. "What is it?"

"It's a wish. You can wish for anything you want. Go anywhere you want to go, be anything you want to be."

"Can I take my mom to Disney World?"

"You can wish for anything."

"I wish to go on vacation with Mom!" Abby lifted her fists into the air.

Macy shook her head. "This is all too much."

"You'll hear from the wish planners after the holidays," Kimberly told her.

Sterling leaned close and whispered in her ear. "Did you fund that?"

"I simply reached out to the appropriate people to set the wheels in motion. But Make*A*Wish of Louisiana did receive a sizable donation as well. What can I say? It's a favorite organization of mine."

"I love that about you," he murmured. "Okay. Back to your gift!"

She lifted the top, pulled away the tissue paper, and gasped.

A photo album sat inside. The cover was a photo of her grandparents' house here in New Orleans, where her mother had grown up. She ran her fingers over it, then opened the book. The first pages were filled with a family tree, photographs of her mother as a child, and black-and-white pictures of her grandparents. Her mother's high school picture came next, alongside her father's. A wedding photo of the two. Kimberly in her mother's arms.

"Is that your mommy?" Abby asked.

"Yes, that's my mommy," she whispered. A tear escaped her blinking eyes as she pressed her hand to her mouth.

Abby patted her shoulder.

She reached for Sterling. "Where did you find these?"

He squeezed her hand. "I know your family history is important to you. Between Elise and Georgia, we tracked down the photographs. And we got onto an ancestry site to see what we could piece together for you."

She leaned into him. "Thank you so much."

Flipping another page, she discovered a picture of her as a child with both parents. She didn't have the words to tell Sterling how much this meant to her. But his idea to "share some energy" sounded even better. She took his hand, ready to sneak off to his room.

Before she could try to express her deep gratitude, a burst of blue light issued from a fissure. A window cracked open between the living and spirit worlds. She could see all the spirits—Bo, Violet, and Maud—waving good-bye, all of them smiling. Bo was now young, free of his chains, and able to cross.

One by one they stepped into the light, crossing the Veil.

"Good-bye! Merry Christmas!"

The portal shrank, slowly closing.

She turned to Sterling. "Now, how about—"

Movement at the portal caught her attention. It hadn't closed completely. A grotesque figure rushed forward from the blue light, decaying arm reaching through the shrinking portal and forcing it back open. Kimberly's hair and clothing blew backwards.

Sterling shrank from the sudden gust. "What the hell?"

Before she could intervene, before she could even think, the thing caught hold of Sterling. His eyes bugged as he was dragged forward.

She knew she couldn't cross. But what choice did she have? Sterling would lose his mind in the Nightshade. His logical thought processes would short out in the otherworldly environment with its own set of physics. The distorted reality would not click with his views.

Just as she reached for him, someone shot past her.

Bram.

He grabbed Sterling, shoved him into Kimberly's arms, then launched himself at the monstrous spirit.

As he tumbled through the gaping hole between realities, Bram turned his head and looked directly at her.

"Don't leave me in here forever."

The portal snapped closed.

MORE BY ADMISSION PRESS

Looking for your next great read?
Visit www.admissionpress.com

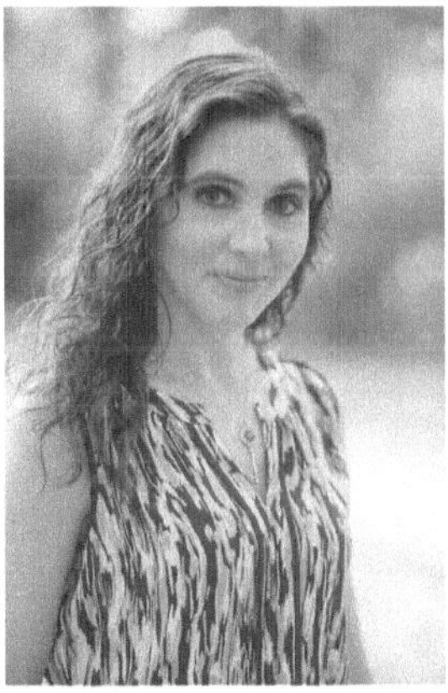

ALSO BY LARA BERNHARDT

The Wantland Files series

The Wantland Files

The Haunting of Crescent Hotel

Ghosts of Guthrie

Halloween in Hannibal

Women's fiction

Shadow of the Taj

Red Rain

www.ingramcontent.com/pod-product-compliance
Lightning Source LLC
Chambersburg PA
CBHW060928190726
48286CB00002B/678